# The Chaste Wife

*By the same author*

Spa Partners
A Touch of Town Bronze

# The Chaste Wife

DELIA ELLIS



ROBERT HALE · LONDON

First published in Great Britain 2002

ISBN 0 7090 7036 5

Robert Hale Limited
Clerkenwell House
Clerkenwell Green
London EC1R 0HT



2 4 6 8 10 9 7 5 3 1

Typeset by
Derek Doyle & Associates, Liverpool.
Printed in Great Britain by
St Edmundsbury Press Ltd, Bury St Edmunds, Suffolk.
Bound by Woolnough Bookbinding Limited.

# Acknowledgement

I offer my grateful thanks for all the assistance received from the Archive Services in Chester, Crosby and Dolgellau, and from the Ellesmere Port Boat Museum.

I am also indebted to the staff at Dolgellau, Tywyn and Barmouth Public Libraries for their unceasing patience and help, and to my husband John for his inexhaustible supply of encouragement and advice.

# Chapter One

IT IS A source of wonder that, much as the upper classes seem to abhor idleness amongst the poor and lowly, they are quite addicted to it in themselves. But so it has ever been and so it was in the year of 1816, when Britain was still basking in the sunshine of its victory against the French at Waterloo, and the London rich were eagerly trying to outdo each other in matters of ostentation and display. Being of their number, the Dowager Countess of Reyne, in her opulent box at the Haymarket Opera House, was entertaining a small party of guests. Earlier in the evening, the National Anthem had been sung on stage by the performers to welcome no less a personage than Princess Charlotte, with her young husband, who had chosen the Opera House as the venue for their first social appearance since their wedding at the beginning of the month. Charlotte, for once on her best behaviour, smiled and bowed, and from their seats in the five tiers of blue and gold painted boxes, the *beau monde* applauded enthusiastically, all eyes, in the candle-lit auditorium, eager to see how the marriage was progressing.

It was an exclusive audience: indeed it was rumoured that any box not already taken for the season was tonight being hired out at the exorbitant fee of ten guineas and more, just so that fashionable gossips could see the princess. The dowager had not to dig so deep: it would have been unthinkable that she should not have a box at the Opera House for the season, though she was still in half-mourning for her husband and was known to prefer the ballet or a farce. Tonight, however, it was a comic piece, *La Cosa Rara*. Naldi was singing, and Lady Reyne expected to enjoy herself, so she was naturally irritated to hear a disturbance at the back of her box, just as the curtains were drawing back. She turned round, frowning, to see a tall, broad-shouldered young man in military uniform standing in the shadows just inside the rear curtain. There was something familiar in his stance, and in the outline of his head, and, to the surprise of her guests, she shot up from her chair, holding out her hands, a look of pure joy spread across her plump face.

'My darling boy,' she hissed, so as not to disturb the other boxes. 'Is it you indeed? I hardly recognized you.'

'Mama!' said the Earl of Reyne warmly, enclosing her portly frame in his arms. 'Let me look at you. I cannot tell you how much I have missed you.'

'But dearest, when did you return? How did you know I was here? Goodness, how tall you have grown! Have you eaten? Oh, my dear, I shall go distracted with joy!'

Recollecting his whereabouts, Lord Reyne pulled his mother after him out through the velvet curtain and into the lobby, where stood another young man, similarly clad in military costume. 'Mama, you must let me introduce you to Captain George Radleigh,' said Reyne. 'Poor fellow, he has had to put up with me all across Europe so you must be especially kind to him. I said he must stay with us while he is in Town.'

Lady Reyne beamed at Captain Radleigh. 'Of course you must stay with us, dear boy,' she said graciously, extending her hand. 'I shall want to hear everything from both of you.' She turned back, lovingly, to her son. 'Six years, my dear! Six years since you have been home,' she said, tracing his face with her fingers. 'You can have no idea how I wanted you when your poor father died. Not to have been there for his funeral, Marcus, that was so very . . . so very. . . .' Her voice trembled and she trailed off.

'I know, darling,' he said, taking her into his arms again. 'You must know that I felt it too. But I didn't hear of it for more than two weeks afterwards, while we were at Albuera with Beresford. You remember how desperate things were. How could I ask to come home? Someone had to look after the men.'

Reaching into her reticule, Lady Reyne searched out her handkerchief and dabbed her eyes. 'I did understand, dearest, of course I did, but when you couldn't come then, I was sure you would come home when we sent that monster to Elba,' she said, trying hard not to sound reproachful. 'And not even to return after Waterloo, though it seemed to me that everyone else did. I confess that did disappoint me, for I so wanted to show you off. And now it is too late, for you have quite missed all the celebrations.'

'I'm sorry, love,' he said, hugging her again. 'Were you very upset? Someone had to deal with all the diplomatic wrangles, you know. And I'm home now.'

'So you are.' she sighed, 'though not for long, I dare say.'

'Why? Are you so eager to be rid of me?' said Reyne, mildly surprised. 'I'm selling out of the army as soon as possible, for with Boney safely locked away they have no further use for me. Don't tell me I'm not welcome?'

'Don't be silly, Marcus, of course you are. I'd keep you with me for ever had I only my own wishes to satisfy, but you will surely wish to go into Cheshire? It will be thought a slight should you not. Indeed, I am not sure you shouldn't have gone there first.'

'Before seeing you, Mama? Nonsense!'

'My dear boy, you will surely wish to see your wife?'

At her astonishing words, Captain Radleigh choked. 'Your wife, Marcus!' he exclaimed, smiling incredulously. 'Good Lord! We've been friends for six years. We've saved each other's lives more than once. Nobody could accuse you of not being able to keep a secret, could they, dear boy?'

Ignoring him, Lord Reyne, who for the past few years had been called by the epithet major, said, persuasively, 'But they would not expect me to go to Cheshire without first paying my respects to you, Mama? They know I haven't seen you since Father died.'

'You know Lady Reyne better than I do,' said the dowager, 'What did she say in her letters? Did she not mind that you would be coming here first?'

'Her letters? Ah!' said Reyne, with a painful expression. 'There's a small problem about letters, Mama, for we haven't actually exchanged any. Not since I left London.'

'But that was six years ago, my love!' cried his mama, horrified by the disclosure.

'I know that, but you must make allowances for the exigencies of warfare: the difficulties in writing and so forth, and then getting the letters home,' he pleaded, hopefully.

'I am sure that Lady Reyne did not expect a letter every day, dearest. None at all might seem just a little remiss. After all, you wrote to me.'

'Of course I wrote to you, darling, for you would have been furious had I not.'

'Don't you think your wife might be a touch cross too, Marcus?' said his mother, shaking her head.

Lord Reyne felt his collar, uncomfortably. 'But I knew that Father exchanged regular correspondence with Lord Cornford, Mama. And I knew that, after he passed away, I might rely on you to do so.'

'I?' said the dowager, her eyebrows reaching almost to her hairline. 'When did you ever know me to keep up a correspondence with anyone?'

'You wrote to me!'

'Of course I did, Marcus, you are my son. I thought you might be killed.'

'When I go to Cheshire, I might very well be,' he said, grimly.

'But how was I to know that you weren't writing whilst you were away? You sent letters before that, from London; I naturally assumed you would continue to do so.'

'Did she never tell you that I hadn't written, when you visited them?' he said, in a perplexed tone.

'Did you think we had visited, dearest? But we never did. We certainly intended to, but the brother – Guy, was it? – well, whatever he was called, he chose to contract some sort of an ailment. Whooping cough? Yes, I think so, and you would not have wished me to enter a house with whooping cough? My dear, even for you I couldn't do that. That must have been the year you went to Spain, for I remember that much was talked of our going later, but that Papa's health began to suffer just about that time. Barbara did come to Town for a brief visit, but not to *us*. We were at *Chelling*, so that Papa could convalesce, poor love, so she stayed with an aunt instead. After that, your father's health continued to worsen and we simply could not attempt the journey to Cheshire.'

'But did you not visit the Cornfords after Papa's death, dearest?'

'Oh, my love, I am sure that I should have, but you know how uncomfortable it is to travel anywhere north of Berkshire! And, really, they were your father's friends more than mine.'

'But Barbara is my *wife*, Mama!' cried Reyne, seeing a chasm of misunderstandings open up before him.

'My dear, perhaps you should have remembered that before. I am sure that she will have been more surprised not to have heard from you than she would have been not to have heard from me.'

The delicate matter of Reyne's bride having been discussed without any satisfactory conclusion being reached, they moved on to the safer subject of the late war. Lord Reyne and Captain Radleigh sat up with the dowager late into the night in the elegant Berkeley Square house which, since his father's death, now belonged to his son, imparting all she could wish to know of the six years which had transformed Reyne from the unripe youth who had dismayed her by going off to war, to the brawny young man who had returned. Reluctant as she was to leave them, eventually even she had heard enough for one night about battles and marches, advances and retreats, bivouacs and hardships, and, having first made a hundred and one arrangements for their comfort, she went happily off to her bedchamber, leaving the two young men sitting up over a tray of port.

They appeared very comfortable together, sitting in the half-light of a branch of candles and the dying embers of the fire, a natural consequence of their having undergone the numerous trials and tribulations of long years campaigning. Though both were tall, and they shared a roguish sense of humour, they were otherwise quite dissimilar. Lord Reyne was rather an athletic, loose-limbed, thoughtful young man, with an open, pleasing countenance and good features. He had a frank, easy manner, which made him friends wherever he went, and a healthy sense of loyalty, which helped him to keep them. He described Captain Radleigh as almost a brother: they had endured together most of the rigors and misfortunes of warfare, and, in spite of their youth, each had a look about the eyes of men who had seen more than their portion of the ills of the world.

Despite this similarity, Captain Radleigh's character was generally more light-hearted. He was of a slenderer build, had a rangy frame which seemed for ever on the move, and never seemed to tire. Even for the heir to a viscountcy, he was very self-possessed and he had an easy, rather impertinent charm, which, while it infuriated a few, was quite irresistible to most people who met him. He would never have been pronounced handsome – one Spanish *señora* had described him as bearing a strong similarity to a monkey – but his face, under an unruly mop of dark, curly hair, had a life and a spirit which could hardly be seen without pleasure, and people were used to thinking of him as well-looking. It had been said of Captain Radleigh that it was quite impossible to keep a secret from him, for, as soon as he suspected anyone of so doing, he would not rest until he had winkled it out of him. It was natural then, that as soon as the door closed behind the dowager, he should pounce on her son, saying, 'Well now, you secretive devil, tell me all about this wife of yours.'

Reyne sighed. 'It is no very great story, and I am tired. You don't want to hear it tonight?'

'Do you jest? I'm the man who has been beside you while you have flirted your way across Europe, old fellow. I'm the man who has had *señoras* by the half-dozen filched from under his very nose. I now find you have been married all this time. Do I want to hear about it, he asks?'

'Very well,' said Reyne, with resignation. 'But I don't want any laughter. And, if we are being completely accurate, you should know that I am only *nearly* married, in the strictest sense of the word.'

'No, *that* I don't understand. *That* you will have to explain to me,' said Captain Radleigh, pouring two generous glasses of port from a cut-glass decanter and passing one to Marcus.

'I daresay you will think it rather an odd start: indeed, I can scarcely believe it myself, looking back,' said Marcus, examining his fingernails. 'To state it baldly, eight years ago my father arranged a marriage for me with the daughter of a friend of his, Lord Cornford. It was their wish that the families should be united. Barbara – my wife – was suitable: rank, fortune appropriate, and after a little persuasion I agreed to it. She, being just sixteen, had no thought but to obey her parents, I'm sure, and I was but eighteen, myself. We did not meet until two days before our wedding day.'

'Abominable!' cried Radleigh, horrified.

'As you say, abominable. Strangely, it did not seem so at the time. My father, I knew, thought only of me. He had an absolute conviction that only people of similar rank and fortune could be happy and that he should get me safely married before I met someone less suitable. Believe it or not, I was perfectly willing to humour him.'

'You would not do so now?'

'Probably not,' Marcus agreed. 'I find that, after six years of war, I am not too worried if the person with whom I sit down to dine is of the same rank. But, to continue: we were married at the church on their estate in Cheshire. Having had many years to reflect on it, I realize now that Lady Cornford, Barbara's mother, was less happy about the marriage than her husband, for she persuaded him that it should not be consummated until Barbara was eighteen.' He laughed shortly. 'I wish you could have seen me that day, George, for I doubt you'd have believed your eyes. May, it was, and bitterly cold. I had caught a bad chill, or some such thing, and I seem to remember shivering in church while I was waiting for Barbara, and my father telling me to buck up. I couldn't tell if I was ill or simply terrified, so, when Lady Cornford said she wished her daughter to remain with them for two more years, I was nothing loath to agree: indeed, I was so completely embarrassed by the whole affair that I just wanted to get away. I think Barbara thought me rather feeble. To cap it all, my chill worsened as the day wore on and I had to take to my bed. A pathetic thing to do! Mama, bless her, was certain I was at death's door. In those days she was always convinced that I was sickly, and on that occasion I was glad of it, for she insisted on bringing me back to Town with her so that she could consult her physician. She wrapped me in a fur cloak, tied a piece of red flannel around my throat, and stuffed me in her carriage. It was quite humiliating.'

'What was she like, this wife of yours? Was she such an antidote?' said Radleigh, fascinated by the whole affair.

'I hardly remember,' Marcus confessed. 'No, of course she wasn't: not an antidote. Father wouldn't have done that to me. I rather fancy she was a little dab of a thing: ordinary. I recollect a pair of huge, pleading green eyes, begging to be left where she was. It was no very great thing for me to oblige her, I assure you.'

'What a sorry state of affairs. And not to want to consummate the marriage! I think some of those piquant little morsels you were so friendly with in Spain might be surprised to hear that you were so reluctant, dear boy.'

'No, I'm not sure it puts me in the best light,' said Marcus, laughing. 'Now you know why I've never mentioned it. Paltry stuff. Besides, we never met again. We wrote stiff little notes to each other, in our best copperplate, for nearly two years: I'm sure her mother dictated them, and I just wrote about hunting and the weather! But as the time drew nearer when I was to claim my bride, I got more and more alarmed. Oh, not just of the marriage itself, but the fact that we had to set up our own household, and I had to buckle down to learning how to manage a large part of the estate, which Father intended to hand over. It was all rather too much for a twenty year old. Father even started talking about Parliament: maiden speeches, the whole thing. I'm ashamed to say that I flunked it, and persuaded him to let me join the army instead. Mother, naturally, didn't want me to go, but I nagged and nagged, until my father said that I should get it out of my system. I confess I've stayed away all this time without taking any leave so that I didn't have to see Barbara again. It is about eight years since I last saw her: six, since I left England. She must be about three or four and twenty by now. Now that the war's finally really over, I can't possibly stay away any longer. Nothing for it, but to bite on the bullet. So I shall sell out and become a regular married man. Indeed, I am even ready to think of Parliament. I saw enough of the way the poor live while we were in Europe, and it's no better here. I'd like to see if I could make a difference.'

'Good Lord, Marcus, don't tell me you've become a Whig, too? You're full of surprises this evening.'

'For which I don't intend to apologize,' said Reyne firmly. 'As I say, I shall sell out of the army and become a regular pillar of the community, look after my lands, try to do something in the House and take my wife to Almack's.'

'Like a real, grown-up person, do you mean?' said Radleigh, pulling down the corners of his mouth.

'Put like that, I suppose it is a bit nerve-racking. I say George, old fellow, you've seen me through enough scrapes: I suppose you couldn't be persuaded to come up to Cheshire with me? It feels a bit like going into the lion's den after all this time.'

'Persuaded? I'd like to see you try to stop me. I wouldn't miss this for anything,' said Captain Radleigh, without hesitation.

'Excellent fellow. And we don't need to rush things, you know. I've plenty of people I want to see while we are in Town, and surely we owe ourselves a bit of a spree before we have to go and do the pretty at Hurst Park. Lady Reyne – which I still find it difficult to think of calling her – has waited this long: a little longer can't hurt. I have a distinct feeling that, when I get there, they might just have something to say to me about my qualities as a correspondent.'

# Chapter Two

HURST PARK, LORD Cornford's noble mansion, set in many acres of lush, Cheshire countryside, was a happy marriage of old-fashioned Jacobean features and the carved stone, wood and plasterwork of a later age. Arriving at the Park for the first time, few could help but admire the harmony of its diapered brickwork, carved stone ornamentation, and great panelled chimneystacks.

The three gardeners, however, at present employed in shaving to perfection the lawned area in front of the house, and who had lived and worked on the estate all of their lives, noticed none of this, for it was a warm day for so early in the year, and they were already looking forward to their luncheon of bread, cheese and small beer. Had they cared to look upwards, however, and peer through the stone-built mullion-and-transom windows, thought to be one of the house's most handsome features, they could not have failed to see the short, stout figure of the viscount, hurrying up the long gallery, grasping in his hand the latest copy of the *Gazette*. Reaching the end of the gallery, Lord Cornford burst, without ceremony, into his wife's dressing-room, just as Pratt, her maid, was putting the finishing touches to Lady Cornford's toilette.

'My dear!' cried his wife, seeing his face. 'Whatever is it? You are as white as a sheet!'

'Edith, prepare yourself! He has come home!' he said, holding out the newspaper. 'Finally he has come home.'

Lady Cornford did not pretend to misunderstand him. She pressed a hand to her throat. 'Oh Edward,' she breathed, turning as pale as he, 'however shall we tell her?'

Recalling the presence of Pratt, Lord Cornford waved her away, pulling up a spindly little chair beside his wife. 'She must be told of it without delay,' he said, once Pratt had gone. 'After all, Barbara must have realized it would happen one day.'

'Recollect, Edward, she hasn't seen Reyne for eight years. *Eight years*, my dear! That is a third of her lifetime. I fancy she hoped she would never see him again.'

'Nonsense! He's her husband. How should she not?'

'But he has spent more than six of those years fighting across Europe. And Waterloo, Edward. *Waterloo*! It is not unreasonable, with so many fine young men having been killed, that he should have been one of them.'

'You sound as if you wish he *had* been killed, Edith,' said Lord Cornford, reproachfully.

'Of course I don't wish it. Bad enough that the poor dowager has lost her husband, without losing her son as well. I only say that it is possible that Barbara may be a little . . . unprepared for his arrival.'

The two sat silent, their minds working, then Lady Cornford, as if the words had been torn from her, cried, 'Oh Edward, I can't help thinking that you and the late earl have been very wicked in this!'

Her husband flushed darkly. 'She might never have received another offer as good as Reyne's, my dear,' he said, trying to justify himself. 'It was my duty to see her well disposed of in marriage.'

'Your duty? To whom? Certainly not to Barbara. She could have her choice of half-a-dozen young men, today, if she wished,' said her mother acidly. 'All perfectly eligible. She could have had her own choice, and no harm to you.'

'How was I to know she would grow up to be so beautiful and

be able to pick and choose? You must admit she showed precious little sign of it at sixteen. And now she must make what she can of it, as other girls have done before her. Besides, none of her other admirers is an earl. You could not expect me to pass up such an opportunity.'

Lady Cornford put a hand on her husband's arm and brought her face close to his. 'Couldn't you have the marriage annulled, if she wished it?' she pleaded. 'It is surely not too late, even now?'

'Annulled! Have you taken leave of your senses?' he cried, appalled at the very idea. 'Do you want to have us all held up to ridicule? No, I cannot have the marriage annulled. On the contrary, it must be consummated as soon as possible. Don't you understand, woman, it is a great match far her? Indeed, since his father died and Marcus took the title, it is an even better match than we thought. Why, the lands alone must yield something like fifty thousand a year. And his papa was heavily involved with canals and mining and I don't know what else. Not that that affected my choice, naturally!'

His wife snorted to show how much she believed that, and Lord Cornford said again, 'Not that that affected my choice, but I should be a fool to try to get my daughter released from such an advantageous match. And you may believe me or not as you choose, but there will come a time when she will realize that she wouldn't like to have been married into a lower rank than she is used to, whatever she thinks now. Would you have liked to see her as a Mrs Jones or Smith, living above a butcher's shop or going out to milk cows?'

'Oh, don't be ridiculous, Cornford,' said his lady, crossly. 'There was never any idea of such a thing, as well you know. But she could have had a choice: married from affection, as we did.'

Silence hung heavily between them for several moments, for Lady Cornford rarely disagreed with her husband, at least not outwardly: besides, whatever she might say, there was much to recommend Lord Cornford's point of view, for there was no denying that Barbara had been brought up in a particular style, and to expect a certain consequence. But on this occasion she had a very particular worry, and eventually she could not help but say, 'What of Mr Falconer, Edward? What is to be done about him?'

'Mr Falconer? Do you mean Falconer?' he said, sharply. 'That fellow who has been spending so much time here recently? Why, what has he to say in the matter? My good woman, I hope you have not encouraged anything of *that* nature. Nothing can come of it. And besides, he must be getting on for forty.'

'Of course I haven't, husband. But it cannot have escaped your notice that Mr Falconer has been attentive to Barbara. And he is only thirty-four, my love, which is very different from forty! It would not be so very wonderful if she had become attracted to him. He is a vastly handsome young man, and very charming. The contrast between Mr Falconer and Reyne is unlikely to have escaped her notice. You must admit that Reyne rather let himself down on his wedding day.'

'That was merely unfortunate. Anybody can be taken ill. Besides, contrast or not, what has that to say to anything? A married woman cannot become fond of another man.'

'Tell that to Lady Hertford, my dear,' said Lady Cornford, drily, thinking of the Regent's mistress.

'My daughter is not such a woman as Lady Hertford. You may tell Falconer as much, before I do.'

'Who said she was?' said his wife, patiently. 'I merely tried to remind you that it is not unknown for married women to be attracted elsewhere. Mr Falconer has such manners, I am sure that, were I a girl again, I would like him, too. And remember, the marriage was never consummated.'

'And whose fault was that? Barbara might have been safely with child while he was away in the army had you not thought her too young. That would have given her something to think about, Edith. She wouldn't have had time for Falconer then.'

'It is not my fault that Reyne stayed away for eight years, Husband. I did not think it was unreasonable to stipulate that my child should be eighteen before the consummation.'

'And see where that has got us,' he said, irritably.

'Well, I always knew that you were ready to throw my child to any wolf that happened to be passing as long as it had a title. I was not going to let my little girl be frightened at sixteen!'

'I am not going to argue with you, Edith. Whether she likes Mr Falconer or the man in the moon, she already has a husband. You must remind her as much, and you must acquaint her of his homecoming, my dear, before luncheon if you please. I don't want him arriving at the gates and her still in the dark as to his whereabouts.'

Lady Cornford knew where her daughter would be at that time of day, and she walked the Long Gallery and upstairs to the schoolroom, where, on opening the door, a charming picture met her eyes. In amongst the shabby schoolroom furniture, Lady Reyne was seated at a small upright pianoforte: beside her, on the long stool, sat her brother Guy, a youth of twelve, (or twelve and three-quarters, as he was wont to describe himself!). The two were playing duets, and Barbara was singing. They had been practising *The Cambrian Lullaby*, newly translated from the Welsh, and it was so nearly ready to be heard, that it gave their mother a good deal of pleasure to listen to them.

Lady Cornford was very proud of her children, and wondered constantly how such a very commonplace couple as she and her husband had produced such a handsome-looking pair: in truth, she counted it in the light of God's recompense for taking from her, in infancy, her two other babies. Barbara she adored, but her son Guy was the apple of her eye, for he, too, had nearly died of whooping cough in his seventh year. From that moment, she had watched over him like a mother hen, hardly allowing the breeze to fan his face. Since she could not bear to be parted from him, she employed a tutor instead of allowing him to go away to school: he had only to catch the hint of a chill for his family to send at once for Mr Wytchett, their physician, and if he ever had the chance to play anything strenuous with other boys, such as a game of cricket or battledore, his mother was on tenterhooks until he was safely restored to her again. Indeed, she tried very much to keep him from such temptations by rarely inviting boys to Hurst Park at all, and refusing, whenever her husband would allow it, any invitations he received elsewhere. The result of this treatment was quite the opposite to what was intended: having never been allowed as much exercise as other boys, Guy was rather a slight lad, a fact which his mother deplored, yet used as her excuse to cosset him even more. Most boys would have chafed at such treatment, but Guy had a very gentle disposition, and patiently endured it. He was a very handsome boy too, having a fine-boned, sensitive face, and large brown eyes, which showed everything he was thinking. His mother was sure that he would break hearts one day.

His sister was already doing so. Lady Cornford had mentioned Mr Falconer to her husband, but she could quite easily have included virtually every young man in the neighbourhood on the list of Barbara's admirers. Just now, she was on the last verse of her song, and, since her voice was very sweet, Lady Cornford waited until she had quite finished before reminding Guy that Mr Marchbanks, his tutor, would be waiting for him. Then she sat next to Barbara on the stool he had just vacated.

'My love,' she said, as soon as Guy was out of earshot, 'your father has asked me to speak to you on a matter of some urgency. I won't prevaricate, Barbara. It is needful you know that your husband is back in England.'

Her daughter's stunned gaze went to her heart.

'My love, you must prepare yourself,' she said, pulling Barbara into her arms. 'It is in the *Gazette*. He is certain to come into Cheshire very soon.'

Lady Reyne, her face now devoid of colour, said in a hollow voice, 'Must I see him, Mama? You won't make me, will you?'

'My love, he is your husband,' said Lady Cornford. 'What else can I do? Can you not try to look upon it as a joyful occasion?'

'Joyful! How can you, Mama? I don't even know him. He hasn't even *written* to me! How can you expect me to feel *joyful*?'

'But the war, dearest. Think about that. The difficulties in writing in the midst of all those battles. How can we possibly know what he has had to endure?'

'We know very well what he has had to endure, Mama. Lady Thackeray's son was with the army for almost as long as Reyne, and she heard from him nearly every week.'

'But not all gentlemen are such good correspondents, my love. And really, Barbara, it is as well not to dwell on it, for what is past is past. Surely I do not have to remind you of your duty? You are the Countess of Reyne: nothing can change that now. And, indeed, I hardly know why you should wish to. It is such a great position as you were meant for. Nobody that I know of could grace it better than you will, once you are used to it. I know that I shall have no cause to be ashamed of my good girl.'

# Chapter Three

OUTWARDLY SUBMISSIVE, INSIDE, Barbara raged against the injustice of the world. All very well for her mother to say that she must receive Lord Reyne now that he had finally come home, but Barbara had had eight long years to consider every aspect of their marriage, and she had little enthusiasm left for it.

When her mother left her, anxious to report Barbara's compliance to her husband, their daughter went to her bedchamber, not daring to speak to anyone else until she had her feelings under control. That she should have been so summarily disposed of to a man who had so little interest in the arrangement that he stayed on the Continent long after all the other officers had come home, and who hadn't sent her a single letter while he was there! Why, he hadn't even written to her on the occasion of his father's demise, but had left it to her mother to explain to her that she was now a countess! It was six years since he had stopped writing even the stark little notes which were his part of their stilted correspondence; six years, from the time he went into the army, in which to regret ever allowing her parents to persuade her to take him. Dismissing Stowe, her maid, then throwing herself face down across the peacock silk coverlet, she leaned on her elbows, cupping her chin in her slender hands.

Thinking back, it seemed incredible now that, when she was sixteen and her father had first hinted at his marriage plans, she had even been mildly excited. She had been a very shy little thing then, and it had seemed only proper that her father, so much wiser than she, should choose a husband for her. That was before she had met Reyne – Viscount Searle as he had been then – and when she had only her father's description to colour her opinion. When he had described the viscount as 'a fine young man', her imagination had translated that to mean 'well-favoured'. By the time he was expected for the wedding, she had worked up his frugal description so that, in her mind, he was handsome, witty, fashionable: everything a young girl dreams of. Reality disabused her of any such hope: instead, she was introduced to a thin, slight, pale-faced young man, with little conversation, no wit, a great deal of embarrassment, and very much under his mother's thumb. What was much worse, he was hardly any taller than she was herself; his skin still had the blemishes of a boy, and he was a clumsy dancer. It was a humiliating disappointment, especially as she could tell that her friends had no very great opinion of him either. She wished the ground would swallow him up and could only be relieved that she hadn't to live with him until she was eighteen. When he had caught a chill in church, and his mother had whisked him back to London to consult her physician, she could only be thankful to be rid of such an encumbrance. And now he was back, having lived, she was sure, a horribly disproportionately charmed life! Her cheeks flamed hotly as a dreadful thought struck her. She'd grown quite a lot taller since she had last seen him: suppose he should actually be shorter than she was now. She couldn't bear it!

Barbara spent the afternoon thinking up several improbable schemes to save her from her fate, which included packing a portmanteau and running away to become a lady's maid; offering herself as a governess to anyone who would take her; or becoming an actress like Miss Kelly, who had become one of her idols after she had seen her act Ophelia at the Theatre Royal during her one brief visit to London. She even considered throwing herself on her father's mercy, a plan she was forced to reject, having just finished reading *Tom Jones*, and remembering still, how little such a ploy had served Miss Weston. All was lost! Her father was as bad as Squire Weston and had married her to a thin – *short* – weak, halfling, whom any one of her friends would have scorned, had they been so miserable as to have been offered him.

Her thoughts drifted gradually, and inexplicably, to Mr Robert Falconer, their near neighbour, and she sank into a wistful reverie. Surely there could be no greater contrast than between her husband and Mr Falconer. *He* wasn't short: when she wished to catch his eye, she had to look up a gratifyingly long way. He was, too, an excellent dancer – she had cause to know that because, at any assembly or ball they both attended, he always claimed her for the first two dances: and at the last Tarsall Assembly, he had taken her into supper and had then asked for the last two cotillions as well, which had scandalized all the chaperon's. For the past year, since he had taken the lease at nearby Garthwaite Manor, she had spent more time than was good for her in thinking about Mr Falconer. She had not yet decided whether or not she was in love with him, but he was fearfully handsome, and it was very pleasant to have him sighing over *her*, when most young women she knew were sighing over *him*. In this she had received ample encouragement, since very few days passed without Mr Falconer finding an excuse to call on Lady Reyne, though he knew that she was a married lady, and he rarely came without bringing some little trinket to amuse her. Neither was his skin blemished. Indeed, he was far past the age of such things, being in his thirties, which was the most gratifying circumstance of all. That Mr Falconer, handsome, mature and, some whispered, very experienced with ladies, should like *her*, seemed positively delicious. She continued, therefore, to think her father the wickedest parent in the world.

There was little sign of cruelty when she met him at dinner early in the evening, for Lord Cornford, a genial man so long as he was not thwarted, was in excellent spirits. She was his 'good girl'; he had known he could rely on his Barbara: he gleamed at her in gratitude.

But it was not enough that she was obeying him, he was determined that she should be brought to *like* the match as well. During dinner he became expansive, reminding her what a fortunate thing it was that he had proposed the marriage to his old friend, the late earl, for 'Mark my words,' said he, 'everybody would have been on the catch for his son now, had I not been sharp enough to secure him for you. He is one of the richest men in England, my love – not that that weighed with me, of course. Mark you, I should think the fathers of any number of young women will be champing on the bit to think that you have caught him, for they'd like the opportunities it would give them to join in with some of his projects! His estate manager is up to every rig and row in Town. Making money hand over fist, I hear. There'll be flutterings in all the dovecotes. You'll be much envied, my dear.'

His wife, wondering that so much of the merchant blood which had coursed through his family's veins a couple of centuries earlier still remained in him, despite their having long since given up all connection with trade, and noticing anxiously Barbara's unenthusiastic face, tried to catch Lord Cornford's eye and cool his ardour. But he was too taken up with visions of future opportunities to notice. He had a bright thought. 'You'll want to see the *Gazette*,' he said, smiling. 'I've brought it in to show you.'

Barbara reached across and took it. The piece about Lord Reyne was very prominent: it bore the information that *London rejoiced to see the handsome young Earl of R. safely returned to the bosom of his family*, adding coyly that there would be *celebrations, not only in B. Square, but at H. Park in Cheshire, as well.*

Handsome! thought Barbara, with a sigh. They obviously call every earl handsome. They forget that I have seen him. I shan't be taken in by that promise again!

Lord Cornford continued to gloat. 'I daresay we shan't have to be patient for more than a day or two before he waits on us, my dear,' he said, looking Barbara over, with undisguised benevolence. 'Indeed, did he but know how beautiful you have become in his absence, I doubt he'd still be in Town now.'

*

Lord Cornford's estates were situated a few miles south-east of the county town of Chester, its southernmost gates being only half a mile to the north of the large village of Tarsall, on the outskirts of which lived a respectable family by the name of Waverley, with whom Barbara's family was particularly intimate. So pleasant and genteel were they that Lord Cornford had long forgotten that their fortune had been made in trade, and he allowed his daughter to visit them as often as she pleased, which was fortunate since Barbara counted Miss Mary Waverley, the eldest daughter of that family, as her particular friend.

After an almost sleepless night, it was very necessary for Barbara to discuss her problems with Mary away from the other members of the family. On the pretext of returning a book, she called on them at their large rambling house, and persuaded Mary to walk with her into Tarsall.

As every best friend must, Miss Waverley, a pretty young woman of excellent principles and good sense, sympathized at once with every aspect of Barbara's plight. She already knew of Lord Reyne's return, for her father had seen the *Gazette*, and she was eager to know how Barbara felt about receiving him, for she had been the foremost recipient, for several years, of all her hopes and fears.

'It is so unfair,' Barbara grumbled, as they walked into the village along lanes thick with hawthorn blossom and billowing clouds of lacy cow parsley. 'With all those young men dying, I'd begun to feel almost optimistic.'

'Indeed, yes!' said Mary, her mouth turning up into an infectious grin. 'So thoughtless of him not to take a bullet on your behalf. I simply cannot think what he was about. They don't make gentlemen the way they used to, do they? I hope you mean to impress upon him how he has disappointed you, when next you meet.'

Barbara had the grace to laugh, for she shared her friend's sense of the ridiculous. 'Of course I didn't really want him to be killed,' she said, with a droll grimace, 'I just didn't want him to come back to *me*! I kept on hoping that he would meet somebody on his travels whom he wished to marry and that he might ask my father for an annulment. But if he couldn't have accommodated me in that fashion, and I had to choose between him being shot and me having to marry a man I don't like, I still think it would be a difficult choice to make. Any girl would find it so, I suspect.'

'Oh certainly,' said Mary, resuming her satirical smile, 'The number of girls who would wish to reject a peer of the realm, who also happens to be one of the wealthiest men in the kingdom, with a house in Berkeley Square, estates in Berkshire, Sussex, Northumberland and Ireland, and who undoubtedly has access to the best society in the land, must be prodigious. It must be miserable, indeed, to be married to such a man. If only you might be left on the shelf, like me, how much happier you would be!'

Barbara laughed. 'Goose! You aren't on the shelf! You are barely twenty-one. And you are so pretty that you are bound to get a husband before long. Indeed, it is incomprehensible to me that you haven't already been snapped up.'

It was hardly for Mary to point out that she probably owed much of her bad luck to being the best friend of Viscount Cornford's daughter, and being in her company whenever they were at a ball or an assembly, or whenever gentlemen were likely to be around. Men liked Mary, for her dark prettiness and her wit; but tall, elegant Lady Reyne they adored, for she was one of fortune's darlings. Certainly she was beautiful: her long heavy auburn hair falling almost to her waist; her eyes a brilliant green; her nose, small and straight; her full, expressive mouth, made for kissing. But these were but the trappings of her beauty, for Barbara had something more, that certain, indefinable *something*, which, for want of any better word, we call *charm*. It was an embarrassment of riches but she was, as well, lucky in her mother for, despite the fact that she, too, thought her daughter very lovely, she had the sense to bring her up to believe that appearance was of little importance and that a good-humoured disposition was far more to be admired by gentlemen of understanding than mere good looks. It did her no disservice in the eyes of others when an excessive compliment was met with incredulous laughter, and resulted in her being almost as popular with females as she was with gentlemen.

It wasn't altogether surprising, therefore, that Mary was inclined to be overlooked in the general admiration of Lady Reyne, though in any other company she must have been thought a very pretty and charming young woman. But Barbara wasn't Mary's only problem. 'You are forgetting one slight obstacle which stands in the way of my getting an eligible partner, aren't you love?' she said now. 'However generous Father is with regard to my dowry, in some people's eyes, it could never be enough. Blood counts!'

'I've never heard anything so ridiculous!' cried Barbara, indignantly. 'Any man would be fortunate to get you.'

'Of course it isn't ridiculous, Ba. You must have noticed how, when people find out that Papa was in trade, they cool towards me – some, at any rate – and they are very careful to keep their sons away from me. Oh, not you! Never you. Nor your family; though I think Lord Cornford might not welcome me so readily were Guy nearer to my age. But others certainly. And who can blame them? I should do just the same, no doubt, were I in their positions. We musn't have the best blood in the land polluted, must we?'

'Rubbish! You'd do no such thing,' cried Barbara, fanning her indignation. 'Nor would anyone with any sense. And, anyway, we have no right to feel superior to people in trade: our own ancestors were merchants.'

'But that was centuries ago, love. You have been a titled family for more than a century, so you cannot possibly put yourself in the same boat as me. Remember, I should never get invited to Almack's if I went to Town for the season, or be presented at Court, or, oh any number of things you take for granted. What gentleman wants that?'

'Since I have only ever been to London once, Mama and Papa disliking it so much, you might have my share and welcome if you would take my husband, too, with all his lands and houses. You cannot think how quickly I would present him to you were I to be able to get my freedom.'

'I suppose it is Mr Falconer. That is why you wish you were not married to Lord Reyne. But, surely, he is just such a case in point. Remember, Ba dear, if your family had been so recently in trade, like mine, Mr Falconer's mama would do anything to prevent him from marrying you, whatever your dowry.'

'And if he should obey any such dictate, I should not want him,' said Barbara, dismissively. 'Not that I think you are right,' she continued, reflecting carefully on what she knew of him. 'Mr Falconer is so mature that I am sure, were he to fall in love, he would be quite capable of handling his family.'

'Do you think so, indeed?' said Mary, wistfully. 'I wonder. Are any men capable of doing so.'

'Certainly, they are,' said Lady Barbara, failing to notice the faint blush which had spread across Mary's cheeks. 'Not that it makes much difference to me, of course. I have given my word to Papa that I will go through with it. And, even worse, to Mama! When she spoke to me of the great position I was born to, the deed was done. But I cannot help wishing that Reyne were better favoured. And he is such a weak little being, I shall be for ever having to quack him, I make no doubt, just as Mother does Guy.'

'Try to be a little more optimistic, Ba. Eight years is a considerable period, you know. He might very well have altered.'

'Would that you might be right, but I doubt I shall have such luck.'

'And then, you are so beautiful that he will very likely fall in love with you the first time you meet; then you may wrap him around your little finger – which, for sure, you would like.'

'But it is not the first time we shall meet, is it? We have already met, and I didn't take his fancy then, else he would not have raced back to Town as soon as he saw an opportunity.'

'But in those days you were quite different. You are far more beautiful now.'

'I was different, that's true. But Mary, even if he thinks me attractive, I could never like a man who admires a woman solely for her looks.'

'My dear Ba, for goodness sake, think what you are saying, I implore you!' said Mary, with one of her sudden rushes of humour. 'Surely, in admitting so much, you are cutting yourself off from almost every member of the male population!'

A hoot of laughter burst from Barbara's lips. 'You are very right! Oh Mary, what a sad lot they are,' she said ruefully. 'To have to be beholden to such creatures, it is very lowering. And can you imagine me as a wife, and trapped by one of them? I am sure I shall do it very ill, for I hate being ordered about, even by Papa. I shall have to begin at once to practise meekness, and being housewifely. If he is still sickly, I shall put in my order for a goodly supply of red flannel and get on with it. I shall ask his mama what sort she buys. Do you think he will expect me to carry *him* across the threshold?'

Mary giggled, glad that Barbara was now in better spirits. They had come by now to the edge of the village and, in the necessity of looking in at Woodcock's the draper to see what new patterns had come from London, at Scarfe's the bookshop to enquire whether a parcel of books ordered had yet arrived, and calling on one or two dependents, all intimate conversation had to be suspended. It was not until they were on the way home, that Mary said anxiously, 'And Lord Reyne, Ba, when does he come? How much time do you have?'

'Papa thinks he is bound to be here in two or three days at best,' replied Barbara, with a depressed look. 'Not that I am in any hurry, as you may suppose. Dear Mary, you will not let this marriage come between us? I shall need all your support in this if I am to be able to bear it.'

# Chapter Four

BUT REYNE DID not come to Hurst Park within two or three days, nor was a letter of excuse received from him to intimate when such was his intention. During that week, the only news the Cornfords had of him was from reports in the *Gazette* and other London newspapers which Lord Cornford had brought to him by post coach. But at least there were plenty of those! Every other paragraph seemed to include tales such as that which reported the *handsome young Earl R. and his friend Captain Radleigh* being entertained at the races *by the beautiful Lady C. and a crowd of ladies from the beau monde*, or the piece which had him *in the Green Park on a fine hunter, accompanied by the dashing Lady L. and some of her friends.*

He's certainly making his mark, thought Barbara, when, in another edition she read a particularly sycophantic account of *this indefatigable young man, who, in one day, managed to attend no less than eight events, including a balloon ascent, two breakfasts, a dinner, a visit to the opera and a ball*, and which ended, *One wonders how Napoleon managed to remain at large so long with such fine, energetic young men as this ranged against him.*

'One wonders, indeed,' snorted Barbara to herself, 'I'll bet his mama was close at hand to administer the laudanum when he went up in that balloon!'

But by now, far from being pleased to be spared his company, she began to be just a little cross. 'Good Lord!' she exclaimed bitterly to Miss Waverley, when she opened yet another newspaper, 'Have you seen this, Mary? Have they nothing better to do than report everything that absurd man does? Does he go out of his way to appear foolish?'

Miss Waverley took the newspaper and read the article at which Barbara's finger stabbed. *A wager by Lord R. on the probable outcome of a race between a pig and a goat.* Mary quickly read it through, and laughed. 'You are not surprised, love?' she asked. 'All young men make silly wagers. You are not to expect them to be grown up!'

'He is twenty-six, Mary,' said Barbara, in hollow tones. 'Most men have set up their nursery by then.'

'And most men still act as if they are in them, dearest! But you are not in a hurry for him to come?' asked Miss Waverley, anxiously watching as she strode furiously around the room.

'Nor do I want him to make me a laughing stock,' sighed Barbara, tearing the newspaper from Mary's hands and throwing it on the floor.

But worse was to come next day, and this time it was Lord Cornford's turn to explode. Until then, though a little disquieted by his son-in-law's non-appearance, he had preferred to make no comment about his prolonged sojourn in Town. As he had explained to his wife on many occasions, it took time to sell out of the army, and there were bound to be many affairs to occupy himself with concerning his estates, having been away so long, and being new to his position. But when Lord Cornford opened the *Gazette* at the breakfast-table and read the latest *on dit* concerning Reyne, he banged his fist on the table and his wife was afraid he would have a seizure.

'Well, my lady,' he shouted at her. 'I hope, when you read this, that you will be pleased you would not allow the consummation of your daughter's marriage at the proper time!' and he threw the newspaper across the table, where it landed on a silver chafing-dish full of buttered toast.

'Husband!' she cried, aghast at such a display in front of the servants.

His wife's reminder seemed only to infuriate Lord Cornford

even more and, jumping up from his chair, he waved his hand at his footmen, telling them brusquely to leave the room.

'Now read it,' he cried, once they had gone. 'No! On second thoughts, let *me* read it, just so that you may get the full flavour and see where your mamby-pambying of your child has led.'

Barbara went to leave the table. 'No!' shouted her father. 'You remain where you are, my girl. It will do you good to learn where coldness leads.'

'That is unjust, Edward,' said Lady Cornford calmly. 'Barbara has done nothing. If you wish me to hear the report you shall calm down first, else I shall take my daughter out of the room so that she shall not see this disgraceful exhibition. It is Reyne you should be annoyed with.'

'But we shall *lose* him, Edith,' cried her anguished husband. 'After all my efforts. And just when I wanted to interest him in becoming involved in a little venture of my own!'

'Read it, if you please, so that we may at least have an inkling of what's amiss,' she ordered.

'I hope you will be as calm when you hear it, Edith. This scoundrel in the *Gazette* has written, *Although the fashionable world has watched in amusement all the diverting pursuits and idiosyncrasies of the fascinating young Earl of R., this newspaper cannot help but imagine the feelings of a certain young countess, left to kick her heels at her father's house, instead of being asked to share in the general celebrations for her husband's safe return. Enjoyable as it may be for a young gentleman to be made so much of by some of the most beautiful ladies in Town, a word should be dropped in our hero's ear about the claims of duty above pleasure. Should he not already be in Cheshire?*

As Lord Cornford completed the final sentence, both ladies gasped in unison.

'How dare he! How *dare* he make me the butt of such an insult,' cried Barbara, rigid with anger. 'Every one of our neighbours will have seen this!'

'My dear, this cannot go on,' said Lady Cornford. 'You must make him come at once.'

'I won't receive him if he does,' cried Barbara.

'You will be lucky if you ever get the chance to do so,' said her father, continuing unconsciously, to split the wafer on a letter which had been brought in with the newspaper.

'So be it,' said Barbara, her eyes spitting green fire. 'I'm sure I don't care.'

Lord Cornford, who had meanwhile been allowing his eye to run swiftly down the letter in his grasp, looked, of a sudden, much more cheerful. 'My dear,' he said, his voice transformed. 'We have been precipitate. All is well. There is no need for any of us to be cross. Read this. It will make you feel so much better.'

He handed the letter to his daughter, obviously much happier. On her, it had a quite different effect. She read, with mounting anger,

*My Dear Cornford*

*Accept my compliments, if you please. I write to inform you that I am now arrived back in England and, having attended to some small matters of business in Town and satisfied a natural and important desire to visit my maternal and paternal relatives, it is now my wish to attend you at Hurst Park. This letter gives my intention to wait on you on Monday of next week. Trusting to your forbearance, I shall be attended by my friend, Captain Radleigh. I shall be travelling by curricle and assume that you will have stabling, too, for my hunters, which will follow.*

*I remain, etc.*

With every word she read, Barbara's chin went up. That he should write so coolly, in such a tone as if he conferred the greatest honour. Eight lines after six years! And not even to mention her name! Her head buzzed that such a wet rag of a man should dare to send that sort of peremptory message. Her father had begun to speak again, but she caught only the end of his words. Anxious not to show how furious she remained, she forced an answering smile when he said, with a beaming grin,

'It will be your day, Barbara, my love, but I think it might be much the best thing to have a quiet day on Monday, when he arrives. A neat little dinner, just for the family. Or, stay. We shall invite the Waverleys. Then, should the conversation become a little strained, they can fill the breach. That will be admirable. Waverley always has something to say for himself, and you will like Miss Waverley here to support you, I daresay?'

Lady Cornford held her breath, to see what Barbara would say, for she had not appreciated, quite as had her husband, the tone of Reyne's letter. To her surprise, she appeared all compliance. With deceptive meekness she agreed at once with her father's plan, and even thanked him for his thoughtfulness in allowing her to have Mary by her. But inside, indignation welled up.

So it is Reyne's intention to wait on me on Monday. His wife! thought she, a grim smile setting itself on her face. After he has visited all the *important* members of his family, naturally. And having undertaken all his small matters of business. His urgency is staggering. Arrogant, graceless, fleshless, *short*, little man! He will learn that I am no more eager to see him than he is to see me.

'Father,' she said sweetly, 'I think a small dinner on Monday will be just the thing, as you say, on top of Reyne's long ride from Town, but I should not like him to think that we consider his arrival merits *no* celebration.'

'My dear, you think just as you ought,' said her father anxiously. 'Perhaps, after all, we should invite more guests?'

'No, Father. I agree entirely with Monday's plan. But I do wonder if it would not be a good idea to arrange for a ball as well, in order to introduce him to our neighbours again after so long. Perhaps on the following evening, when he and his friend have had time to rest?'

Lord Cornford beamed. 'An excellent scheme, my love. You are always right. But it will be a good deal of work to get things arranged. The invitations will have to go out tomorrow if we are to have them returned in time.'

'Leave all to me, Father: invitations, everything. I promise you it will all be done as you would wish.'

Lord Cornford was delighted with his daughter: her mother, who hadn't liked the letter herself and remembered enough of a young woman's pride to know that it must have wounded Barbara, wondered what she was up to and feared the worst. Had she been able to read her mind, Lady Cornford would have been even more apprehensive.

Thinking he conferred a welcome treasure, the viscount gave Barbara her husband's letter to take away with her. Back in her bedchamber, as she read through the brief lines again, a mischievous, and most enchanting smile transformed her face. 'Certainly I must introduce Reyne to our neighbours,' she said to herself. 'Mr Falconer will be back from Tunbridge Wells by Monday. Reyne must meet *him*. And I shall have Josh Baggeley, Lord John Wynnon and some of the others. I wonder if Reyne is still such a wretched dancer?' she speculated, hugging herself. 'Mr Falconer dances so well, and even Josh Baggeley is better than my dear husband. We shall have cotillions and quadrilles and country dances and waltzes until they are coming out of his ears. I pray to God that he is still as clumsy as ever! And Mr Falconer always asks me for the cotillions, so my husband shall have the pleasure of seeing how well we dance together. That will give the *fascinating young earl* something to cut his teeth on!'

At the same time that Lord Cornford was raging against the article in the *Gazette* pitying his daughter for being neglected by her husband, it was seen in London by Captain Radleigh, who rushed off to find Lord Reyne, eating breakfast with his mother in the garden-room. Laying the *Gazette* on the table in front of him, Radleigh said drily, 'You'll be popular at Hurst Park, I shouldn't wonder. Have you seen this?'

When Reyne had read down the column, he closed his eyes, and rubbed at a crease which had appeared between them. 'Blast! Which busybody is responsible for that?' he groaned. 'They will think I am only going to Cheshire in response to this. They will never believe we had already made our plans to do so.

It is too bad! Things are awkward enough already, Indeed, they could hardly be worse.'

'Oh, if I know women and she has seen this, I think you'll find they could,' said Radleigh, with a fit of laughter.

# Chapter Five

'MY DEAR, I'VE been thinking,' said Lady Cornford to her daughter, as they were writing the last few invitation cards, 'you must have a new gown for the ball: perhaps you should have several new gowns? Your riding habit, too, is sadly shabby; and perhaps some new morning frocks? Mrs Fanshawe tells me that Madame Thiers recently brought back dozens of new patterns and fabrics from Town, all in the latest styles. Shall I send for her? She will surely have time to make something by Monday. You may have a complete wardrobe, if you wish it.'

Barbara stiffened. 'A second trousseau, Mama! What a novel idea. But I should have thought any of my gowns quite good enough for Reyne's visit.'

'As you wish, my dear; but reflect a little, for he has come recently from Paris, and every Frenchwoman is stylish. Remember, too, that if the *Gazette* is to be believed, he has been mixing with very *tonnish* women since his return.'

'While I am a dowd, I suppose?'

'Of course not. You always look charmingly, but a few new gowns cannot hurt. Don't look a gift horse in the mouth. It is not every day that your father can be brought to spend his money, but even he won't begrudge it in such a cause.'

Reminded of what she had read in the *Gazette*, Barbara could only agree, since making Reyne regret his decision to stay abroad so long had become something of an obsession. 'If it will make you happy, Mama, of course Madame Thiers shall make some gowns for me,' she said, kissing her cheek. 'Send for her by all means. Only we must get all these invitations sent before I have to spend hours being pinned in front of a glass, or we shan't have a ball at all. It wouldn't do if, by the time the invitations reached their destinations, everybody were already engaged elsewhere.'

'My dear, they would all break their engagements on an instant so as to meet Reyne. Knowing what servants are, you may be certain that news of the ball has spread by now. I expect everyone is already anxiously awaiting an invitation.'

Barbara finished writing to the final person on her mother's list, then shuffled through the cards, searching for a particular name. 'Mama, I do not see a card for Mr Falconer and his mother,' she observed. 'Have you written one?'

'My dear, didn't you say they were at Tunbridge Wells?' said Lady Cornford, blushing, very conscious that she was betraying herself. 'It seemed rather a waste of time.'

'Yet you sent one to the Lorimers, and they do not return from Town for a month. Mr Falconer is expected home at any moment. You did not mean to leave him off the list?'

'Of course not, my dear. I did not realize. Naturally, send a card,' said Mama, in failing tones, feeling a headache coming on, and wondering how she would explain herself to her husband.

'Good,' said Barbara, satisfied, 'for he is much the best dancer hereabouts, darling. If I am to start the ball with Reyne, as I know I must, the least we can do is to invite someone who knows the steps for all the other dances. If I remember correctly, Reyne will tread all over my slippers.'

'You don't know that, dear,' said Lady Cornford, anxiously. 'Give him a chance. He might yet surprise you. He could have changed out of all recognition by now. You have. Mr Falconer is charming, Barbara: I like him myself, but you will remember, won't you, that Reyne will not expect you to dance more than two dances with anyone other than himself? All is different now he is home. I give you a hint, no more than a hint, that your behaviour at the last Assembly in allowing Mr Falconer to have all these dances and to take you into supper, was thought rather fast by some of our friends. If your father had heard of it, I dread to think what he would have said!'

She saw Barbara's pout, and added, quickly, 'Not that I allowed anyone to say so to *me*. I told them that you are a married lady, not an unmarried girl, and that, anyway, since I was your chaperone, I was the best judge of what was proper.'

'Good for you, Mama,' cried Barbara, leaning across to kiss her mother's cheek again. 'Only you don't believe a word of it, do you, darling?'

'Oh, Ba,' said Lady Cornford, desperately hoping that Mr Falconer would be detained at Tunbridge Wells. 'I am so fearful that you mean to do something dreadful.'

The rest of the week saw Hurst Park thrown into a frenzy of preparations. Usually, Lord and Lady Cornford enjoyed a very quiet existence, and their servants were quite unused to arranging for very large gatherings. So long was it since they had held a large ball at the Park that the housekeeper and steward were quite put out at being expected to cater for such an event. Extra help was drafted in from the village, and the corridors rang with the sound of servants opening up state apartments; setting up chairs, card tables and corners for musicians in and around the ballroom; checking champagne supplies; denuding hothouses and flower borders: the list was endless. The servants even worked through Sunday, and by late evening the house shone like a new pin. The housekeeper and the steward began to be hopeful that all would go smoothly.

Lord and Lady Cornford, too, were hopeful since, for most of the week, Barbara had been steadily calm. She seemed to have accepted her fate and to be prepared to make the best of it.

There had been just one moment when this new peace looked like being shattered. On Sunday, when they returned from the morning service at Chester Cathedral, Barbara went into her bedchamber to fetch a handkerchief. Taking a few steps inside, she thought she must have come into the wrong room by mistake: her bedchamber now looked completely changed. Gone were her ornaments, her tambour frame, the dolls she had had as a child. Missing were her perfumes, her jewellery and dressing cases, her slippers and even her maid. In some confusion, she went off to seek Mama, only to be told that her things had now been moved into a new, and much larger bedchamber.

'Let me show you, my love,' said Lady Cornford, taking her into a room which led off from the Long Gallery. 'See, I have had Stowe move you in here. You have all your things, but this has always seemed a much pleasanter room: the view of the gardens is lovely.'

'But I like my *own* room, Mama,' said Barbara, very annoyed at having her things moved without anybody consulting her. 'I can hardly see the lake from here.'

'It is a pretty room, but I'm afraid it wouldn't do now, my love,' said Mama, choosing her words carefully, yet hardly able to refrain from blushing. 'This room has a dressing-room which leads into another bedchamber. When your husband arrives, it will be more suitable.'

As the implications of her mother's words became clear, Barbara paled, while colour continued to riot through her mother's cheeks. 'You are not suggesting that we . . . *share* the dressing-room? Mama!'

'My love, it is perfectly proper for you to do so, I assure you. Papa and I share a dressing-room.'

'But you're married!' she cried, holding her hands to her face.

Lady Cornford patted Barbara's cheek. 'So are you, darling,' she reminded her. 'It will not seem strange once you are used to it.'

It was a bitter shock. She had a wild desire to rush to her father and beg him to save her! But it wouldn't do, of course: he was on the side of the enemy. Pride came to her aid. She was married and must bear it. And if she had to suffer, she would do her best to see that Reyne had his share of it.

On the day of his arrival, Lord Cornford had calculated that

Lord Reyne and Captain Radleigh would be with them by late afternoon. In consequence, he and his family repaired, at five o'clock, to the blue salon, where a cold collation had been laid out on a large mahogany pedestal sideboard, ready for their guests.

It was then that Lord Cornford began to have doubts as to the wisdom of yielding to Barbara's wish for a ball. On reflection, he rather thought that Reyne would have preferred to spend his time in Cheshire amongst a simple family group, giving him time to reacquaint himself with his wife. He had a sudden flash of memory, seeing Reyne, as he had been eight years before: a pale, sickly young man, shy and lacking in social address. What if he hadn't altered? Might he not find the ball too much of an ordeal?

He walked across to where his wife was sitting with her daughter on a Grecian sofa of carved mahogany. 'My dear, this ball, I'm sure it's a bad idea. I don't know why I didn't realize before. He was such a timid young man: it is improbable that he will have changed to any large extent. Suppose the journey makes him ill again? The last thing he will expect will be a ball. And I'm not sure he will want any other guests this evening. I think I shall have a hot brick put in his bed in case he should wish to retire, shall I?'

'I wouldn't be at all surprised were he to be ill when he arrives,' said Barbara bitterly, looking up from her piece of eimbroidery. 'I hope you have asked for an extra room to be prepared, for he will almost certainly bring his physician with him as well as his friend.'

Just then Guy, who had been looking out, down the long path towards the south gates for the first sign of his brother-in-law, turned to his family and said, with an ironic smile, 'I don't think he will want a hot brick, Ba. Come and look from the window.'

Barbara refused to oblige him, remaining seated, but the viscount and his wife went across and peered out. In the distance, racing hell for leather up the Long Ride in a cloud of dust, they could see a sporting curricle, drawn by four handsome greys, and carrying two men: one in military uniform, hanging on to the side of the rolled-down hood, like grim Death, the other in a caped greatcoat, standing up to drive, cracking his whip over the head of his leader.

Lord Cornford called in delight, 'Well, I'll be . . . Barbara, do come and see. He looks like a charioteer!' But Barbara remained very intent on her embroidery.

As the curricle swept round the circular path, and the horses were brought to a standstill, loud sounds of laughter rang out.

They heard the carriage led away, heard the outside doors being opened by footmen and waited for Bragg, their butler, to announce her husband. She had a brief moment of terror before they entered, then mentally shook herself. She wasn't the milk-and-water miss she had once been. She could surely deal with a halfling like Reyne.

She heard Bragg announce, 'The Earl of Reyne,' closely followed by 'Captain Radleigh'. Looking up she saw, standing by the door, two tall gentlemen, one in military costume, and the other in a well-fitting coat of blue superfine, dove-coloured pantaloons and a pair of gleaming Hessians. No trace of nerves seemed to assail either of them: they came in with the ease of those who were at home wherever they might find themselves. Barbara took one look at them, and then looked back at the door, expecting her husband to follow them in. Neither of these gentleman could be her husband, surely? Each was a picture of health. But nobody else entered. She looked back at the two gentlemen again, and stared hard, Even so, it was several moments before she recognized Lord Reyne, so altered was he.

She was not the only one who was surprised, but her father recovered more quickly.

'My dear boy,' said Lord Cornford, shaking hands, first with his son-in-law, then with Captain Radleigh. 'Let me welcome you back to Cheshire. I should say, welcome *home*.'

Lady Cornford, too, shook hands, saying pleasantly, 'And here is Barbara, Marcus. You will wish to introduce her to Captain Radleigh.'

Taking her cue, Barbara laid down her embroidery and stood impassively as her husband, a very different husband than she remembered, walked towards her. He was quite as shocked as she was: he remembered a little girl, pretty enough, but nothing had prepared him for the lovely woman who stood before him. His eyes flicked to Captain Radleigh, who watched the scene with undisguised amusement, then they turned back to Barbara appreciatively.

She felt him surveying her from head to toe and blushed, furious at having done so. Quite easily, he took her hand, and in a voice which showed that he, at least, was not disappointed, said warmly, if not quite truthfully, 'Lady Reyne, what a long time it is since we met. I've missed you.'

Barbara looked up at him and said coolly, without a touch of expression, 'Indeed, My Lord, you must have, I am sure. What a pity, then, that you have been obliged to spend these weeks in Town. We read all about you. You had so many *important* things to do, didn't you? Naturally, you could not come before.'

*Sotto voce* so that only Reyne could hear him, Captain Radleigh murmured, 'Brrr. Has someone left a window open in here? I could swear I felt a draught.'

# Chapter Six

'I'M GLAD YOU told me she was a poor little dab of a thing, Marcus,' hissed Captain Radleigh, as they followed Lord Cornford up the Great Staircase to the rooms off the Long Gallery, which had been prepared for them. 'I didn't know they looked like *that*. Perhaps if I ask nicely enough, my father will get one for me!'

Lord Reyne mouthed at him to be quiet, praying he would keep his unfortunate sense of humour damped down until they were alone. The two young men had adjacent bedchambers: Lord Cornford left Captain Radleigh at the door of one room, showing Reyne into the next, and the captain waited until he heard their host go back downstairs, before joining Reyne next door, without so much as a 'by your leave'.

The room he entered was a fine, large apartment containing an alabaster chimneypiece and over-mantle, a large four-poster bed, a Neo-Classical wardrobe, a mahogany serpentine chest of drawers, a pair of mahogany tables and several smaller pieces of furniture. Blue silk wall-coverings lined the walls, which were liberally sprinkled with paintings by Van Dyck and other masters. In the background, Reyne's manservant was unobtrusively unpacking his master's trunk, and Reyne himself was looking out of the mullioned windows at the pleasant garden below. He swung round as he heard the door open.

'You could try knocking, George,' he protested, as Captain Radleigh barged in.

'Sorry old fellow,' he apologized. 'Got out of the habit while we were over there. We so rarely had a door.' He looked around him. 'I say, Marcus, they've done you proud here. Mine's much less grand. All this comes from being the fatted calf.'

He flung himself down on the bed. 'Much softer than mine.' Then he sprang up again, looking all around him, curiously. Seeing a door in the corner of the room, he went over at once. 'What's in here?' he said, turning the knob. 'Hm. Dressing-room.' He noticed that there was another door on the opposite side of the dressing-room. 'I say, Marcus, is that where *she* is?' he said, in a loud stage whisper. 'Do you share this?'

'Ssh,' said Marcus, fearful of being overheard. 'She might be in there!' he hissed.

It was too much for Radleigh: he fell about laughing, and had to be manhandled out by the earl, to the obvious disapproval of his valet, who was trying to pretend he wasn't there.

'I can see that you're going to be a great help,' said Marcus.

'You didn't say anything about helping,' said Radleigh, portentously. 'I'm here to observe. Besides, what help do you need? Seems to me that everything's been thought of. Your bedroom: dressing-room: her bedroom.'

'You build an attractive picture, George, but, whilst I have no wish to cast a fly into your ointment, would you say that my wife welcomes my attentions with all the enthusiasm we'd hoped for?'

'Ah, the lovely Barbara, do you mean? Well, you can't have everything, old fellow,' he said, with a huge grin. 'How many words has she spoken since we arrived? Ten? But look on the bright side. You won't need an icehouse now you are married. Just draw a trough full of cold water and get Barbara to speak to it.'

'I'm glad you're amused, George,' said Lord Reyne, stiffly. 'You can afford to be: she's not your wife.'

'And it's a source of considerable regret, as you might imagine,' said Captain Radleigh, convulsed with laughter.

'Don't, George. It isn't funny. I tell you what: we'll stay here for a few days, long enough for me to do my duty by the girl, and then its hotfoot back to Town as fast as the horses will take us. It won't be so bad. It's fashionable for couples to live separate lives, nowadays. Some of those women in Town hardly ever see their spouses. And I certainly can't stand much of dear Barbara. I need somebody a little more encouraging.'

'Pity, though,' reflected the Captain, pensively. 'Such an exquisite creature. Those eyes; that hair! It seems a terrible waste.'

'Indeed, yes. You've no idea how she's changed. When I first saw her I thought my luck was in. She soon disabused me of that hope.'

'Pretty decent of the old chap to hold a ball for you, though,' said Radleigh. 'I was afraid we were going to be holed up with only the family. That would have been bad.'

'I like them, though, don't you? The mother's charming, and the boy's a pleasant young lad, too.'

'*They're* all right, it's Barbara who scares the hell out of me.'

'Cornford said he's holding the ball so that his neighbours can get a good look at me – his words, not mine.'

'Well, that's a big disappointment for them,' said Radleigh, his ready grin appearing again as Reyne threw a pillow at him.

With Reyne and the captain upstairs out of the way, and Barbara having gone to dress for dinner, Lord and Lady Cornford took the opportunity to discuss how things were progressing.

'My goodness, Edward,' said Lady Cornford, at once. 'I could hardly recognize Reyne. What a delightful young man he has become.'

'He certainly has,' said her husband, glowing. 'I think Barbara must be pleased with him, don't you? Who would have thought he would have grown so tall and so manly? Yes, I think we may congratulate ourselves on everything going so well, don't you?'

'Going so well! My dear, you're blind. Did you not notice that she hardly spoke two words to him?'

'It is rather a delicate situation, Edith. I daresay she is shy.'

'She has never been shy. Well, not for years, anyway. If you ask me, she is still smarting from that account in the *Gazette*. I do hope she is going to behave.'

'What do you mean, *behave*? My dear, you said she understood her duty and was ready to do it!'

'Before you showed her the *Gazette*, she was. Not the wisest thing you've ever done.'

'So, he remained in Town a little longer than he *should*,' said Lord Cornford, reasonably. 'He's here now. And he is such a handsome fellow. I thought she would be delighted with him, and willing to forget any fancied slight. I am sure I should be.'

'A pity you cannot marry him then, my love.'

'I mean, if I was a young girl! Please, Edith, this is serious. He is a fine strapping lad: perfect bloodstock. I own that I was not always quite happy at betrothing Barbara to him when he was such a sickly fellow – one thinks, naturally, of the succession – but now, why he's a picture of health. What reason have you to think Barbara dissatisfied?'

'I did *mean* to mention it to you, Edward,' said his spouse, in failing tones. 'When we were sending out the invitations, Barbara insisted on sending one to Mr Falconer. That makes me just a little apprehensive.'

'Falconer!'

'I don't, for one moment, expect him to come, my dear, else naturally, I should not have permitted it. But they have been in Tunbridge Wells these past few weeks, and nobody expects them back for another week and more, so I thought there could be no harm in it. Certainly . . . *almost certainly*, they won't be back. I just mention it on the off chance, the very *slender* off chance, that they are.'

'But this is extraordinary, Edith. Barbara had no right to concern herself with Mr Falconer. My dear, I hope she really does know what's expected of her. You have had a proper talk to her?'

'I certainly tried to, Edward, but she was so embarrassed, and I was so embarrassed, that, well, we sort of . . . gave it up. But she did assure me that she knew her duty.'

'We must hope she knows her duty better than you appear to know yours, Edith,' said her husband, frostily.

Barbara, meanwhile, in her room on the other side of Lord Reyne's dressing-room, was being fitted by Stowe, her maid, into one of Madame Thiers's modish new gowns: an exquisite creation of white muslin over jonquil silk; cut very low; short at the waist and delicately trimmed at the hem with embroidered primroses and seed pearls. As Stowe finished fixing the clasp of the row of fine pearls, which completed Barbara's toilette, she sighed with the air of a job well done.

Barbara sighed too, but it had nothing to do with her appearance, for she had found the afternoon to be very much of a trial. It did not come easily to her to be cool towards guests, and she was aware that, not only were her parents watching her anxiously, but that, several times, when she had answered Reyne shortly, Guy had been puzzled that she, who was normally a byword for good-humour, should disgrace herself. But if the afternoon had been unpleasant, she approached the coming evening with mounting dread. She shivered as she recalled the talk she had had with Mama, and looked apprehensively towards the door, which led to her dressing-room. She had heard distinct signs of occupation while she had been dressing for dinner, and could only be pleased that she had earlier had the forethought to order Stowe to bring all that she would need into her bedchamber so that she would not be obliged to invade their mutual territory. Stowe had had the slipper bath brought in and filled at her request, but all the time she was bathing, she lived in dread of the communal door opening. So fixed was her mind still, on such a fearful contingency, that, when a light tapping was heard to sound, it took a few moments for her to realize that the noise came, not from the dressing-room, but from the door leading from the Long Gallery. Her hands flew to her bosom, her heart hammering wildly. In an unsteady voice, she told Stowe to see who wished to enter, holding her breath in case it should be her husband. When her maid opened the door and only Miss

Waverley stood there, Barbara's breath came out in a rush and she sank, shaking, on to a nearby chaise.

'Thank heavens it is you,' she cried, with relief. 'Come in quickly and close the door before anybody else comes past.'

'You did not mind my coming early, Ba?' said Mary, anxiously. 'I couldn't stay away any longer. Oh my dear, I was at my window earlier and I saw Lord Reyne riding past on the turnpike with his friend – at least, was it Lord Reyne? It wasn't anyone from these parts: the curricle was so smart, and I was sure it had a crest. When it came into view I was certain it must be them, but then I saw the two gentlemen and I wasn't sure. Neither of them looked as you described your husband. The one in uniform certainly didn't look small and sickly from where I was. In fact, he looked as if he must be rather tall, though it is difficult to tell, sitting down. And the other one was actually driving the curricle *standing up*! The most dashing thing I've ever seen! He was definitely tall. And very well made, and good-looking. Well, they were both good-looking. My dear, it was fearfully exciting. They passed Mr Colebatch's gig with only inches to spare: they didn't even slow down. Was it Lord Reyne and his friend? Ba, you said he had a delicate constitution: those gentlemen—'

'Are not delicate! You are very right, Mary. I was never more shocked in my life.'

'Which was your husband? The military gentleman, or the other?'

'Reyne has sold out of the army, apparently: the one in regimentals is Captain Radleigh.'

'They are both vastly handsome, dearest. Neither seemed sickly to me, which must be a relief to you. After what you told me, I had pictured Lord Reyne wrapped in a large flannel waistcoat and cravat. To see him springing his horses so recklessly. . . !'

'Ssh,' warned Barbara, looking anxiously towards the dressing-room as Mary's voice became louder.

'Why? What?' said Mary, opening her eyes in a question.

'We share that dressing-room,' mouthed Barbara, keeping her voice to hardly a whisper. 'He might hear us.'

'You *share it*! But why? Why could you not have stayed in your own bedchamber? You have a perfectly good dressing-room there.'

'Mama said we must share a suite of rooms as we are married. His bedchamber leads off from the other door. It is the most embarrassing thing in the world. *I'm* not using it. I had Stowe bring my bath and my dressing things in here.'

'I should *think* so! Oh, Barbara. Intolerable! Haven't you a key to lock the door?'

'Mama says I may not as Reyne is my husband.'

'But do you like him, dearest?'

'Would you like a man who has made you a laughing stock? On his arrival he came into the house without a care, as if it was the most commonplace thing in the world to have married someone and then to stay away for eight years, six of them without making any contact whatsoever! I swear he hasn't a nerve in his body. He was perfectly at ease. He had the temerity to say that he had missed me! He actually flirted with me! I suppose he thought I would forget that he has left me here alone for so long if he paid me a few compliments. I daresay he expected me to be eating out of his hand by now. Well, I am not.'

'But Ba, do you not think that it may be as I said and he may have been attracted to you at once, and that is why he flirted with you? You are so very beautiful: men fall in love with you all the time.'

'Don't be silly, Mary, of course they don't. Men only say such things because they like to be thought romantic. They always have to be making a fuss about someone: it means nothing. Besides, Reyne had altogether too much presence of mind for me to think he was really attracted to me. More like, he wanted me to be in love with *him*, and that I vow will never happen. I shall soon show him that it takes more than a few compliments to attract *me*.'

'What will you do?'

'I intend to make him realize that he is by no means the only fish in the sea,' she said, firmly. 'Do you know whether Mr Falconer has come home yet? It would be so provoking should he arrive too late for the ball. I mean to give him as many dances as he asks for, whatever Mama says. And I hope some of the others are there too. Lord John Wynnon would help greatly, in putting Reyne's nose out of joint.'

'And the cat among the pigeons, if you are not careful,' said Mary. 'You will take care that Mr Falconer does not upset Reyne too much by his attentions, won't you?' A look of anxiety spread across her face. 'I should think that, after all those years on the Peninsula, Lord Reyne must be an expert with swords and pistols. You would not wish Mr Falconer to come to any harm?'

'Of course not, silly. I only want Reyne to go away again for another eight years. I also want him to feel as foolish as his behaviour has made me look. My love, you must stay very close to me this evening. I do not mean to give him any more opportunities to flirt with me. It probably works very well with ladies in Town: I am determined that he won't get his way with me.'

# Chapter Seven

When lady Reyne and Miss Waverley went down to the drawing-room, the rest of the household was already clustered around the fireplace, waiting for Mary's parents to arrive. Barbara's eyes were drawn irresistibly to her husband, who had dispensed with his travelling clothes and looked very handsome in a plain, well-fitting, rather military-styled black coat and knee breeches. His shirt points were elegantly starched; his neck cloth was tied in an intricate fashion of his own, his hair arranged à la Brutus, a style made fashionable by Mr Brummell.

She would not give him the satisfaction of seeing her notice him, however, and did not allow her glance to rest on him for more than a brief moment, then passed on to Captain Radleigh, who, looking very much at home and rather rakish in his dress uniform, was standing making Lady Cornford, with whom he was already on excellent terms, laugh at his ridiculous jokes. He broke off his conversation with her in mid sentence on seeing the ladies, and gave them instant gratification by staring with undisguised admiration, before offering each an arm and drawing them over to join the others.

And now it begins, thought Barbara, fighting panic, as she moved towards the fireplace.

'My dear,' said her father, obviously in an expansive mood, 'How well you look. Doesn't she, Marcus my boy.'

'She does, sir,' returned Reyne warmly, saying no more than

he felt. When he had arrived at Hurst Park, Barbara had been dressed in a modest, sprig muslin frock, and she had looked lovely, even then. Now, in the charming, *décolleté*, jonquil gown, which accentuated her creamy skin and the auburn glints in her hair, she was quite dazzling.

'And Mary, my dear, you look quite delightful,' added the earl, conscientiously, for he was very nice in matters of etiquette. 'I think, you know, that you grow prettier every time I see you.'

By the time Mary had thanked him for her part in the compliments, and Captain Radleigh and Lord Reyne had echoed his sentiments, the noise of a carriage was sounding, and in only a few minutes, Mary's parents were ushered in.

Their host went to greet his old friends, pumping Mr Waverley's shoulder, and paying his wife the old-fashioned courtesy of kissing her hand. He wasted no time before introducing them to his son-in-law, sure they would approve of each other. They were a very sociable couple, very much at ease in company, and it was a comfortable gathering, with no uneasy silences, which filed into dinner, half an hour later.

Naturally, Lord Reyne escorted his wife and, as they walked through the wide doorway, he took the opportunity of murmuring to her, 'I wish you will let me say again, how remarkably well you look this evening, Lady Reyne. It is very strange, but I didn't remember you as being so beautiful.'

'Didn't you? Surely it is not altogether surprising that you had forgotten what I looked like, My Lord,' she returned, sweetly. 'Or do you pride yourself particularly on your memory? I should have thought that most memories blur after eight years.'

'Yes, eight years is certainly a period. I begin to regret having stayed away so long.'

'But you are back now. And fully in time to spend a year or two with me before my looks finally fade entirely,' she said, with heavy irony, sweeping before him into the body of the room. Lord Reyne felt his collar and followed her in.

Lord Cornford had intended to dine, that evening, in the elegant banqueting hall, which formed part of his state apartments, but his wife had vetoed his suggestion, thinking that a more intimate atmosphere would answer better than ostentatious display. Instead, they were to dine in the family dining-room, rather a small, dark, panelled room, made homely by the presence of a huge fireplace and a vast collection of family treasures and favourite portraits. Although it was now well into June, the day had been unseasonably cool, and the chill which evening brought with it, had encouraged Lady Cornford to order that a fire be lit. She had arranged for as neat a dinner as Reyne was likely to find anywhere; their wine cellar was second to none; the room glowed in mellow candlelight, and her daughter was probably one of the loveliest young women Lord Reyne had ever seen. Lady Cornford had great faith in the power of good hospitality, and where it could lead. In her view, a convivial gathering of excellent conversation, handsome company and relaxed surroundings was the best hothouse for any romance. Surely here the poor start her daughter and Reyne had made might be speedily forgotten? And it was increasingly urgent that the two be brought into greater harmony, since tonight, to all intents and purposes, was their wedding night.

At dinner, Barbara found herself seated next to her husband and determined to say as little to him as possible within the bounds of politeness. From their respective places at the head and foot of the table, her parents watched anxiously as the company worked its way through two full, and very fine courses, which included a white soup, a boiled salmon in a shrimp sauce, a saddle of mutton, a ragout of beef, a couple of chickens, a rice pudding, some roasted sweetbreads, some jellies, a dish of eggs, some frilled oysters, and a host of tempting side dishes. They could not flatter themselves that the couple were getting on, a circumstance for which their daughter seemed entirely to blame. Time after time they heard Reyne trying to instigate some topic or other of conversation: just as often though, their daughter answered politely, but with little more than a monosyllable. When the gentlemen, including Guy, who was at his first grown-up dinner, were finally left to their port,

Lady Cornford could not wait to get her daughter to one side.

'Barbara!' she hissed, while Mary and Mrs Waverley were settling themselves into chairs by the fireside and adjusting some small, delicately painted screens to protect their faces from the heat. 'My dear, you are being impolite to your husband. Do you wish to create a scandal?'

'I don't know what you mean, Mama. I am sure I am always polite to any of our guests,' she said, turning away.

'So you are, my love,' said her mother, touching her arm, 'which is why I find your behaviour to your husband so distressing. My dear, if you will take advice from your mama, and, incidentally, one who has been married for more years than she cares to remember, you would do as well to humour Reyne. Husbands are always more malleable when they are entertained: as they are when they are treated with a little respect.'

'As is everyone, Mama, as I should be the first to know,' said Barbara, bitterly, moving over towards the piano.

'My dear, you must not keep looking back. Your duty now is very clear, When Reyne comes from the dining-room, I shall expect you to be more congenial.'

Mary, who had caught the tail end of this exchange, sent Barbara a sympathetic smile, and would have gone over to offer what comfort she could, had she not received a silent negative from her mother.

Much to Lady Cornford's delight, the gentlemen lingered but a short while over their port, during which time Reyne and the Captain had been asked by the others to relate their part in some of the battles in which they had been engaged. So colourful and well drawn were their accounts, not only of battles, but of their time in between, that Lord Cornford had decided that, if Barbara could only hear them too, even she might be inclined to view Reyne more favourably. At the earliest possible moment, therefore, he had persuaded them back into the drawing-room, where the ladies were waiting.

Nobody wanted music that evening, and the two young gentlemen needed very little encouragement to continue where they had left off. In describing their adventures, they both became very animated. Lord Reyne, in particular, had an engaging way of conjuring up, in a very few words, accurate representations both of hardships and delights. In spite of every wish to the contrary, Barbara found herself listening, spellbound. Without realizing it, she moved from the piano to a nearby stool, so as to hear him better. Whilst he was entertaining the company, Reyne could not help but notice the effect he was having on his wife, and being eager to improve matters between them, it rather went to his head, spurring him on to enliven his narrative even more.

Without wishing to make excuses for him, it must be remembered that, after their long, tiring journey, Lord Reyne had had a particularly good dinner and a deal of excellent wine, and he was now in a glow of good humour. When he reflected on it the next day, it was his only explanation for not being careful enough to curb his tongue. But curb it he had not. In his enthusiasm that night, he had no idea how many times his tales of adventures included the mention of the ladies he had met during his travels. Captain Radleigh did notice, and began to feel a trifle hot under the collar on his behalf. He saw, too, that, though the rest of the company was still highly amused, Lady Reyne was far less so. In vain did he try to catch Marcus's eye to warn him, but Marcus was fully launched and not to be brought back into port, completely impervious to his signs and grimaces. By the time the Waverleys were getting into their carriage and the rest of the party were ready to separate for the night, he had managed to give his wife the impression that he had spent the whole of his time on the Peninsula in chasing foreign young ladies. Barbara's head throbbed with indignation that he should actually boast of it.

Confident that he had helped his cause, and that his wife was learning to look on him more kindly, Lord Reyne made sure that it was he who stood at the foot of the stairs to hand Barbara her bedtime candle, for he was eager not to omit any of the attentions which, in his experience, ladies enjoyed so much. Putting the silver candlestick into her hand, he gave her a meaning look, extremely glad now that he had come into Cheshire. So elevated was his mood that he failed to notice the scornful look she returned, or her lack of enthusiasm.

Now that the evening was coming to a close, Lady Cornford and her husband were in a bit of a quandary in knowing how things should be arranged. Had it actually been their daughter's wedding night, it would have been rather a simple matter. On such occasions, one's daughter left with her husband immediately after the wedding feast, to spend the initial honeymoon period elsewhere, usually at a house, or a lodge, loaned by friends. None of that could happen here. Nonetheless, though their daughter had been a married woman for eight years, this evening was as much her wedding night as that first night should have been, and they were uncertain how the occasion should be treated. In years past, the household would simply have been collected together to put the young couple to bed. Things being now less savage, that would not do. In fact, if the thing could be achieved without anyone else being much aware of it, Lady Cornford would be very well pleased.

Knowing how anxious Barbara would be, her mother was determined to give her ample time to compose herself upstairs before her bridegroom attended her. She called her husband to one side and whispered to him that she wished him to ask Lord Reyne and Captain Radleigh to join him for a late game of billiards. Startled, he protested that surely Reyne would be eager to join his bride?

She squeezed his forearm. 'My dear,' she whispered, 'let us give our daughter an opportunity to change into her nightgown in peace. I well remember what wedding nerves are like.'

Marcus was a little taken aback when his father-in-law suggested billiards at that particular moment. Much as he liked him, he was eager now, to go up to his bride, for he flattered himself that he had made considerable headway with her. But he had no wish to alienate his father-in-law, and he dragged Captain Radleigh after them to keep score. After one game, Lord

Cornford considered he had done his duty by his daughter and declared himself ready for bed, recommending the young gentlemen to follow his example.

Marcus was by no means loath to do so, but Captain Radleigh pulled him back, letting Lord Cornford go up without them. As soon as he had gone from the billiard room, Radleigh said, tersely, 'What do you think you were playing at this evening, Marcus? Have you got a death wish or something?'

'What do you mean? What have I done?' said Reyne, completely in the dark.

'What have you done? Didn't you notice me trying to catch your eye? I was trying to prevent you from getting any deeper into hot water than you had already plunged. Don't you realize how many different women you mentioned tonight? Señora Cuesta: the contessa: have you no notion of tact? You have returned to your wife after having been away for years – an insult in itself – and all you can do is draw attention to the number of women you have had dealings with in the interim. I suppose there must be some women who would not be resentful, just as we are told there are saints on earth, but I've never yet met one. And now, I suppose, you will expect her to welcome you to her bed!'

# Chapter Eight

LADY CORNFORD FOLLOWED Barbara upstairs, catching up with her in the Long Gallery.

'Barbara, dear,' she said, anxiously, 'I wanted to make certain that you were all right. You were so quiet downstairs.'

'I'm perfectly well, Mama. Why should I not be?'

'No reason in the world,' said her mother, glad that she was calm. 'I should have known that my sensible girl would not fail her family by being *missish*. And you have plenty of time to prepare yourself. I have told Papa to keep him downstairs. They are in the billiard-room, so it will be half an hour or more before he comes to you.'

'Comes to me? Who? Mama! You cannot mean. . . .' Her words petered out, her eyes stricken.

'But darling, we spoke of it the other day when your things were moved. You must have realized that you would share a . . . room?'

'Well I didn't,' said Barbara, baldly. 'Not so soon. You said nothing about sharing my bedchamber. You only said that we would share the dressing-room. And, heaven knows, that's bad enough! I had Stowe move all my dressing things into my bedchamber rather than use it. And even then I was on tenter-hooks for fear he might come in. Why, I've hardly spoken to him. Are you sure he will expect. . . ? No, I cannot think he will. Won't he want to get to know me first?'

'It's possible, I suppose. But men are very odd creatures. My understanding of them leads me to think that you ought not to rely on it. Besides, darling, he's really very nice. And awfully handsome. I am sure he will be kind. Come now, you must go in. Your poor old mama won't get a wink of sleep tonight in worrying about you.'

Squeezing her tightly, Lady Cornford turned Barbara towards her bedroom door and gave her a final little pat to send her on her way.

As soon as she went into her bedchamber, it was obvious that everything had been explained to Stowe. An air of concern hung about her like a pall, and she greeted her mistress breathlessly.

'Oh, My Lady,' she said at once, her eyes as round as saucers, 'only look at the beautiful nightgown your mama has left for you.'

She drew her over to the four-poster, where lay a nightgown of the finest cambric, trimmed with exquisite point lace. There was no denying that it was a beautiful garment, but when Stowe helped her out of her evening gown and into the nightgown, she could not help thinking of herself as a lamb being prepared for someone else's feast.

It was Barbara's custom to read a chapter or two of her book before going to sleep, but on that occasion she didn't allow herself that luxury. Instead, she draped her shawl over the back of her bedside chair and snuffed out her candle, for surely, if she could but get to sleep before he came up, or even if he thought she was asleep, Reyne would not disturb her? Snuggling down among the crisp, lavender-scented sheets, she was certain that sleep would not come easily. It was something of a shock, therefore, to find that, not only did she fall asleep, but that she suddenly found herself being woken out of it again by an insistent voice.

'Who is it?' she called drowsily, staring over at the figure, holding a lighted candle, which stood in the doorway, and not immediately recalling her circumstances.

'It's me. Reyne. Who else should it be?'

His voice jerked her into wakefulness. 'What are you doing here?' she hissed, anxious that nobody else should hear them.

It was so obvious what he was doing there that Reyne didn't

quite know how to answer. For a terrible moment, he wondered if he had made a *faux pas* and the family didn't expect him to claim his bride so soon. He had assumed, having been given an adjoining room, that they and she would expect him to join Barbara that night. Were they, in fact, expecting him to wait? And, if so, for how long?

'I . . . I thought you *expected* me,' he said lamely, seeing her pull her cashmere shawl from the bedside chair and wrap it closely around her shoulders.

And, of course, that was exactly what she had expected! But she had heard the doubt in his voice, and she wondered if she could exploit it. It was all very well for Mama to say it was her duty, but actually to have a gentleman in her bedchamber, and that gentleman a virtual stranger, was so shocking to her that she determined to get rid of him if she could, at least for tonight. She decided on attack rather than defence.

'Are you saying, sir, that after all that I have discovered about you this evening, you expect to come into my . . . room,' she said, freezing him by her tone.

'*What* have you discovered?' he asked, dismayed at such an unexpected turn of events.

'I have learned why you took so long to come back to England, sir,' she said, with no lessening of frost. 'And from your own mouth. All those women . . . I can hardly call them ladies . . . I was never more shocked. No wonder you didn't find time to write to me.'

With Captain Radleigh's words ringing in his ears, he felt his face redden, and was glad that she couldn't see him clearly in the candlelight. He *had* been clumsy. He remembered battle tactics, and began to wonder if it would not be wise to withdraw until a more favourable encounter seemed likely. Moreover, it was very late; he'd been up since dawn, and he *had* drunk an unconscionable amount of wine. Truth to tell, he had the very devil of a headache. He was about to make a dignified retreat when a vision flashed across his mind and rooted him to the floor. Even now, Radleigh would be picturing him in his wife's bed. He could just imagine how he would laugh if he heard that Marcus had left his wife's room so tamely. He had to try again.

'I . . . I didn't mean to shock you, Barbara,' he explained, gently. 'Perhaps you misunderstood me?'

'I think not, sir,' she said, frostily. 'You did all those things, yet you were a married man!'

'Yes, I know,' he said, wryly, thinking that perhaps it was best to be open with her, 'but it didn't particularly feel like it then. To speak plain, it doesn't even feel much like it now. Truth to tell, I hoped for a warmer welcome.'

'I thought I might trust you to say something unspeakable, sir.' said Barbara, ever more coldly. 'After all that I heard you say, you expected a warmer welcome? Are you lost to all sense of shame?'

'What has shame to do with us?' said Reyne, coming further into the room and closing the door behind him. 'You are my wife.'

'As, indeed, I was when you were jaunting with these other women. And don't *dare* come any closer!' she warned, pulling her bedcovers up to her chin. 'Leave me alone.'

By now, Lord Reyne was angry. He was ready to tell her that he had every right to get as close to her as he wished, when he noticed her eyes, which looked huge in the candlelight, and full of fear. Whatever he had intended, that look stopped him. He knew, then, that he must leave her. How to do it and still keep some dignity for himself, puzzled him for no more than a second. Coming even closer to the bed, he stood over his wife. In response, Barbara shrank even further away, until she was almost hidden in the bed hangings.

'This may come as a dreadful blow to your vanity, ma'am,' he said, balefully, 'but I am by no means loath to do so. You may consider yourself the most beautiful woman in the neighbourhood, but in the wider world you might find yourself no very great thing after all. I am here, this evening, because I have a very great sense of duty, not because I expected any particular entertainment. I honour the arrangement made by my father, that is all.'

His words mortified Barbara. 'I suppose, sir, that you expect to be considered a gentleman for doing so,' she said, impassively. 'I might tell you that no *gentleman* ever uttered such ungallant sentiments as you have just expressed.'

'If you think I have been ungallant, Lady Reyne,' said Marcus, with a crooked smile, 'it is as well that you cannot read my thoughts.'

And with that, he left Barbara, by way of the dressing-room.

Barbara sank down into the pillows, her heart racing, though she couldn't decide if it raced from fear or indignation. That he should speak to her like that! That he should admit that he thought her *no very great thing*! It was insupportable. A burning sensation blazed at her breast. Were it the last thing she did, she would bring that man to his knees!

She was still entertaining herself in thinking up plans for his undoing when she finally fell into an uneasy sleep, where she tossed and turned to the accompaniment of oversized dreams of Reyne, on his knees before her, pleading to be allowed to kiss the hem of her gown, as she walked away with Mr Falconer, who was appearing, for some odd reason for which she couldn't account, in a crown, and holding a sceptre.

She was awoken early, by birdsong. The shutters were still closed; the room in semi-darkness, and she lay there with her eyes closed, gradually coming back to life, until the events of the previous evening gradually seeped back into her consciousness. She gave a silent groan, imagining the complications which that encounter would surely produce. For some reason, she ached all over, and she stretched her shoulders and her arms in a languorous movement. To her horror, her hand felt a form beside her and she was sitting up in a flash, her legs half out of bed. As she got to her feet, she felt her nightdress being jerked, uncompromisingly, backwards, and she landed inelegantly, flat on her back on top of the bed. Looking up startled, she saw her husband leaning over her, and she started to cry out. Before she could manage more than a whimper, one of his hands was over her mouth, his other catching hold of her wrist.

'Ssh!' he hissed, shaking her. 'Do you want to waken everyone? I'm not going to touch you, don't worry.'

In view of his presence in her room, Lady Barbara was not inclined to trust to his assurances, and she went to scream again. This time, as well as putting his hand over her mouth, he pressed his whole weight on top of her. She could feel his body through the thin fabric of her nightgown, his bare legs against hers, and she struggled to free herself.

'Madam, will you stop that,' said Marcus, breathlessly, now getting very annoyed. 'A moment's consideration should have made you realize that, if I am not in your bed when your maid comes to waken you, everyone will know that we haven't . . . *slept* together. I have absolutely no interest in your person, but I don't intend to upset the apple cart by advertising the fact all over the county. Of course, if you want everyone to know that you are unwilling to do your duty, that is different.'

He looked down at her, frowning, and she shook her head. Only then did he release her, at which she rolled away in order to get as far from him as possible.

'No, that won't do, Lady Reyne,' said Marcus, taking her wrist and pulling her back nearer the centre of the bed. 'Your maid will never believe that you have had a proper wedding night if you are hanging off the edge of the bed. She shall find you on your pillows, next to me, and you shall give her – which means the whole household – the impression that you have had an agreeable night.'

Barbara pulled her wrist out of his clasp and rubbed it. 'I shall certainly do no such thing,' she said, moving away from him.

'Madam,' said Reyne, jerking her back again, and hanging over her. 'You have two choices: you may engage in this charade, or I shall take you in earnest! I care not which.'

Barbara looked up at him and saw such determination in his eyes that she could not doubt that he would keep his ward. Although she did not answer him, she stopped pulling away and he took that for his assurance.

'Very well, My Lady. I shall come into your room each night, while your maid is still in the room, and she shall see me ready to get into bed. I shall also be there when she wakes you up.

Keep to your side of the bargain and your person shall be sacrosanct – a relief to us both, I have no doubt.'

With that, he turned his back on her and lay on the pillow beside her. So shocked was she at having a man in bed with her that her mind was numbed. She could still feel the hardness of his body on top of hers, and the strange sensation, which had been stronger even than her fear. She hardly dared to breathe in case he should touch her again.

It was a huge relief to hear Stowe's knock. She called at once for her to enter, anxious to have someone else in the room.

It was clear that Stowe thought the situation highly romantic. Along with the hot chocolate and toast, a red rose in a vase had been placed on the breakfast tray, and Stowe, herself, exhibited such an expectant expression that Barbara itched to slap her.

To Barbara's embarrassment, instead of remaining decently hidden under the covers, Reyne sat up in bed the moment Stowe entered. He stretched his arms luxuriantly, and his face exhibited such a look of contentment, that Barbara could well imagine what Stowe must be thinking. To make matters worse, and to her intense annoyance, he lifted her hand and kissed it. Then he picked up the rose from the tray and handed it to her, saying aggravatingly, 'A rose for a flower, my love.'

Embittered though she was by such provocation, she was also very much aware of him. He had on only his nightshirt – his dressing-gown was draped over a chair – and she could see clearly his masculine frame.

Casually, he helped himself to toast from her breakfast tray, and then said, matter-of-factly, 'I need more than toast, darling. I'll go down to breakfast. Radleigh will like me to join him, I'm sure. And you'll like time to dress.' And with a further kiss, this time on her cheek, he got up, put on his dressing-gown, and went next door, leaving Barbara to regain her composure amidst Stowe's tender ministrations.

And this fiasco we must go through every day, she fumed, inwardly. I shall kill myself!

# Chapter Nine

BREAKFAST AT HURST Park was generally a family affair so, when Marcus strolled into the sunny breakfast-room, Guy and his parents were already there, entertaining Captain Radleigh.

Surprised to see him come down so early, having fondly imagined that he would be too comfortable with her daughter to wish to leave their bed, Lady Cornford excused herself almost at once, to see if she could glean anything from Stowe about how the night had gone. Servants knew everything: she would certainly know if there had been any discord.

Once she had left the room, the conversation, which had been general, turned inevitably to sport, as it is wont to do when men gather together. Lord Cornford, himself a trifle taken aback at having breakfast with a son-in-law who should have been safely tucked up with his daughter, was nevertheless mindful of his duties as host and began at once to search through the *Chester Courant*, to see if he could find anything for their amusement.

'What a pity you didn't come into Cheshire earlier in the year, my boy,' he said gloomily, as perusal of his newspaper failed to fetch up anything very interesting. 'We have a very good winter season hereabouts. Now, if you'd only come a few weeks ago, you'd have caught the races: and you've missed the regatta, too. Dashed if I know how you'll entertain yourselves. Apart from a cocking match at the Close Pit – which I know I can trust you not to mention to the ladies – I can see precious little else to suit.'

'Don't worry about us, sir. We don't need to be entertained,' Marcus hastened to assure him. 'A little fishing, a little riding: that will suit us perfectly. We've had enough excitement for a lifetime, and we're used to fending for ourselves.'

'I say, sir,' said Guy, looking shyly across at him. 'I hope you don't mind, but I went to have a look at your curricle this morning. Your groom said I might. It's a regular dasher, sir, isn't it!'

'It is a bit flash,' said Marcus, agreeably.

'Oh no, sir, I . . . I . . . didn't mean, I mean, I would never think *that*, sir. Indeed, it must be the handsomest carriage I've ever seen! And your greys too. Complete to a shade. I never saw such a well-matched team.'

'Do I understand from that that you are keen on horses, Guy?' interposed Captain Radleigh.

'I *am*, sir,' said Guy, earnestly. Then, seeing his eyebrow quizzically raised, he added, with a grin, 'Oh sir, you are roasting me!'

'I?' said Radleigh, breaking into laughter.

'Would you like to drive out with me this morning?' said Marcus, enjoying his enthusiasm. 'I've a mind to see a little more of the country hereabouts.'

Guy's eyes gleamed at the offer, then faded anxiously. 'Won't Captain Radleigh wish to go with you?' he said, looking across at him, his heart in his eyes.

'Oh, I think I can bear the disappointment,' said Radleigh, indulgently. 'As a matter of fact you'd be doing me a favour. After all that driving yesterday, I was thinking of wandering into that little village we passed yesterday on our way in. Tarsall, was it? Give my legs some exercise. I could do with buying some . . . er . . . Hungary Water. My man forgot to pack it.'

'What, no Hungary Water, George?' said Reyne, trying to keep a straight face. 'Well, you certainly can't do without that.'

'You are very good, sir,' said Lord Cornford. 'Both of you. But you really must not let my son be a nuisance. I am sure you can find better company.'

'But I asked *him*, sir,' said Marcus, gently. 'I should not have done so, you know, had I not wanted him, but he seems just the fellow to show me about the place. I saw nothing of it, remember, when I was here last.'

Guy was radiant. 'Oh sir! Do you indeed mean it? I should like it of all things. May I go, Father?' he asked, anxiously. 'You said I hadn't to have any lessons while Reyne is here, remember, so Mama let Mr Marchbanks go home for a holiday.'

Lord Cornford was left with nothing to do but agree. Looking out of the window, he said, 'Well, it is a good deal warmer today, so I doubt your mother will object. Ask her, mind. No doubt she'll quack you before you go, but I won't let her stop you.'

Guy was almost incoherent, trying to thank all three at once: Reyne for agreeing to take him, his father for letting him go, and Captain Radleigh for giving up his seat in the curricle.

'Why should Lady Cornford quack the boy, sir?' said Captain Radleigh, once Guy had gone off in search of Lady Cornford. 'Is he sickly?'

'Thank God, no,' said his host. 'Not now. These past few years he's been tolerably stout, I thank you. But he nearly died of whooping cough when he was younger, so my wife's always anxious.'

'Poor little chap,' said Marcus, feelingly. 'But surely, sir, if he's been pretty stout recently, he needn't be quacked? My mother used to force all sorts of concoctions down me for the same reason, only it was typhoid fever that nearly did for me. It wasn't until I joined the army and she couldn't do so any more, that I began to toughen up.'

Lord Cornford looked very anxious at that. 'My boy, for goodness sake don't say so to my wife. She lost two babies to whooping cough before Guy had it, and she likes to think she's doing something to prevent it from happening again. And it can't do him any harm, you know.'

'If Guy doesn't object, why should I?' he said, with a shrug. 'I doubt, though, if I'd be so patient.'

Lady Cornford, meanwhile, had caught Stowe between duties, and had learned from her that Lord Reyne had certainly been in his wife's room during the night. So why had he come down so early, and why wasn't Barbara with him? She was not one to approve this new romantic trend in which couples spent every moment of the day gazing into each other's eyes, but surely Reyne's willingness to be separated from Barbara so quickly did not augur well. She decided she must see Barbara and judge for herself. Tapping on her door and waiting a mere second before she entered, she found her daughter all but dressed, and reading her post.

'There you are, my love,' said Lady Cornford, without preamble. 'I thought you would come down with Reyne. Is everything all right?'

'Certainly, Mama,' said Barbara, remembering Reyne's instructions.

Her mother waited expectantly, hoping for enlargement, but when it failed to materialize, she added, 'And Marcus? Is he all right too?'

'He seems well enough, Mama,' said Lady Barbara coolly. 'Why don't you ask him?'

Lady Cornford looked into her daughter's face, anxious to discover some small sign that here was a woman who had known bliss. Sadly, she saw none. She began to have her suspicions that things had got off on a wrong foot.

Now Lady Cornford was not a woman who found it easy to allow her family to fall into difficulties without making a push to help them out again, but on this occasion she couldn't think of anything she could do or say to help such an unsatisfactory situation. With the ball on the horizon, and all their neighbours coming to see how much the couple liked each other, catastrophe surely threatened. Pausing only to recommend that her daughter should wear the new coral round dress which had been delivered from Madame Thiers only last evening, and which she thought could only help matters, she scurried off again, determined to report her suspicions to her husband, and get his help in thinking up any little ways in which to encourage the newlyweds towards a better understanding.

Meeting her son on the way down, big with news about the

promised curricle ride, Lady Cornford was exceedingly put out that Marcus should have suggested anything so dangerous. She had begun to have a better opinion of him than that. To take him out in a *racing* curricle was surely not to be thought of, for she had seen the reckless way that Marcus drove his carriage up the long drive, and, though it was certainly very dashing, and she wished she might have persuaded Barbara to watch his arrival, it would not do for Guy. In this she thought she had an excellent reason. Lady Cornford had once read a treatise which had cautioned people of the unwisdom of riding on the new steam trains, which were being vaunted as a future means of travel, and on which it seemed that speeds of twenty miles an hour would soon be reached. The treatise had stated categorically that to travel so fast would be injudicious to the human brain, and in her mind, she had immediately applied the danger to fast carriages as well, especially open ones, for surely, if the head was exposed, the danger must be vastly increased? She did just what most women would do at such a juncture and said to Guy that she was sure his father would never let him go.

'But Mama,' Guy protested. 'Papa says I *may* go.'

'*Really*!' said his mother, shaping her brows into a frown. 'How very odd of him, my dear. Depend upon it, he does not realize he means the curricle. If Reyne will but take you quietly in the landau instead, I shall be very much obliged to him, for it will put some colour into those pale cheeks. I should not have a moment's peace were you to go out in the curricle.'

'Oh no, Mama! You mustn't ask him! Not the landau. Why, he will think me the veriest *flat*!'

When Guy returned to the breakfast-room, all the pleasure had gone from his face, which was enough to make Lord Cornford stick to his guns, for once. On Lady Cornford being assured by Reyne that he would be in safe hands, her husband insisted that Guy should be allowed to go. He mitigated her disappointment, by allowing her to feed Guy some Galls pills recently purchased from Mr Monk the apothecary, knowing that Guy would count that an easy payment for such a rare outing.

As soon he had swallowed the second of the noxious pills, Guy lost no time in persuading Marcus to walk with him to the stables, instead of waiting for the curricle to be brought round, so as to prevent his mama from thinking up any more cures.

They were crossing the hallway ready to go outside at the very moment when Barbara chose to come downstairs. Thus, Reyne was treated to his first sight of her, not in the coral dress recommended by her mother, but in a dashing riding habit of royal blue velvet, over which she wore a tight jacket, braided across the front and finished with a military collar and epaulettes. Lord Reyne stepped forward instinctively, but before he could reach her, Guy moved in instead, anxious to share his pleasure with his sister.

'Ba,' he cried, his face aglow. 'Reyne is taking me out in his curricle. And Papa says I may go! It is of all things great. The neatest rig you've ever seen, and his greys, bang up to the mark.'

Lord Cornford, who had followed them out into the hall, saw the admiration in his eyes when Reyne looked at his wife, and decided he had been precipitate in allowing his son to take up Reyne's time. He said, bracingly, 'Guy, my boy, now that I recollect, I am sure Reyne would prefer to drive your sister out. On this occasion, you know, it's being his first morning. Perhaps he can take you tomorrow.'

Barbara saw Guy's jaw drop and had, in any case, no intention of driving out with Reyne, for she had other plans. 'On no account in the world, Papa,' she said at once, and very firmly. 'I am taking Cobweb out for a canter towards Garthwaite. I haven't had her out for two days. I certainly don't want to upset any plans Reyne might have made.'

Her father's surprise was apparent to all. He was shocked to hear his usually compliant daughter sounding so waspish, nor did he like the sound of her destination, since he remembered that Garthwaite Manor was where Mr Falconer resided.

He said faintly, 'I don't think he had actually *made* any plans, Barbara, my dear. And besides, if he had, I am sure he would prefer to take you out, instead.'

Infuriated that her father's words might suggest that she was hurt by Reyne's indifference, Barbara's face showed her disdain.

'If Lady Reyne prefers to exercise her horse, sir,' said Reyne, registering obstinacy in every line of his wife's body, 'I am the last person to stop her. My own and Radleigh's hunters arrive today, and then, perhaps, Barbara and I might ride out together. Meanwhile, I have promised this young man a turn in my curricle. If I'm not mistaken, he is not to be gainsaid.'

Then with a casual farewell, he went off towards the stables, with Guy at his heels, calling back to Captain Radleigh, (who had watched the whole with his usual wry sense of humour, and mentally shook his head at Reyne's inept manner of dealing with his wife), that he would see him at luncheon on his return.

Left somewhat stranded in the hallway, looking like a child left out of a party, Barbara had nothing left to do but take herself and her smart new riding habit out to where her horse was waiting. Holding her chin high, she acted as if she had no greater felicitation in life.

Meanwhile, Reyne and Guy had gone to the stables where His Lordship's curricle was being harnessed. Taking Guy up beside him, they were soon out of sight of the house, on the cindered track, which wound its way around the estate. They hadn't gone very far when Guy, who was in seventh heaven, said effusively, 'I say, sir, I'm so glad that you are married to Ba. Thank heaven you married her before you went abroad.'

Reyne took time to digest this before he answered, 'Do you think I might have been unsuccessful in my suit had I applied later?'

Guy laughed outright. 'Oh sir, you are funny,' he said. 'You'd never have won her if you'd left it until you came back from Spain. Ba might have been married any number of times by now. Had you not married her then, she'd never have had to wait until she was twenty-four.'

'Popular, is she?'

'What do you think, sir?' said Guy, with a mischievous lift of his eyelids. 'She's my sister, and even I can tell she's pretty, so you can imagine what other fellows think.'

Anxious not to appear too interested, Reyne decided to leave the subject in abeyance while he manoeuvred a tricky bend, and he contented himself with asking questions on aspects of the estate, which came to his notice as they drove on. They were almost a quarter of the way round before he said, casually, 'And has your sister any *special* admirers? Any she favours more than the rest?'

'Oh, Barbara could have her choice amongst them all, I should say,' Guy said, artlessly, unaware that he was giving anything away. 'I know that Lord John Wynnon likes her, and he is reckoned about the most well-favoured man hereabouts.'

'And does your sister admire *him*?' he asked, in measured tones.

'It's clear she likes him,' said Guy, anxious to be strictly fair, 'but if I had to plump for one of her admirers whom she has favoured most, I should say it was Mr Falconer, though he is not as handsome as Lord John. He certainly likes *her*. We can't get rid of the fellow – so Papa says. He's been in Tunbridge Wells these past few weeks, but when he's at home, he comes to the house almost every day, bringing her some little gift, or a poem for her collection. It's so droll. He's quite old, you know, and he knows full well that she is married to you and that there's no chance for him, but he still comes. I should not be so stupid.'

Chewing on what Guy had told him, Reyne brought the curricle to an abrupt halt. 'Come on, young'n,' he said, peremptorily. 'Off you get!'

Guy looked up at him anxiously, his face bearing all the hallmarks of a puppy who knows he has done wrong, but doesn't remember in which bedroom he did it.

'Come on, out, and in the other side. It's time you took the reins.'

With a heart bursting with gratitude, Guy wasted no time in obeying him.

# Chapter Ten

BARBARA, MEANWHILE, DISDAINED to follow her husband's route, and rode instead across the fields towards Garthwaite. She had no intention of calling at the Manor, such behaviour being rather too transparent, but the servant grapevine had worked with its usual efficiency and she knew from Stowe that Mr Falconer had returned from Tunbridge Wells late on the previous evening. It was not unlikely that he, too, should be out riding, and if so, she intended, *accidentally*, to meet him.

Barbara found herself in something of a quandary. By now, Mr Falconer must surely have heard that Reyne had come to claim his bride and she was unsure how he would take it. It was just possible that he might take the most virtuous action and, now that her husband was actually on the scene and not merely a far off phantom, retire entirely from the lists of her admirers. She caught her breath at such an idea. It simply was not to be thought of: not when he was so important to her plan. It was imperative that she should contrive somehow to meet him before the ball – and without losing her dignity. She had to know if he intended to desert her, for if he did, she would be forced to bring on one of her reserves – perhaps Lord John Wynnon? Certainly she did not intend to chance meeting Mr Falconer for the first time under Reyne's eye and perhaps give her husband the satisfaction of seeing her ignored.

Lady Reyne rode for more than an hour along the bridle-paths which criss-crossed the lands close to Garthwaite Manor without seeing anyone she knew, and getting more and more frustrated. By now, since he usually rode out every day, she might have been supposed to have met up with Mr Falconer, and she was beginning to feel rather vexed at having been led to get so close to the house. So desperate was her situation, that she was hesitating between actually calling at the Manor or returning home without seeing him at all when, to her profound relief, she spotted him in the distance, riding towards her. That he had seen her was immediately apparent, for he raised his whip in salute.

She waited for him to come to her, almost sure of her power, but when he was just a few yards away, she feigned surprise, crying, 'Why, Mr Falconer, what a start you gave me. I'd no idea I was so close to Garthwaite. I seem to have been riding barely any time at all.'

It was not entirely surprising that Barbara prided herself on catching Mr Falconer's fancy for, though he was not the most handsome of her admirers, he would certainly be accounted attractive by any but the most exacting of tastes. Tall, dark and in his mid-thirties, he was a very self-contained man, of considerable charm, elegant bearing and an excellent leg, much suited to the existing fashion for skin-tight pantaloons. His face might have been considered ordinary were it not for the possession of a very square, cleft chin, and a dimple, which appeared in one cheek when he was happy or amused, which took it away from the commonplace. The dimple appeared prominently on seeing Barbara. Taking his hat and his riding crop in one hand, he used the other to rein in his horse until its head was almost touching Cobweb.

'My Lady,' he said, showing his pleasure. 'I was just riding over to the Park to see you before the ball. We must talk!'

'Indeed?' said Barbara, feigning surprise.

'Well of course we must,' he said, with one of his quizzical smiles. 'Don't I always have to speak to Lady Reyne when I am at home? Three weeks away from her is far too long for this poor fellow.'

Barbara blushed, but said, anxiously, 'I thought you must have heard about Reyne returning.'

'I must confess, I did hear something about him being back in England,' said Falconer, showing some concern.

'Not only in England, sir, he is here in Cheshire!'

'That, too, I have heard. I was never more shocked than when my steward mentioned it last night. I had not heard a word of it until then.'

'Then you are luckier than I, sir, for I have known of it for these three weeks. And indeed, I am surprised you did not hear of it even in Tunbridge Wells, for the newspapers have been full of him.'

He caught a hint of impatience in her voice, which led him to believe that she hadn't been altogether impressed by her husband's notoriety. 'I've seen nothing, My Lady. We have been staying with my great aunt, you know,' he said with a grimace, 'and since she is short-sighted, she never takes a newspaper, it being too much bother to read. And Mother has been ill again while we have been in Tunbridge Wells. You know how she needs her spirits kept up at such times, so I have spent much of my time in her sickroom. It always seems to do her good to have me nearby. I have been reading one of Mrs Radcliffe's novels to her. The most frightful tosh! Between that, and taking her for her treatments, and visiting members of my aunt's family, I had hardly a moment to myself. Naturally, I wasn't able to get to the reading lounges to see the newspapers as I usually do when I am there.'

'How fortunate your mama is in her son,' she sighed, seeing the picture in her mind. And as an afterthought, she added, rather less sincerely, 'I hope Mrs Falconer is better now,' – for Mr Falconer's mama was not one of her favourites. Being a valetudinarian by habit, who liked to keep her son very close when she could, Barbara had long known her a force to be reckoned with. She could not pretend to be fond of her, but it was typical of Mr Falconer not to have noticed it, for he had a tendency to see things as he wished, which probably accounted for the fact that he had undoubtedly been paying court to Barbara, though he knew she had a husband elsewhere. His answer illustrated this tendency very well.

'She's pretty stout now, I thank you, Lady Reyne,' he said, taking the hand she held out to him. 'It is just like your sweet self to ask. I left her in Tunbridge Wells with one of her sisters, for my great-aunt's servants didn't seem to understand her little ways. Her new doctor has recommended a lengthy stay for a regular course of treatment at the hot bath, poor thing.'

'I am glad your mama takes his advice,' said Barbara, with complete honesty, while he beamed at her. 'She could not do better. Indeed, I have heard people say that a six-month treatment is needed if one is really to benefit.'

'Six months?' His eyes widened. 'I doubt she'd agree to that, My Lady. But this business of Reyne,' he went on. 'After all these years, you must have been shocked. Had I known sooner, illness or no illness, I'd have come back at once. When I returned last night and read your father's invitation for the ball *in honour of my son-in-law's homecoming* you have no idea how I felt. My favourite lady in the world, and an irate husband back on the scene.' His tone was the caressing one he always used with her. 'Is he ready to call me out, do you think, for looking after his wife so well?'

'I pray you will not joke, Mr Falconer!' said Barbara, anxiously. 'You cannot know what it is like for me. You know what my hopes have been. It was bad enough to learn that Reyne was back in England, but when he remained in Town so long before coming to Cheshire, I began to entertain hopes that, like me, he might not wish our marriage to stand. But when he finally arrived yesterday, any idea that I should not be called upon to honour my father's marriage plans was quite at an end.'

'What is all this about him remaining in Town? I do not understand.'

'Apparently it was not so very important for him to see me as to attend to his other plans.'

'What?' said Mr Falconer, an incredulous smile playing

around his mouth. 'Are you trying to tell me that he was here in England and didn't come to you straight away? What a fool he must be to know that Lady Reyne was awaiting him and to waste his time elsewhere.'

His words were as soothing balm to her wounded sensibilities. 'Apparently it was necessary for him to visit all his family first – every last one of them. Then he spent time being entertained in Town – by every attractive lady he could meet, it seems. He appears to have been determined to attend every breakfast, rout, ball, horserace, balloon ascent and card party in the whole of London. Indeed, had he been determined to give me a reputation as being the most boring woman in England, he could not have done more. Anything was preferable to coming back to his wife.' She laughed shakily, annoyed at how much it still rankled. 'I think he only came into Cheshire at all because he was actually admonished in print by a newspaper proprietor for neglecting me. You may imagine what that has done to my self-esteem.'

'Detestable! What a dashed idiot!' said Mr Falconer, taking her hand and stroking it gently. 'My poor little Barbara. How cross you must have been. Would that I had been here to chase away that frown. And what had your parents to say to all this? They must have been very angry.'

'You'd think so, wouldn't you?' she said, with a shrug of her beautiful shoulders. 'But, no! My parents think he is all that is wonderful. Apparently, I should forgive every slight and welcome him with open arms, just because he is handsome.'

'Oh, so he's handsome?' said Mr Falconer, his face falling. 'You think him handsome, do you?'

Barbara was tempted to repudiate entirely any claims her husband might be said to have as to looks, but she decided to be more equivocal.

'I hardly know, sir,' she said, looking away from him into the distance. 'He has certainly *altered*. Miss Waverley thinks him improved, but, after the way I have been treated, it is difficult for me to view him dispassionately.'

'What a relief!' said Mr Falconer, laughing openly. 'You cannot know how happy I am to hear so little in his favour. I wished him as ugly as Satan. You must realize, though I have never said it, so shocking does it sound, that all my hopes depended on his never returning from the wars. When he didn't come at once, I allowed myself to hope. . . .'

'Hush, Mr Falconer!' said Barbara, opening her eyes very wide at such a bold assertion. Until now, though always attentive, he had been sufficiently discreet not to have made it necessary to keep him at a distance.

'You are very right,' he said, annoyed with himself for having alarmed her. 'But, forgive me, have you been thrown very much together since his return?'

Barbara blushed, remembering that morning in her bedroom. 'Far more so than I have wished, I can assure you,' she said, understanding where his questions were leading, and anxious not to be trapped into revealing more than she intended. 'But I must say no more. I hope, sir, we may have the pleasure of your company this evening. I feel I need all my friends about me at such a moment.'

'Your friends? I hope I am more than that, My Lady,' he said, with meaning, 'and, of course I shall be there. Shall you save me the first two cotillions, as usual? I shall not take no for an answer.'

She nodded her agreement and went to turn her horse away, but he caught her bridle. 'Not yet,' he said, meeting her eyes. 'Don't let us part so quickly. Who knows when we shall be allowed to talk freely, after this? At least let me escort you home. Castor has been eating himself fat in his stable while I've been away. He needs a good gallop. We'll race, shall we, as we always do?'

Barbara, an excellent horsewoman, was more than happy to oblige him and, as they raced back together, remembering that Reyne would be sure to be there, she asked him to take luncheon with the family. After the cold of yesterday, the sunshine was so exhilarating that, by mutual agreement, they took the long way back, by the circular route. By the time they reached the house and had their horses taken to the stables, it was well after noon, and when they went into luncheon, the whole family were already assembled and helping themselves from a table heaped with choice viands of cold meats and fruit.

Seeing Mr Falconer follow his daughter into the luncheon parlour, Lord Cornford could hardly contain his indignation. His wife did rather better and went over to draw him cordially towards the refreshments, where the rest were gathered with their plates.

Mr Falconer had only a brief moment to wonder which was Reyne and to reflect that neither of the two young gentlemen matched Barbara's description of him, before he was being introduced by her as, 'one of my dearest friends'.

Captain Radleigh was amused to see that Reyne's wife displayed the look of a cat who had the cream: it was obvious to him that, in making a point of bringing Falconer to meet Reyne, she was throwing down the gauntlet. He was not to know that Reyne had been forewarned of his rival and had had time to prepare himself for such a scene, whenever it should happen. Much to Barbara's disgust, he came forward to meet Falconer with every appearance of friendliness. Even so, beneath his pleasant manner he was irrationally annoyed with himself to think that his absence had given Falconer an opportunity to get so close to his wife. Certainly his ideas of what constituted *quite old*, differed widely from Guy's.

Captain Radleigh knew Reyne well enough to have a good idea what was passing through his mind, and he watched the two men size each other up: saw that Falconer, tall as he was, was irritated at having to look up to Reyne, even those few inches, and decided they were pretty well matched. Indeed, the expression 'rutting stags' refused to be banished from his mind.

Once the introductions had been made, there was a distinct atmosphere in the pretty luncheon-room, which was, fortunately, quickly dissipated by the return of Guy, who had been sent off by his father to fetch a book from the library. Seeing that his sister had returned, and pausing only to make his bow to Mr

Falconer, he could not wait to tell Barbara how he had spent the morning.

'Ba!' he blurted out, breaking what had become an uncomfortable silence, 'You will never guess! Reyne let me tool the curricle! It was the greatest thing. I drove it all along the edge of the South Wood. You can't think how nervous I was, but Reyne said I did quite well, didn't you, sir?'

'I said you did *very* well,' Reyne corrected, with an engaging smile.

'Thank you, sir,' beamed Guy, his face pink with pleasure.

He turned back towards his sister, and hugged her. 'I am so *glad* that you married Reyne. He is the best of good fellows.'

Mr Falconer, jockeying for position, said, more for Barbara's benefit than for Guy's, 'I wish I had known that you wished to learn to drive a carriage, Guy. I should be happy to take you out any day and give you some lessons.'

'Oh, there is not the least need, sir,' said Guy, beaming. 'Reyne says he will take me out for an hour every day.'

'Guy,' said his mother, reminding him of his manners. 'It is very good of Mr Falconer to offer such a treat, when he is such a busy man.'

He was immediately aware that he had uttered a *faux pas* and blushed violently. 'I mean, it is very good of you, sir, but I particularly wished to learn to drive a curricle.'

As soon as the words were out of his mouth, Guy knew that he had made matters worse and got tangled in a muddle of apologies in trying to make things better.

Mr Falconer, himself red from embarrassment, was anxious to reassure him, aware, in fairness, that, in the eyes of a boy, the landau he habitually drove, must make him cut a less dashing figure than if he drove a racing curricle. Since his only reason for choosing a landau over a curricle was that he knew that ladies liked to be comfortable, and he enjoyed their company, he had always been happy with his sacrifice. But when Guy said, kindly, that he probably drove a landau so that he could take his mama out driving, it was too much.

He was actually on the verge of lying to Guy by saying that he had been considering buying a curricle for some time, but had not yet seen one he liked, when Barbara made it unnecessary by announcing tartly, with a sideways look at Reyne, 'In a few years' time, Guy, my love, when you are less juvenile, you may realize that travelling uncomfortably at speed has little to recommend it and is only undertaken by very *immature* people.'

Barbara was congratulating herself on saving her favourite's face and, incidentally, getting in an excellent thrust at Reyne, when she chanced to glance back at her brother. He wore a look of hurt incredulity. In that moment, she thought she understood how Wellington must have felt after Waterloo, on returning to the blood-soaked battleground. Maybe she had won that round with Reyne, but perhaps it had not been worth the price she had paid.

# Chapter Eleven

LORD REYNE WASN'T the only person intrigued to meet Mr Falconer at luncheon: Captain Radleigh too, had been eager to see him, after having a very instructive morning.

In the army, whenever he and Marcus had gone into new territory, they had gone off together to reconnoitre. Having been left to his own devices somewhat unceremoniously that morning, Radleigh had made up his mind to walk into Tarsall, in order to get his bearings and see what he could scout out. Since he was of a rather flirtatious disposition and knew that his red coat always found favour with ladies, he thought he could depend on being very well entertained for an hour or two.

He had almost reached the outskirts of the village when, fortuitously, he spied ahead a familiar figure in the shape of Miss Waverley, going the same way as he. She carried a shopping basket in one hand, and with her other, clasped the hand of a little girl, perhaps nine or ten years old. Since Miss Waverley had seemed to him a very pleasant, good-humoured young lady, possibly ripe for a little innocent flirtation, he had no hesitation in calling out to her and asking if he might join them.

The little girl was Betsy, Mary Waverley's youngest sister, and at first she was rather frightened by Captain Radleigh's colourful uniform. It did him no harm in Miss Waverley's eyes, that, on their way, he spent time in joking Betsy into a happier frame of mind, and by the time they had reached the centre of the village, all three were getting on together very well indeed.

It was Miss Waverley's intention to go into Mr Woodcock's shop to buy some nankeen to make into breeches for her young brothers. Everyone shopped in Woodcock's, Mary told him artlessly, for he sold *everything*. Captain Radleigh readily accompanied her inside, curious to see what composed *everything* in that part of the world, since there was little window space, and few goods on display from outside. As some of Mr Woodcock's rolls of material stood around the doorway, the shop appeared, at first, very dark. Once inside, however, he was pleasantly surprised to see the space open out and, beside an impressive display of linens, muslins, calicoes, threads, ribbons, buttons, and hat trimmings, there was an area where Mrs Woodcock had set out some comfortable-looking chairs around a few tables covered with white linen tablecloths, so that the ladies could partake of tea and cakes while they were shopping. It was a very welcome addition, and once Mary had chosen some nankeen of excellent quality and some matching buttons, it was not difficult for him to persuade her to take some tea before they walked back home.

Having settled Betsy with ratafia and macaroons, Captain Radleigh began to sound out Miss Waverley about Lady Reyne, but since his questions were heavily interlarded with anecdotes, which made Mary laugh, she had no idea that she was being pumped for information. Besides, she *liked* Captain Radleigh. There had been one or two moments on the previous evening when there would have been an atmosphere had he not been on hand to mask them with his nonsense. Instinctively, she recognized him as a soulmate in the difficult business of reconciling Barbara and Lord Reyne to their singular marriage.

Unaware that she had given anything away, Captain Radleigh soon confirmed, from Mary, the interesting, but not unexpected information, that Lady Reyne was very angry indeed at her husband. When he sympathized, Mary leaned closer and said, confidentially, 'I know that she behaved coldly last evening, Captain Radleigh, but surely one cannot blame her, her position being so invidious? In general, she has the sweetest disposition:

full of fun, you know. And she is kind, too: especially to me. She seems quite unconscious of any dissimilarity between us.'

'I am very glad to hear it, though, I must confess, I don't find it too astounding,' he said, with a droll laugh. 'But, tell me now, why should she be?'

Mary smiled, but could not entirely prevent her embarrassment from being apparent. 'Oh, we are very far apart in the pecking order, sir,' she explained, with a satirical lift of her brows. 'I am very proud of my father, so I don't want you to misunderstand me, but there is no denying that he is a self-made man, which seems to be a sin of some magnitude. He has made his fortune, but we have none of the family connections of many of the houses hereabouts, and in some eyes, we simply will not do. Lady Reyne has never made the slightest difference between us, nor has her family. Some others are not able, so easily, to ignore the merchants from which we stem.'

'Then they must be very stuffy people indeed – and foolish beyond reason. I trust you do not allow yourself to be discomposed by such idiots?'

'They are not *all* idiots, Captain Radleigh,' she said, with a short laugh, 'and, no, I don't allow myself to be discomposed.'

'With respect, Miss Waverley, anyone who places so much emphasis on family connections must be an idiot. Look at Reyne, now. He comes from one of the best families in England, and I have never seen *him* uppish.'

'Yet his father made his marriage with someone of his own rank,' she reminded him.

'Ah, but that was his father, Miss Waverley. That wasn't Reyne.'

'And what of *your* family, Captain?' asked Mary, pressing the point. 'You are the heir to a viscountcy: how would they like to see *you* drawn into friendship with a merchant's daughter?'

'Oh, my family is not at all *nice*, Miss Waverley,' he assured her, a charming grin robbing his words of any insult. 'Why, they even tolerate me!'

Mary Waverley laughed out loud at that. 'You are very

gracious, sir,' she said, mildly, 'but you cannot possibly understand.'

'Tell me then, which families must I be on my guard against? For, if they don't like you, they surely won't tolerate me, so I'd best be ready for them.'

But Mary withdrew at that. 'This is a very improper conversation, sir,' she said, mortified that she had said so much. 'Of course, I do not speak of anyone in particular.'

'Oh no, I can't have that. It's too cruel. It's like giving me a sorbet then taking it away again. You can surely give me one name?' he said, persuasively, putting on a little-boy face which reminded her so much of her brother that she could not resist him.

'Very well, then, just one,' she said, giving in. 'But it is very wicked! Now, let me see. Mrs Falconer, for example. At Garthwaite Manor. She thinks us very poor creatures indeed. She deigns to speak to us at church, but poor Mama is never invited to her tea parties.'

'I dislike her already. Who *is* she, pray?'

'You won't have come across her, for she and her son have been in Tunbridge Wells.' Her eyes crinkled as she burst into laughter. 'Mama suspects that she is only haughty with us because she is but one generation removed from us herself. But you must not say so. Mr Falconer is a great friend of Lady Reyne. You will certainly meet him this evening, for he returned home last night and is sure to come to the ball.'

'I can't say I look forward to meeting his mother,' said Radleigh, with a grimace. 'She sounds like a dragon. May she rot in hell!'

'Captain Radleigh! You should not say such things! And you may leave your sword at home tonight for I understand that Mr Falconer left her taking the cure at Tunbridge Wells.'

'It sounds much the best place for her. And Mr Falconer? Does *he* like you?'

At this, the colour rioted in her cheeks. 'Don't be absurd, sir,' she said, in some confusion, 'Mr Falconer would not *look* at me while Barbara was nearby.'

The words had slipped out before she could stop them, and she instantly wished them unsaid. 'Not that Mr Falconer thinks of Barbara in that way,' she hastened to assure him. 'They are simply very good friends.'

'Known her all her life, has he?' said Radleigh, helpfully.

'Not precisely,' Mary was forced to admit. 'He took the lease at the Manor about a year ago.'

'He does know she's married?' asked Radleigh, gently.

'Certainly,' Mary replied.

'Then, *should* he be such a very good friend to her?'

'Really, sir, you have caught entirely the wrong end of the stick. I assure you that there is nothing untoward between them,' she assured him, indignantly. 'Mr Falconer is far too much of a gentleman to do anything of *that* nature. He is always most *correct*.'

'Oh, I know what you mean,' said Radleigh, wilfully misunderstanding. 'Bit of a slowtop.'

'Indeed he is not!' she cried, jumping instantly to her favourite's defence. 'Oh! You do not understand.'

But, seeing her indignation, and building on what she had already said, Captain Radleigh thought he understood very well.

Later, when he had taken Miss Waverley and Betsy home, and was making his way back to Hurst Park, he digested all that he had heard. 'So Miss Waverley is in love with Falconer; she knows that Falconer admires Lady Reyne; and, Lady Reyne. . . ? What of the beautiful Barbara?' He would just have to wait and see whom *she* liked. But what a *nice* little conundrum to set before a man.

Little wonder, then, that he could not wait to meet the famous Mr Falconer. Nor was it surprising that, having been allowed at luncheon to satisfy his curiosity, and having then seen Mr Falconer make his departure, on a promise to return for the ball, he was anxious to get Reyne to himself and thrash out the whole matter.

When Barbara retired for a nap, so as to be fresh for the ball, he took the opportunity to drag her husband off for a spot of fishing, not wishing to be in the way while the servants had their hands full with all the last-minute preparations.

Although he was too busy to join them, Lord Cornford accompanied them down to the lake, in order to show them some of the best fishing spots, but as soon as he left them, to go back to the house, Radleigh said, with an infectious laugh, 'Alone at last!'

'Fool!' said Reyne, casting his line far out into the lake.

'Well?' said his friend, after Reyne had been sitting, without speaking, for some minutes. 'Aren't you going to tell me how it went? I nearly came to your room this morning, but I decided to be discreet.'

'Discreet! Now that's not a word one usually associates with you.'

'On this occasion you are maligning me. I decided not to come because I wasn't sure you'd be there, or, if you were, whether you'd be alone. And if that isn't discreet, I'd like to know what is.'

'I *wasn't* there, if you must know,' Reyne hastened to assure him, keeping his eyes on his float. 'I was next door, with my wife.'

'So, that's good, isn't it?' he asked, searchingly.

'Apart from the fact that my wife is the most infuriating, cross-grained, cantankerous, *unsociable* person of my acquaintance,' said Reyne, bitterly.

Radleigh picked up on the last of his adjectives. 'Oh! So she didn't welcome you, after all. I simply don't know how to account for it, do you?'

'Very well, so you warned me; there's no need to crow about it. But you were too late by then. You shouldn't have let me drink so much.'

'Yes, silly of me, wasn't it? How could I fail to spend all evening counting your drinks? By the time I did notice, you were too much on the fret to catch any of my signals.'

'Yes, well it's too late now. The die is cast.'

'I thought you said you were in her room. It can't have been all bad.'

'Well it was,' said Reyne; then, suddenly breaking into laughter, he added, 'It was *very* bad. You have no idea how bad! First I spent, oh I don't know how long in listening on my side of the dressing-room door for her maid to leave, which was the most nail-biting thing I've ever done. Never mind Waterloo: that was nothing to this. Then, having decided to be considerate, I thought I should give her a little time to compose herself before I barged in on her, so I left it for the quarter-hour before deciding to try my luck. I was just about to turn the door handle, when I had the most fearful thought that if I came in via the dressing-room and she wasn't expecting me, she might scream or something.'

'Good God, man! You're her husband. She's supposed to be expecting you.'

'Yes, well, when you put it like that it sounds easy. Believe me, it isn't when you do it in cold blood. So, I decided that I should go into the room from the gallery. And then I had the most nerve-racking ten minutes of my life. Every time I went to open my door, some servant or other came along, snuffing out candles and closing windows. I nearly got caught about three times!'

Captain Radleigh had collapsed on the bank by now, convulsed with laughter, an attitude in which he was soon joined by Lord Reyne.

When, eventually, the two of them could stop laughing, Radleigh, keen to hear the round tale, said, 'But you got in eventually?'

'By the skin of my teeth, for I swear another of the wretched maids came along carrying a mop! Thank heaven she didn't notice me.'

'And what did Barbara say to all these shenanigans?'

'She was asleep, would you believe it?' said Reyne, unable to hide his indignation.

This was too much for Radleigh, and again he fell backwards into a heap.

'I called out to her and woke her up, and she acted as if I was a robber-bandit or something. Then she threw all those *women* at me, as if I had been Bluebeard, or something. She said I was *unspeakable.*'

'Unspeakable? Oh that's a bit strong, even for you.'

'After that, I decided to call it a night, but not before I gave her a piece of my mind. I told her that I didn't want to sleep with her any more than she wanted to sleep with me. That I was only there out of a sense of duty. And I tell you, at that moment I meant it! I'd have rather have slept with Medusa.'

'Oh, surely not. All those snakes!'

'Then I left, but I think I kept my dignity,' said Marcus, pulling his shoulders back on a deep outward breath.

'But I thought you said you were still in there this morning? That can't have taken all night.'

'Oh, that's easily explained. I realized that if the maid came in and didn't find me there, all hell would break loose. I didn't want her parents to have an embarrassing situation to deal with, so I crept in through the dressing-room at about half past five and sneaked in on one side of the bed.'

'What did she do when she realized you were there?' said Radleigh, fascinated.

'You don't want to know, believe me. Suffice to say that we have agreed between us that I shall be seen every evening and every morning in her bedroom, so that nobody shall find out.'

'So, basically, you're saying that you made a mull of it. My dear fellow, what a disastrous situation. You don't stand an earthly now, after all that. Just as well you've decided not to remain in Cheshire too long. You'll just have to grit your teeth for a couple of weeks, as we agreed, then come back to Town with me.'

Reyne looked rather sheepish at that. 'I know we *said* that's what I'd do,' he murmured, rubbing his hand across his chin, then bending down to put a new grub on his hook, so that Radleigh could not see his face.

'Yes,' said Radleigh, with a knowing look, 'we certainly *did* say that. Am I to understand from this reluctance to meet my eye that you have changed your mind?'

'The thing is, George,' said Lord Reyne, finding it very difficult to put his thoughts into words, 'she's a dashed beautiful woman: and we are married, after all. I'm not altogether sure that I shouldn't make a bit more of an effort, with both families being so keen, and all. The thing is. . . . .'

'I think I'm beginning to know *exactly* what the thing is,' said Radleigh, with a grin. 'If I'm not very much mistaken, the *thing* is, old fellow, that you are finally beginning to appreciate the finer points of Lady Reyne! I wondered how long it would take you.'

'All right, so I admit it. She's ravishing! If you were me, wouldn't you feel honour bound to take your husbandly duties a bit more seriously.'

'If I were you, I think I'd already be taking my husbandly duties seriously, but then, I'm not an idiot. I only hope Lady Reyne appreciates the huge effort you are willing to undertake on her behalf.' The grin, which had spread across his monkey features, disappeared, and he suddenly looked serious again, as he added, 'And, if I might say so, not a moment too soon, if what Miss Waverley told me is true. Your wife, in case you haven't already guessed as much, seems to have been thrown into the way of being a mite too friendly with this character Falconer. I met Miss Waverley in the village this morning, and the way she assured me what a perfect gentleman this Falconer is, and how he'd never do anything dishonourable, convinced me that he's just the sort of fellow you need to keep an eye on. She as good as told me that Falconer has been chasing after Barbara ever since he came here, nearly a year ago.'

'For once you are behindhand with your news,' said Reyne, looking despondent. 'Guy told me much the same while we were out.'

'He did, did he? I'm glad somebody is useful about here. So what are you going to do about it?'

Reyne sighed, reeling in his line for a better cast. 'I haven't an inkling,' he said. 'I can't knock him down for liking her, can I?'

'Got to do something, old man,' said Radleigh, patting him on his forearm. 'Can't have your wife making sheep's eyes at the fellow. Bad *ton*. The sooner you can get this marriage consummated, the better.'

'Consummated? At the moment that seems as likely as a three-legged Derby winner. If you can think of something – anything! – I'd be glad to hear it. I can't.'

'As a matter of fact I do have the inklings of a little plan which *might* help. It was something Miss Waverley said. But I'll keep it to myself if you don't mind, in case I don't bring it off. Tell you about it when I'm sure.'

'Now why doesn't that exactly give me a warm sense of well-being?' said Reyne, wryly.

# Chapter Twelve

REFRESHED FROM HER afternoon nap, Lady Reyne dressed for the ball in a gown of white tissue gauze over a white silk slip, edged on the bodice and on the hem with tiny, richly embroidered silver oak leaves. Stowe was in ecstasies over her little flat, white silk evening pumps, similarly trimmed with silver, and she was so voluble that, neither she nor Barbara heard the knock sounding on the door leading from the gallery. The visitor was obliged to knock again. This time, Barbara heard it and she carried out her usual vanishing trick into the dressing-room in case it should be Reyne. Listening out, she soon realized that it was her brother and not her husband who had come to see her.

'Guy,' she said, coming sheepishly out of the dressing-room. 'What do you want, darling? Shouldn't you be getting ready? Since it is the first ball you have been allowed to attend, shouldn't you be clean and tidy, or you may find it will be your last?'

'Oh, I've plenty of time for that, but I want to talk to you. I mean alone.' He looked apologetically across at Stowe, who quickly made herself scarce.

Once she had gone, Guy said impetuously, 'You do look nice, Ba. That frock makes you look just like one of those tall women you're always looking at in the *Ladies Magazine*.'

His sister kissed his cheek. 'Thank you, best of brothers. Will it sink me in your estimation if I admit that I think it suits me, too?'

'I should think not,' he said seriously, obviously impressed at seeing her look so fine.

'Well, and are you going to tell me what has brought you here, young man? You haven't been in any mischief, have you? Not today, of all days.'

'No I haven't,' he said, insulted that she should so misjudge him. 'I haven't come about me, I've come about you!'

'About me? I'm sorry, darling, only you looked so anxious that I thought you were in trouble. Why don't you come and sit by me and tell me what you have come for.'

She dragged him over to the window seat and, as soon as they were seated, he disconcerted her by saying, with a troubled frown, 'Ba, don't you like Reyne?'

She was so taken aback that she hardly knew how to answer. Falling back on prevarication, she said, 'Why do you ask, love?'

'You were so horrible to him at luncheon that it seemed to me that very likely you don't.'

'How was I horrid?' said Barbara, wishing she'd been more subtle.

'That business of the curricle. When you said it was juvenile to drive a curricle, don't you think you might have hurt his feelings?'

If Barbara privately doubted if Reyne had any feelings to hurt, she was not going to say so to a young boy in the midst of a serious case of hero worship.

'I didn't say curricles are juvenile, darling, I said that driving fast was juvenile. I think you will find that most ladies think so.'

'But you said 'uncomfortably' as well, and that meant his curricle, you know it did.'

'Perhaps it did, but Guy, don't you think that Mr Falconer needed someone to take his part too, darling?' she said, gently, trying to sound even-handed. 'You had as good as told him that his carriage wasn't good enough, which wasn't the most tactful thing to say. I thought he needed someone on his side.'

'It didn't seem as if you meant that at all. You seemed really angry. Not like you at all. And I did try to let Mr Falconer know that I didn't mean to be rude. But, oh Ba, he is not like Reyne. I wish you could like Reyne, and be pleasant to him. If you carry on being *offish,* he will never realize how nice you are, and then, very likely, he might not stay. And I do wish he would stay. It's awfully jolly now that he's here. Nobody else could have persuaded Mama to let me go out in a curricle and tool it around the estate. And he didn't seem to get annoyed at all when I was chattering away, as Papa does, though I daresay he must have thought me a regular jaw-merchant. I should think he must have been glad to get back, but he never let me suspect it.'

'Then he is certainly a god,' said Barbara, trying to keep a straight face. 'And we shall obviously have to keep him here, if we have to do so by force!'

'Will you, Ba?' he cried, hugging her ecstatically. 'I know you can do it if you set your mind to it, for everybody likes you.'

'Everybody bar one,' said Barbara ruefully to herself, once he had gone away to get changed. 'Nor do I want *him* to change his mind.'

But how to continue to stay aloof from Reyne without hurting her little brother was a matter which would certainly occupy her mind for a considerable period.

When Barbara went downstairs, having first added a spangled gauze scarf, long white silk gloves and a delicately painted fan to her costume, the family was gathered in the drawing-room. Mindful of Guy's strictures on her behaviour to Reyne, she went in looking determinedly cheerful. As soon as her father saw her, he commended her appearance, in order to draw it to the attention of her husband. He had no need to bother, for Reyne – himself looking particularly handsome in a dark blue coat made for him by Stultz – had already noticed that she was in excellent looks. He too, it seemed, intended to be agreeable, since he at once complimented her. To her surprise, however, he said he had but one criticism to make, and that was of her jewellery. Barbara's hands immediately went up to the simple row of pearls she wore and she blushed in confusion, since she could not think how they could offend him. Her confusion mounted when he withdrew from the pocket of his tail-coat, a flat leather case, which, making her a slight bow, he gave into her hands.

'I hope that you will like my alternative choice, Lady Reyne,' he said, with a little smile. 'A small present, which I chose for you when I was in Town, but if you hate them, they can be exchanged.'

Her parents and the others were all delighted by his charming gesture and, aware that all eyes were upon her, Barbara opened the case. There, lying on a bed of black velvet, was the most exquisite pendant she had ever seen. It was exactly to her taste: quite plain, and of very fine sapphires and diamonds hung from a simple chain. Small studs of sapphires and diamonds for her ears accompanied it, and the whole was so precisely what she would have chosen for herself that her pleasure was evident. To add to her confusion, Reyne insisted on putting the pendant round her throat himself. She felt him lift the rope of pearls from around her neck, and, having dropped them in her hand, the pendant was carefully clasped from behind. When he came and stood before her, he expressed himself well pleased, then stepped back for the rest to admire.

It was an extraordinary gesture: after the scenes in her bedroom, Barbara could not account for it, unless he wanted to put her at a disadvantage. She determined to match him in affability and, smiling, this time more broadly, she thanked him again, and begged him to hold her pearls while she placed the earrings in her earlobes. She was still admiring them in a large, ormolu mirror which hung near to the fireplace, when Bragg announced dinner.

It was impossible that Barbara should continue distant even towards her husband, when he had given her such a generous present, and, determined that nobody should be able to accuse her of being either disagreeable or ungrateful, she drew Reyne, for the first time, into her conversation at dinner. She even made him laugh by relating some of the more amusing mischances which she had witnessed previously at balls and assemblies, describing them with a droll sense of humour which enchanted him, and which gave him an opportunity to see why she was so much admired.

In consequence of the coming ball, the gentlemen did not withdraw after dinner, and very little later, the first of their guests began to arrive. Since Miss Waverley and her family were naturally amongst them, Barbara took the opportunity to take Mary to one side before they were swamped by the crowds which would surely follow.

'Dearest Ba,' said Mary, at once, whispering so as not to be overheard, 'let me look at you. Are you all right? Did he come to your room? Oh, love, I have been so anxious!'

'Then I am very sorry for it,' said Barbara, with tolerable composure, 'for you might very well have been saved the trouble.'

'Do you mean that he didn't come to you, Ba dear? Oh, thank heavens! How relieved you must have been. But I was almost sure he would not. Not so soon. You have surely misjudged him, dearest. He must be more thoughtful than you gave him credit for. Sure and he must wish to get to know you better before you enter into any closer relationship. So much more sensible.'

'Before you take steps to have him beatified, Mary,' said Barbara, regaining some of her indignation in the telling of it, 'he did come to my room, if you must know.'

'But didn't you say that I had no need to have been anxious, Ba?' Mary blushed, prettily. 'Oh, but if he came to you, then you must mean that it was not so . . . that you found it not so . . . . I mean, you found that all was well,' she petered off, weakly.

Barbara could not help but giggle at her confusion. 'Would that it were,' she said, with a grimace. 'You quite mistake my meaning: all is decidedly *not* well.'

'Why? What happened, love? Oh! I don't mean that, but, oh my dear, he was not . . . unpleasant?'

'He was decidedly unpleasant. At first I thought he had more delicacy than to come into my room. I had even put out my candle and had gone to sleep. But then, he appeared in my doorway in his dressing-gown! Almost at once we had a frightful disagreement and I sent him back to his own bedchamber.'

'And did he go, Ba? Just like that?' asked Mary, in a voice of awe, everything she had ever heard of gentlemen inclining her to the belief that they were not to be got rid of so easily. 'How did you dare? I should not have had the courage.'

'I dared because by then I was so angry with him that I'd have expelled Lucifer had he tried to come in. My dear, you have never heard *anyone* so ungallant in your life as Reyne was to me. He said that he does not admire my looks at all and that he is only here to honour our fathers' agreement. Now, I don't care whether he admires me or not, but you must admit that it would be odious of any gentleman to say such a thing to his wife.'

'He said that to you, Ba? Intolerable! For shame! I should never have believed he could be so ungentlemanly.'

'Well, he is! Decidedly so. Not that I care a jot if he thinks me unattractive. I did not let him near me after he had been so churlish, as you may imagine,' said Barbara, conveniently forgetting her own share in the argument.

'I should think not, indeed!' cried Mary, indignantly.

'And you will never guess what he had the effrontery to do next,' said Barbara, coming even closer, to put her mouth as near as possible to Mary's ear, so as to prevent any possibility of being overheard. She then went on to describe in full detail, exactly what had happened in her room between the time she had awoken to find Lord Reyne in her bed, and the time he left after breakfast.

'Abominable!' cried Mary, putting her hands up to her cheeks, which were now feeling quite hot. 'Oh Ba, you must surely hate him! But what did he say to you when you met again during the day? That must have been so embarrassing.'

'We've hardly spoken, as you may imagine,' said Barbara; glad that her friend understood how badly she had been used, 'but then, this evening, he did the most unaccountable thing. When I came down to dinner he gave me this pendant and earrings.'

'Oh Ba! They are beautiful! But how very odd of him when he has been so churlish. Do you think he could be one of those eccentric gentleman one reads of in Mrs Radcliffe's novels? Or perhaps he is ashamed of his behaviour last night and this is his way of apologizing?'

'I haven't the least notion, though I suspect he has done it just to make me appear to be in the wrong. It is just the sort of odious thing he would do. But I am determined not to sink to his level, so I have made myself as agreeable as possible in the circumstances. Nobody shall say that it is *my* fault if this marriage does not take.'

Much as Mary admired the jewels, she was horrified that such an embarrassing night should have fallen to her friend's lot, and would have wished to hear more, but that her mother came over at that moment and took her into the ballroom, whilst Lady Reyne was ushered by Lady Cornford into the receiving line to help greet their guests.

There was little chance that Lord Cornford's fashionable neighbours would not flock *en masse* to a ball which gave them the double satisfaction of an opportunity to meet two heroes of Waterloo and a chance of seeing for themselves the intriguing situation which existed between the young earl and countess. Thus, at the appointed time, a constant stream of carriages, led by flambeaux-carrying, running footmen, entirely blocked the long drive, queuing to disgorge their owners before the front vestibule, which quickly became crowded with elegant people, handing their cloaks and greatcoats to servants and moving forward to join the queue greeting their hosts.

Mr Robert Falconer was one of the first to arrive and, pausing only to share a few words with one or two friends, he hurried to join the receiving line, smiling at Barbara before he reached her.

Barbara had looked forward to the ball all day, for she had never been one of the poor unfortunates who suffered the mortification of being a wallflower, and she had no reason to suppose that tonight would be any different: she was certain to have all her dances taken, because she *always* had all her dances taken.

But tonight, she had an extra satisfaction in seeing Mr Falconer pushing his way towards her, her gratification growing as it quickly became clear that he had no intention whatever in disguising his admiration or offering her less than his usual, distinguishing attention.

'My dear Lady Reyne,' he said, as he came up to her, 'I hope you will allow me to tell you that you look most extraordinarily beautiful this evening? How is it that you manage always to look a little more charmingly than when we last met?'

Barbara, who trusted that Reyne had overheard, looked delightfully confused by his praise, but was spirited enough to reply, with a light laugh, 'Do you think that perhaps it might be because last time we met I was windswept from having been riding my horse, sir?'

Ignoring the rest of the crowd pushing forward from behind, Mr Falconer stood squarely in front of Barbara, and looked deeply into her eyes, as if considering her words. Then he shook his head, a very intimate smile on his lips. 'No, that's not the reason at all,' he said, his face taking on an expression which more than one young lady, close enough to see it, wished he might send in her direction. 'I think, you know, that you must accustom yourself to being always thought the loveliest woman in the room. But then, you are used to that, aren't you?'

'Too much, sir,' she said, her colour rising at the extravagance of his compliment.

'On the contrary, ma'am, far, far too little.'

To Barbara's disgust, she distinctly heard Reyne, who was standing on her other side, snort derisively. Her usual reaction when Mr Falconer offered her a compliment which was over-fulsome, was to attempt to dampen his ardour: hearing Lord Reyne's obvious amusement, she was moved to more encouragement. Raising her fan, so that only her eyes showed, she said, flirting from behind it quite outrageously, 'You are very gracious, sir. When one has spent hours getting ready for a ball, it would be lowering indeed not to have at least one gentleman appreciate the effort.'

'For my own poor sake, I should be very gratified were it only one gentleman you had to thank for your share in the general admiration this evening,' said Falconer, bowing over her hand, 'but I dare not hope for it. Lady Reyne is always the most admired woman, wherever she is.'

There was no opportunity for him to say more at present, the general crush of people waiting to be introduced becoming clearly impatient and pushing him forward into the ballroom, but as he moved ahead, reluctantly releasing her hand, Barbara could not resist sending Reyne a triumphant look.

And Barbara had other admirers than Mr Falconer whom she intended to use in order to try to bring her husband to heel, and after an interval of a few minutes, during which time she had greeted a host of friends, another of her favourites, in the form of Lord John Wynnon, stood before her.

It had been a matter of chance which had brought Lord John into the vicinity, for he was the son of Viscount Darenglass, who resided in the county of Derbyshire. Lord John – a rather stocky, very handsome and typically English young gentleman, with heavy straight hair the colour of ripe wheat – had first come into Cheshire nearly two years earlier, on becoming the heir, through the death of a favourite uncle, to a neat little property nearby. He had come intending to put the estate in the hands of a steward and think no more about it, but that was before he had seen Lady Reyne. He still resided sometimes in Derbyshire, but now, much of his time was spent in Cheshire.

He was a very correct, very upright young man, extremely protective of Lady Reyne's reputation, and always tried to keep the outward indications of his admiration well within the bounds of propriety, whatever he might feel within. But, whilst rumours of the losses at Waterloo had been in the process of being speculated upon, inwardly he had ridden high on hope, and, though he hoped he was not an unfeeling man, he was as disappointed as Falconer to learn that Reyne had come through quite unscathed. It was even more of a blow to hear of his arrival at Hurst Park. While he was away at the wars he was easy to ignore: now that he was back, that was impossible. He had not been to see Lady Reyne since he had heard of her husband's intended arrival. Common sense told him that, with Reyne *in situ*, the sensible course would be to withdraw from the lists, but still he lingered. He had the young man's optimism which told him that 'anything could happen', and though he had no very great idea what that anything could be, he could not bear to go back into Derbyshire until all hope was entirely gone. He had decided that, however much it might cost him, he must see Barbara with her husband in order to decide for himself how things stood between them.

As he passed through the hall and took his place in the line, Barbara caught his look of dismay when he first saw Reyne, and felt sorry for him. She remembered having described Reyne to him several times as being rather ineffectual, and she felt a little guilty, for she knew that in her dealings with him, she had often flirted lightheartedly, knowing that, with him, it went deeper. She suspected that Reyne had sufficient pride not to bear with equanimity any attempts to monopolize his wife: Mr Falconer, she was sure, was quite able to look after himself: Lord John, far more sensitive, and indeed, reminding her very much of Guy, she was determined not to have hurt.

'Lady Reyne,' he said, with quiet satisfaction, taking the hand she offered, 'how charmingly you look this evening. I shall ask you at once to save me two dances, else I shan't get a chance later, I know. I missed you at Mrs Crozenor's ball: I'd not have gone had I not been certain you would be there. You were sorely missed. Nobody there could hold a candle to you. I left very early myself.'

'We *were* invited, sir,' said Barbara, pleased that Reyne must have heard him. 'But we were preparing for Reyne's arrival, you know. And you must not flatter me, sir, not an old married lady. I am sure there were many young ladies there who eclipsed me entirely.'

Lord John could not allow that, in his eyes, at least, such a thing was possible, and he tripped over his words in an effort to assure her of it. He had not realized that Lord Reyne was so close, nor that he had spoken loudly enough for him to overhear every word until Reyne's voice in his ear said pleasantly, 'Yes, yes, she knows all that, sir, for she has a husband to tell her so. Do disappear, now, there's a good fellow. I'm going to dance with my wife. If you are very lucky, I might let you take a dance later on. But you can't have her now. It would be unthinkable, you know, were she to open the ball with anyone else.'

Had she not felt so sorry for Lord John, his ludicrous dismay might have made Barbara laugh, but she could not help thinking that he looked like Guy deprived of a treat: besides, he was too good a friend. Excusing herself with a promise that she would certainly save him two dances, she walked off with Reyne towards the ballroom, promising herself that she would give Lord John some small consolation later in the evening when she was free.

# Chapter Thirteen

LORD AND LADY Reyne walked to one end of the ballroom and the set formed behind them as the orchestra started up. To Barbara's surprise, Lord Reyne was now an accomplished dancer, and, after the minute or two she took to discover it, she sent him a mischievous look and said, 'My dear sir, what can you have been up to? Only eight years away and you have already learned to dance. What industry!'

'I know. It's astonishing, isn't it?' he replied, taking up her tone. 'I rushed to learn just for you, as you may imagine. You must know that I take my responsibilities very seriously.'

'I'm sure,' she said, looking up from under her lashes, 'indeed, I am hopeful that one day, if you study hard enough, you will even remember where I live.'

'Oh that is very easy now, My Lady,' said Lord Reyne, knocking the wind from her sails, 'You live wherever I do.'

She took a deep, indignant breath, glad that the movement of the dance carried her away from him at that moment, for she was not certain how to answer such blatant provocation. The dance bringing them back together, and apparently unaware that he had said anything with which they were not in accord, Reyne said, 'I was on Wellington's staff towards the end of the war, you know. He would not have tolerated any one of his officers being ungraceful in the ballroom, so it is him you have to thank for having such an exceptional partner.'

'You are not so exceptional,' said Barbara, crushingly. 'And I could hardly know that you were on the great man's staff when you didn't write to tell me so. I have some talents, but fortune-telling is not one of them.'

'Is it not? Then I owe you an apology for not writing, though you could not have expected me to know that you had not included fortune-telling amongst your accomplishments. I cannot believe that your mama allowed such an omission.'

'It was remiss of her, sir, but then, never having studied the black arts herself, she could not know that I would need it.'

Lord Reyne burst into laughter. 'Very well,' he acknowledged, 'you are too quick for me. I shall admit at once, before I sink myself any further, that I am not a good correspondent.'

'Not a good correspondent? What you, My Lord? Whatever can you mean?' she said, biting her bottom lip to stop from laughing. 'Surely nobody could expect to receive more than eight letters in eight years from her husband? And not even one of those after he had left England. It would be too demanding of any woman to ask to hear more often.'

'You weren't any better,' he reminded her. 'I didn't get a single letter from you either, from the time I left England. Very disappointing.'

'Yes, I am heartily ashamed of myself,' she said, sucking in her cheeks to try and stop herself from laughing. 'Though I do have to wonder a little if that might have had anything to do with the fact that you did not send me your direction?'

'And then, of course,' he went on lamely, 'it was difficult to get letters home.'

This time she did laugh. 'Absurd man,' she said lightly. 'Do you suppose that none of the gentlemen in these parts have been in the war? And every one of their families heard from them very regularly.'

'Well, you have me,' he admitted. 'I am a rogue and a scoundrel.'

'Don't expect me to disagree with you,' she said, with a grimace. 'Odious creature.'

*

There could be few parents happier than Lord and Lady Cornford that evening as they watched their daughter lead the dance with Reyne, and, while they were so occupied, Lord Cornford could not resist taking the opportunity to whisper to his wife, 'I think it is going to be all right, my dear, I really do.'

His wife sighed happily in agreement. 'Oh, my dear, how well they look together. And Barbara is smiling, so she must be content, do not you think so?'

'She would have to be a very fussy young woman were she not. My dear, the necklace and earrings he bought her must have cost him upwards of two hundred guineas. What a charming gesture. And he has told me today that the dowager is happy for Barbara to take possession of the family jewels whenever she pleases. He did not bring them as he considers them unfashionable, but he is happy to have new settings made for them should she wish for it. I should think she must be pleased at that, do not you?'

'I am not concerned with family jewels, Edward, I'm only pleased that Reyne has turned out so well and that they seem to be getting on. Mark you, I cannot help but wish that they had met for the first time this evening, for I am sure they would have taken to each other immediately: she's so lovely, and he's so handsome. I don't see how they could have helped it. And then all these misunderstandings could have been avoided.'

'Are you still blaming me for that?' said Lord Cornford, irritably. 'I still think it was fortunate that his father and I made the match while they were young for, you may depend on it, one of them would be married by now, else.'

'Dear Lord Cornford, blaming you for what?' said a silky voice at their side. In his eagerness to defend himself, and in her eagerness to blame him, neither of the Cornfords had noticed, until it was too late, one of their guests, a certain Mrs Baggeley sidling up.

Mrs Honoria Baggeley professed herself to be a close friend of Lady Cornford: Lady Cornford would have described her to her true intimates as a tiresome acquaintance, whom it was impossible to cut, Mr Baggeley being equally despised by Lord Cornford as a gossiping old bore. In such a close community as theirs, it would have been impossible not to invite the Baggeleys to the ball, but Lady Cornford wished they had not come. They belonged to a lesser branch of an important northern family, but to hear them talk, one could be forgiven for imagining them to be minor royalty. The fact that a distant cousin was a baronet raised them, in their own estimation, to the same rank, and their conversation was larded with talk of their cousin, Baronet Christie. Seeing the simpering features of Mrs Baggeley so close, Lord Cornford excused himself on a very flimsy excuse indeed, and left his poor wife to endure the misery of conversation with her without being able to escape.

'And what were you blaming on poor Cornford, my dear?' asked Mrs Baggeley, in an arch tone which never failed to raise her hackles.

'Blaming Cornford? You must have misheard,' said his wife, lying shamefully. 'On such a happy evening, I think neither of us has cause for blame. Indeed, when I see Barbara and Reyne so radiant, I think I shall never be unhappy again. He is such a dear young man.'

'Certainly they look happy enough, my dear. You must be pleased, finally, to have him return to Barbara. I won't pretend to you, ma'am: some people thought it was his intention never to come back.'

'There are always ill-natured people about,' said Lady Cornford, deceptively mild. 'But thank heavens you are not one of them. Only the very worst-natured people could spread such an ill-founded rumour. That young man has done nothing but give six years of his life for his country, and at much personal cost. Well for us that he, and all those other brave young men concentrated on their military duties instead of coming home, else goodness knows where we might have been by now. Overrun by the French, I shouldn't wonder, and Boney in Whitehall! Some of the more spiteful tongues hereabout probably deserved it.'

'Indeed, it doesn't bear thinking about, though some say that they were surprised not to have seen Lord Reyne come home after Waterloo. Most officers did so, it seems.'

'They obviously don't have such a nice sense of duty as Reyne. When Wellington, himself, asked Reyne to assist with all those diplomatic chores, which naturally arise from warfare, he didn't feel that he could refuse. I was shocked to hear from him that considerable numbers of troops still remain in France and Belgium. Imagine, all those poor women still waiting for their husbands. He tried to get as many of those poor men home as he could.'

'But not himself, apparently. Forgive me, my dear, but did you know that there has been some talk that Lady Reyne did not altogether welcome his return?'

'And what do you think, Mrs Baggeley,' said her mama, with some satisfaction, pointing to where Barbara and Reyne were dancing. 'Do you think she looks unhappy?'

Even the most dispassionate observer must have been obliged to say that she did not, and Mrs Baggeley admitted, again, that they seemed to be on good terms. They were that moment walking down the set, and something Reyne said made Barbara laugh so much that her eyes sparkled. It looked very much as if he was making love to her, and Lady Cornford watched them complacently.

Seeing her pleasure, Mrs Baggeley added, spitefully, 'Some people's noses will be put out of joint at seeing them together, I daresay.' Her hand was pointed languidly in Mr Falconer's direction. 'That gentleman must be disappointed to see Reyne home,' she said.

'Mr Falconer? I haven't the faintest idea why he should be,' said Lady Cornford, stiffly. 'Any friend of Barbara's must be pleased to see her reunited with her husband. We, as you may suppose, are delighted with Reyne. And, really, he has grown so handsome that Barbara could hardly be less so.'

'I wonder whether Lord Reyne will like his wife having so many dances with Mr Falconer as he is used to taking,' said Mrs Baggeley, archly.

'I hardly know,' said Lady Cornford, stiffly, 'but I am sure that my daughter will do just as he wishes.'

Mrs Baggeley realized from her tone that she had gone too far. 'What a sweet head you have on tonight, Lady Cornford,' she gushed.

'Madame Thiers calls it an *African turban*,' said Lady Cornford, quite as willing to find a new topic of conversation. 'Apparently, it is based on a design which is half Moorish, half Persian, which I confess I didn't even know were African, did you? I cannot tell you how pleased I am with Madame Thiers, for I must confess that before she set herself up in Tarsall, I had allowed myself to fall sadly behind in matters of fashion.'

'My cousin, Sir James's wife, says that one can never be considered really fashionable unless one shops in Bond Street. She always goes to Madame Bertin, and my cousin's wife is quite the most modish person I know.'

Lady Cornford held her breath and her temper in the name of hospitality, but, looking deliberately at Mrs Baggeley's head, on which she had stuffed, over her mousy curls, a white net and gold turban known as *l'antique*, very pointedly made no reply.

It was fortunate that at that moment, Mrs Waverley appeared at her friend's elbow. Giving Mrs Baggeley no chance to accompany them, she made an excuse to take Lady Cornford off with her to another part of the ballroom.

So close was their friendship that, despite the great difference between them of rank and fortune, they invariably used their first names with each other. 'Grace, you are a saintly woman!' cried Lady Cornford, as Mrs Baggeley receded behind them. 'I thought I would be stuck with her forever. What an odious creature she is, to be sure. Did you know that to be really fashionable, one simply must shop in Bond Street at Madame Bertin's, for I never did?'

'And I suppose "my cousin, Sir James Christie, Baronet," told her that!'

'Very nearly. It was "my cousin, Sir James's wife", actually,' she said, so nearly matching Mrs Baggeley's tone that Mrs Waverley giggled. 'It is very hard that one should be obliged to invite such people. I would rather spend an evening with my maid. Oh, but my dear, I do not intend to allow anything to upset me tonight. I am so happy!'

'It is Barbara and Reyne, of course. Yes, I've been watching them too. Do you know, my dear, I think they will confound all the gossips after all. After last night, Mary and I have been so anxious, but now I see that we have been worrying for nothing. Barbara looks radiant.'

'Yes indeed,' said her mother, 'though I confess that I am quite at a loss to know how it has come about. I do not hesitate to say so to you, for I know you won't tell a soul, but last night, after you left, she was quite distraught to think that he might come to her room.'

Mrs Waverley's eyes widened with interest. 'And did he?' she whispered, coming close.

However embarrassed Lady Cornford had been to talk over such matters with her daughter, with her friend, a woman of the same age and experience, she had no such scruples. 'Apparently he did, my dear, for he was in her bed this morning when Stowe went up with her tray.'

'And were they. . . ?'

'Good God, Grace, how should I know? You don't think I asked Stowe that, do you?'

'No, of course not, Edith,' said Mrs Waverley, turning scarlet. 'Stupid of me.'

'But then he came down to breakfast without her. And, instead of spending the day with her, as one would expect, this morning he took Guy out driving in his curricle and spent the rest of the day fishing with Captain Radleigh. I don't mind telling you, Grace, that by teatime this afternoon we had just about given up on them.'

'Don't you think that, perhaps, he was just making Captain Radleigh feel more at home, Edith?' said Mrs Waverley, helpfully.

The two frowned, as if considering the matter then shook their heads at the same time. 'No!' they said in unison.

'But now, only look at them. They seem just like any normal newly wedded pair. And did you see the pendant and earrings he bought her?'

Mrs Waverley assured her that she had, and said all that was expected of their beauty and of Reyne's good nature in thinking of it, leaving Lady Cornford so much in charity with her friend that she remembered that it was now her turn to be interested in Mary.

'My dear,' she said, peering across the room in Mary's direction, how well Mary looks tonight. That cream-coloured satin looks charmingly with her dark hair. And who is that she is dancing with? Ah, it is Captain Radleigh, to be sure. I do like that young man, Grace. You know he is the son of Pulteney. What a good thing that would be for your girl.'

Mrs Waverley laughed, not without a tinge of wistfulness. 'It certainly would, Edith,' she said, 'but I am sure that Mary's expectations are more modest. Pulteney will certainly want an older, more established family for his son.'

'You think too much on rank, Grace, and forget all Mary's excellent qualities. And then, you know, she will have an excellent dowry. I am sure that she would grace any man's home, with her accomplishments and her sweet temper. A man who knows what he is about looks for a woman of charm and sense and those she has in abundance. I am certain that we shall both live to see her make a good match, if you will only stir yourself to bring it about. Would you like me to try to promote a match between her and Radleigh? I am certainly ready to do so.'

Mrs Waverley looked horrified at that, knowing how much Mary would abhor such interference. 'On no account in the world, Edith. I can assure you that Mary has no pretensions in that direction.'

Both ladies looked back at the set in which their daughters were dancing: each of them seeming as if she had not a care in the world. Seeing her daughter's flushed cheeks and radiant looks as her husband leaned down to speak to her, Lady Cornford felt a glow of expectation. She was even beginning to speculate on how soon she would begin to see her grandchildren.

Mrs Waverley's daughter looked happy too. Captain Radleigh was clearly taking pains to amuse her, and her expressive face illustrated every nuance of their conversation. Mrs Waverley could not but hope that her daughter would not have her expectations raised by that young man.

# Chapter Fourteen

MRS WAVERLEY MIGHT have been spared that worry: far from building any hopes on Captain Radleigh, Mary was the most miserable girl in the room, and only a huge effort made her appear cheerful. How could her mother know that she had no interest whatever in Captain Radleigh, when Mary had taken such pains to hide the strength of her real attachment, which was to Mr Falconer?

It had been an ambiguous business from the beginning, for in feeling herself drawn to Mr Falconer she knew that she was being false to Barbara. But always, at the back of her mind, had been the undeniable fact that, since Barbara was a married woman, her friendship with Falconer must finally lead to nothing, unless Barbara had been willing to forget all claims to honour, which she could not believe.

At the time when Mr Falconer had left with his mother for Tunbridge Wells, Mary had little hope of winning him away from Barbara, but the earl's unexpected return had encouraged her to hope, especially when Reyne turned out to be so very well-looking. She had begun to think that Mr Falconer would finally have to admit defeat and think of another: perhaps even of *her*. And, really, it was not too great a leap of imagination to make since, though Barbara was quite unaware of it, Mr Falconer always, unaccountably, flirted with *her* when Barbara was elsewhere: indeed, even when he was with Barbara, she often felt his eyes on herself, compelling her to meet his gaze.

She was already in the ballroom, amongst a group of mainly young people clustered around Captain Radleigh, when Mr Falconer entered, the gentlemen wanting to hear about the late war, the ladies happy simply to be charmed by him. As Mr Falconer came over to join them, one young man was in the middle of saying to Radleigh, 'What was it like, sir? It must have been a fine thing to have been with Wellington at the final battle.'

She was near enough to hear Radleigh answer, with a wry smile, having thought back to the noise, and the fear, and the terrible stench of death which had been Waterloo, 'Oh, very fine. The most cheerful fellows in Brussels went to the Duchess of Richmond's ball beforehand: it's rather a pity that most of them are now dead.'

In the cluster of questions which followed, Mr Falconer took Mary aside. 'Miss Waverley, you look very pretty this evening,' he said, with a slight bow. 'You must be sure and save me one of your dances later on.'

Mary blushed with pleasure, though she noticed that, as usual, he hadn't actually named the dance which he wished to take: indeed, it had sometimes crossed her mind that perhaps he did so deliberately so as to keep himself free whenever someone more eligible was available.

'We have been listening to the captain's accounts of Waterloo, sir,' said Mary, casting an eye in Radleigh's direction. 'It seems to have been the most terrifying experience. How much we owe to those brave men.'

'Indeed,' said Falconer, very correctly echoing her serious tone. 'I am afraid such heroic souls cast us mere civilians into the shade. And quite rightly too.'

'Oh no, indeed, sir, I would not wish you to imagine that I think anything of the kind,' Mary hastened to assure him. 'Had Bonaparte's forces landed in England, we should have been in a sorry plight were all our gentlemen to have been abroad.'

Mr Falconer was moved to take her hand between both his own. 'You are extremely soothing to the soul, Miss Waverley,' he said smoothly, 'which is probably why I enjoy your company so much.'

Small wonder, then, after such extravagant compliments, Mary began to feel that anything was possible. It was a hope cruelly dashed only a few moments later when the small orchestra on the rostrum, which had been quietly tuning up, began to play the music introducing the first set of dances. This seemed to be the signal Mr Falconer had been waiting for. Still with the same smoothness, he bowed low over Mary's hand again then, standing upright said, 'I know you'll excuse me, Miss Waverley: you know I always have the first two with Lady Reyne. She'll be expecting me.'

And without more ado, he walked away from her, leaving her absolutely abandoned out in the body of the room, away from the group from which he had plucked her. She felt as if the world rocked at her feet. His behaviour was so ungentlemanly, taking her out of her party and leaving her there, that she could scarcely believe that he had treated her thus, after speaking so intimately just before.

It was then that Lord Reyne escorted Barbara into the ballroom and led her to the head of the set just forming. Mr Falconer was halfway across the ballroom by that time, but even from that distance, Mary could see the crooked grin with which he tried to disguise his mortification.

Mary was sure that since she was the nearest girl to Mr Falconer, and that he had already asked her to save him a dance, he would now return to claim it, for, really, it was the only polite thing to do. Indeed, he had even looked across at her, as if he was considering the matter. Instead, he had frowned, apparently with a certain amount of regret, as if to say, 'No, not her', then his eyes had moved to see who else was nearby. His eyes had obviously alighted on someone else, and without another glance in Mary's direction, he moved away and took a partner from a small group of girls at the edge of the room.

Standing alone near the middle of the room, Mary was looking about her for the nearest group of people she could join without being too conspicuous, when Captain Radleigh stepped out of his circle of admirers and walked quickly across to her.

'Miss Waverley,' he said, smiling down at her and holding out his hand. 'Will you do me the great honour of dancing the first two with me?'

Hardly knowing what she did, she placed her hand in his and allowed him to take her into the set, his rank allowing him to take a position second only to Reyne. To her confusion, Mary found herself placed above many of those she had been used to think her superiors.

Mr Falconer, she saw, was partnering Miss Annabel Chalmers and, knowing him, she wasn't at all surprised. Miss Chalmers was the daughter and only child of Sir William Chalmers, a widowed landowner with many thousands of acres, and recently knighted. Even so, Mr Falconer could do no more than take her to join the second eight. Mr Falconer had to peer a long way along the line to catch sight of Barbara: when he saw that Miss Waverley was now just below her and dancing with Radleigh, he shrugged his shoulders in surprise.

Good for her, had been his first thought: his second, characteristically, that once Radleigh knew the details of her background, Miss Waverley would very quickly find herself back in the second set like himself. Not that he begrudged her that moment of triumph: he was something of an adventurer himself, and his birth, though he had managed thus far to hoodwink the county into believing it something more, was quite as humble as hers.

Just at present, Mr Falconer was in something of a quandary, for his ambition, once he had seen that Lady Reyne was disposed to admire him, had led him to spend the past year waiting to see whether the annulment which the entire neighbourhood had predicted between the countess and her husband occurred. If it had, he had been reasonably confident that, given a little luck, he, perhaps, might take Reyne's place as Barbara's husband. Much as he admired her, Mr Falconer wasn't in love with her, but he knew his own worth, and he knew women. With

Reyne out of the way, he was sure that Barbara would need little encouragement to accept his own proposals: he was also shrewdly certain that, should an annulment take place, with all the scandal that entailed, her parents would be only too pleased to get her speedily settled. And marriage to the daughter of a viscount was far, far higher than even his good looks and charm could take him in a more conventional manner, his fortune being so much less respectable than his style of living had led his neighbours to believe; his family rather more obscure than the lofty Norfolk family to which he had hinted he belonged.

And now, after he had wasted so much time, this tiresome business of Reyne had almost blasted his hopes. When he had met Barbara earlier in the day – surely at her instigation – he had been almost certain that he was still in with a chance, and he was therefore considerably put out to see her husband leading her on to the floor of the ballroom, and the couple apparently on good terms.

It was that which had led him to partner Miss Chalmers. She was not nearly such a prize as Barbara, not quite as beautiful, nor of such standing, but she was still a very attractive girl, and Sir William was undeniably a man of considerable means and influence. In his own way, he had much to offer. It was a very delicate matter, and he set himself the balancing trick of first ensuring that Lady Barbara was entirely lost to him before he committed himself to securing the other.

He caught sight of Miss Waverley again briefly, at that moment in his considerations, regretting not for the first time, that it was Miss Chalmers and not Miss Waverley whose father owned all those acres, since her person he admired more than either Lady Reyne or Miss Chalmers. But it was not to be thought of. His underhand machinations must continue, and he must dance and flirt his way with Miss Chalmers through the first two dances, but not so overtly as to excite indignation in Lady Reyne's bosom.

Captain Radleigh, meanwhile, was watching Miss Waverley very closely as they danced. Indeed, he had been watching her even before he danced with her, ever since she came into the ballroom, for tonight, in view of Falconer's active pursuit of Lady Reyne, he intended to begin his task of rousing Mr Falconer to a proper appreciation of Miss Waverley instead. He had seen the way Falconer had flirted with her, and the way in which he was surely raising expectations he had no intention of satisfying. He had also seen him cruelly abandon her. It had given him a good deal of pleasure to be able to take Miss Waverley so near to the top of the set, a long way above Falconer. It would give him a great deal more pleasure if he could bring Falconer to a state where Miss Waverley could sport with his feelings as he now played with hers.

Mary was all gratitude for Radleigh's neatness in rescuing her, but her heart was overflowing, and she could not speak. They were dancing a quadrille and, after the first few steps, Captain Radleigh said, with a droll smile, 'It is very bad *ton* not to speak during a quadrille, Miss Waverley. They will all think you don't like me, and I simply refuse to believe in that possibility.'

Miserable as she felt, Radleigh's high spirits were infectious. 'Yes, I could tell at once, as soon as we met, that you were a shrinking violet, sir,' she retorted, spiritedly.

'It is very discerning in you, Miss Waverley, to have recognized the retiring personality beneath the outward show I erect so bravely about my person.'

'Absurd man! There is not a soul on earth who would believe you to be bashful.'

'But it is true, I assure you. You don't know how grateful I am to you for agreeing to dance with me, for I don't know who else would take pity on me.'

'First a shrinking violet, now a wallflower. You only have to stake a claim to being an English rose, and you will have a garden full,' she said, impishly.

'Now that would be silly, Miss Waverley,' he said, making her an elegant bow, 'for I am dancing with an English rose, and she is nothing like me.'

Since she hardly knew him, Mary didn't know how to answer

the unaccustomed flattery, and she lowered her eyes so as not to meet his as the dance continued.

'This is too bad,' said Radleigh, putting his mouth very close to her ear. 'Now you won't even look at me! And you, my first partner. Don't you realize how it looks? It is going to be very bad for my reputation as a partner. All the other ladies will wonder what I could have said to deserve such a put down.'

How could Mary help but laugh? 'I am watching my steps, sir,' she said, with a dignified little bow of the head.

'Why? Don't you dance the quadrille often in Cheshire? Oh, but of course you don't. I forgot we are in the country, so I suppose it is all country dances hereabouts.'

'Yes, and I suppose you think we do them all around a maypole, too. I can assure you, Captain Radleigh, that we do nothing of the sort, and we dance everything here that is danced in Town,' she assured him firmly.

'I am delighted to hear it, for that means you waltz too, so you must save me the next two. And you shall let me take you into supper, if you please, for I am well known for always taking in the prettiest girl in the room. It would be ruinous to my reputation to have to take in a dowdy.'

Colour ran through Mary's cheeks. 'You mean to be kind,' she protested. 'You saw Mr Falconer's behaviour, and it is that which makes you ask me. Really, there is no need. Do not waste your evening on that account: I assure you it is of little matter.'

'It might be of little matter to you, but it isn't to me,' he protested. 'I want you to dance with me. And to have supper, else I'll probably end up having to ask one of the many antidotes Lady Cornford seems to have swamped us with. You wouldn't want me to get indigestion?'

'You are very good, sir,' she said, determined to remain calm, 'but I really cannot allow you to have your evening spoilt.'

'But it is you who are spoiling it! Oh come now, Miss Waverley, don't deny me some sport. Do it for my sake, if not for your own. My foot itched to kick that gentleman for you, and I hate to see you let him get away with it so tamely. Dance those dances and have supper with me, or are you really prepared to let that arrogant fellow think he may use you as he pleases?'

She looked up into his face, saw his affability, and a mischievous smile spread across her features. 'Do you know, I don't believe I am,' she said.

'Excellent,' said Radleigh. 'We shall have the whole room talking. I'm not sure if you know it, but some gentlemen find military men an enormous challenge. We are like a red rag to a bull. They will often go to any lengths to steal our partners from us. I just mention it, you know, so that you don't change your mind. I am not at all nice, and am certainly not above subterfuge in getting my own way.'

'Are you always such an avalanche of determination, sir?' she asked, her smiling face robbing her words of any insult.

'Always,' said Radleigh, triumphantly.

By the end of the first two dances, it began to feel very hot in the ballroom. Collars were wilting; gloves had to be changed; and Lord Cornford's excellent punch was drunk in quantities. In the interval before the next two dances, more than one couple drifted out through the French windows and on to the veranda, some being followed by chaperones, but most being allowed this small freedom, there being so many people nearby.

Captain Radleigh, noticing that Mary was heated, first took her fan from her wrist and wafted it near her face to cool her, and then, noticing the exodus, persuaded her that they might very well walk out with the rest, and take advantage of the evening air.

Lady Reyne caught sight of them just as they were passing outside and a secretive smile touched her lips. Reyne saw the look and said, 'I see you approve of Miss Waverley walking in the gardens with Radleigh. I confess I am surprised. The ladies of Cheshire have certainly become bolder since I was last here. You would hardly even speak to me when I was here before.'

'Oh yes, we are very quick to take up the latest mode here,' said Barbara. 'It has only taken us eight years to alter, which, as you yourself admit, is a mere nothing! Of course, one would not be so bold in London, but here, where we know everybody, it is felt quite safe. As for Miss Waverley, perhaps it is the gentleman who is the bolder of that pair. All that training you both had with the Spanish ladies must have helped enormously, I shouldn't wonder. I doubt it was at Mary's instigation that they went outside. Certainly I never saw her do so before: but then, it is an exceptionally hot evening, and she looked very heated.'

'You are a very good friend and do just as you ought in finding an excuse for Miss Waverley. Every couple should have somebody to find a good reason when they wish to be romantic, else how would anybody's suit ever prosper? Fortunately, as a married couple, we don't need an excuse and, since that tiresome Baggeley woman appears to be bearing down on us, I think we owe it to Miss Waverley to go and join them at once. To speak plain, Lady Reyne, it is our duty to chaperone them.'

'Indeed yes,' agreed Barbara. 'Certainly I could not square it with my conscience were I to leave Miss Waverley alone with Captain Radleigh, delightful as I find Mrs Baggeley's company.'

But when they reached the veranda, Miss Waverley and the captain were nowhere to be seen: nor were any of those who had already wandered out anywhere about. On the contrary, the night was so warm, and the moon so full, that they had all taken to wandering about the gardens, some of them even going as far as the lake, an expedition made easier from Lord Cornford's having ordered a multitude of candle lanterns to be hung in festoons between the trees along the pathways to light the way.

Despite these attractions, Lady Reyne and her husband chose not to follow them, but preferred to remain on the veranda, leaning their arms lightly on a low, planted wall, which separated the house from the informal garden leading down to the lake.

'Cooler?' said Reyne, taking her shawl from where it was draped across her arms and wrapping it around her shoulders.

'Indeed yes,' said Barbara. 'It is delightful. I wish Papa could be brought to have some of the windows opened in the ballroom. But I know from experience he will not. Mama is certain that if a breath of night air reaches her she will expire on the spot. And with poor Guy being allowed to stay up, there is no hope for any of us.'

'I can't see Miss Waverley anywhere, so I am afraid our plan to save her from a fate worse than death will have to wait, since we haven't the vaguest notion in which direction they have walked.'

'Oh I do hope not a fate worse than death, sir,' said Barbara laughing. 'In poor Papa's gardens: and Captain Radleigh such a pleasant gentleman.'

'I'm glad you think so. Mary could not be in better hands, I assure you. He is liked everywhere, especially by ladies. I never knew a man so fought over.'

'If that is a hint, there is no need sir, I assure you. Mary won't fight for him. She rates her claims quite as low as others do, and would certainly not expect to attract a viscount. I must say, though, that it seems very odd to me that people of birth and fortune should limit themselves to choosing partners from such a narrow stratum in society. If one is wealthy, one has an opportunity to marry for love: not to do so seems perverse. It is very depressing that people are so worldly that they shouldn't want to marry, well, let us say, someone like Mary, simply because her father was astute enough to make a fortune: yet, if her father had been born wealthy and had never done a stroke of work in his life, people would queue up to get her.'

'If I gave the impression that I suspected Mary of trying to catch Radleigh, it was a very wrong one. The fact that she is your friend would naturally predispose me to liking her, but my own observations lead me to believe that she is a very sweet young woman. I am not her enemy, any more than you are. Like you, I hope to see her make a good match. Indeed, I hope we shall always think alike in essentials.'

'Why should we not,' laughed Barbara, 'for we were certainly in agreement when we were married, in thinking that we would be happier living apart, which showed a surprising degree of consanguinity?'

'I can only hope that we still think alike, My Lady,' said Reyne, putting his hands on her shoulders and turning her to face him, 'because I think we have lived apart for too long.'

'And whose fault is that?' she reminded him, a challenge in her voice. 'Catching a chill only to escape from me?'

'I was very bad, wasn't I?' he admitted, ruefully, lifting her hand to his lips. 'But I was very well served in doing so, for I lost the opportunity of spending all those years with the loveliest girl possible.'

'Very practised, sir,' said Barbara, forcing a light laugh, for she found herself a little out of her depth. 'You said it was Captain Radleigh who charmed ladies. He must certainly have had a rival in you. And does he give such fine presents as you do?' she asked, clasping the locket which he had earlier placed around her neck. Unexpectedly, Lord Reyne touched the smooth skin around her throat on which the necklace lay. Feeling suddenly very shy, Barbara couldn't look at him, but she felt his hands reach for her shoulders and slowly pull her towards him. Her eyes closed and she had even begun to raise her face to his, standing on her toes to reach him, when she felt him suddenly release her, and she fell back on her heels. Her eyes opened and, to her chagrin, she saw Mr Falconer walking out of the ballroom into the evening air. Never had an interruption been more unwelcome: in that moment she wished that she could magic him back to Tunbridge Wells.

'Ah, there you are, Lady Reyne,' said Falconer, as if assured of his welcome. 'I've been searching everywhere for you. The musicians are striking up again, and I came to seek the honour of your hand for the next two.'

'What a pity you didn't come and ask earlier,' said Reyne, denting his assurance. 'My dance again, I'm afraid, isn't it my love'

His smile drew an answering gleam from Barbara, and, pausing only to promise Falconer that he should certainly have the next two if he wished, she gave her husband her hand and let him lead her back to the ballroom.

'Shameless behaviour, My Lord,' she said, with a tremor of laughter, 'Poor Mr Falconer.'

'Nonsense! He is lucky that I let him dance with you at all, the way he behaves. I shall be watching that gentleman more closely from now on.'

'It could hardly be less closely than heretofore, could it?' she said sweetly.

'Little scold,' said Reyne, taking her into his arms, and tightening his arm round her waist. 'I can see that I still have a long way to go before you forgive me. But I shan't give up, you know. We Reynes never do.'

Barbara was beginning to think it the most delightful ball she had ever attended. Reyne had been so attentive and so amusing that she had even begun to think she may have misunderstood him; that, perhaps, he had merely been thoughtless in not writing, or that his circumstances made him too embarrassed to do so. The notion set up in her a glow of pleasure. She pictured the moment when his hand had touched her throat and a delicious shiver ran through her. Her lips curved in a smile of contentment and Reyne chanced to look down at her at that moment. Their eyes locked in an intimate smile. In that instant Barbara began to think that their ridiculous marriage might indeed work itself out: that perhaps all the misunderstandings might be forgotten and that they could start again, this time properly, with all that it entailed. A deep blush rushed over her face as she thought of last night. If he came to her room tonight, surely she would be unable to send him away!

She was about to give him another encouraging smile when, from the corner of the ballroom, a few feet away, a bombastic voice assaulted her eardrums, even over the sound of the musicians. Mr Baggeley had finally cornered her father and she, as well as everybody else in that part of the ballroom, was a party to their conversation.

She heard him say, 'So, My Lord, you must be pleased that that young man finally came home to get your daughter. I don't mind telling you, that if I was in that position with a daughter of mine, I'd have been tempted to take a horsewhip to him. It don't do a young woman's dignity any good to be seen to be left dangling, waiting for her husband to tell her when he's ready for her. Some of those jaunts he got up to in London before he came up here, well, for a married man, I'd have thought they were a bit wide of the mark. Imagine Sir William letting his Annabel be treated so! My son Josh, now, he may not be an earl, but he knows how to treat women. Lady Reyne must be very equable, that's all I say, falling into his arms so easily. Some women would have given him more of a run for his money, I reckon.'

Reyne's arm was still around his wife and he felt her stiffen. The dance took them away and they heard no more, but Reyne had heard Mr Baggeley very clearly and, he realized despondently, Barbara had heard him too.

# Chapter Fifteen

It was not altogether surprising that, after hearing Mr Baggeley's words, Barbara's goodwill towards her husband, which had been building all evening, was now at an end, and her neighbours, with whom she had earlier been so much in charity, seemed little more than a ghastly collection of ghouls, there only to jeer and sneer. She very properly finished her dances with Reyne, but gone was any desire to remain with him when they were done. When Mr Falconer came to claim her for the two cotillions about to begin, she showed rather too much pleasure as she walked off with him, her face wreathed in smiles.

As Reyne watched his wife being taken away by his rival, Guy, who had been on his best behaviour all evening, and making himself useful, came bounding over, like an affectionate puppy. Lifting devoted eyes to Reyne, he said, 'I say, sir, this is a fine ball. Papa says I don't have to dance, and I've eaten my way through a whole blancmange.'

'I'm glad you are enjoying it,' said Reyne, absentmindedly, his eyes noticing the way that Barbara's steps matched Falconer's so well, that it was obvious they had danced together very often.

'You don't want to worry about Mr Falconer,' Guy said anxiously, noticing the frown, which had appeared on his brother-in-law's face. 'I asked Barbara about that landau business, and she said she only took his part because I had hurt his feelings. He's quite old, you know, so I dare say that is why she did it. I heard Papa say that he must be at least thirty-five.'

'As old as *that*? said Reyne, with a wry grin. 'It's a wonder they haven't put him out to graze by now.'

'Oh, sir, you are a one,' Guy laughed.

'And you, young man, should be in bed by now, if you want me to take you out for a drive tomorrow morning. I warn you, I never stay in bed late after a ball. I shall be ready by nine o'clock, if not before, and I shan't wait for you if you're not there.'

The ball was nothing to driving a curricle and he was gone in a moment. Smiling to himself, Reyne could see him, a few moments later, saying goodnight to his parents on the other side of the ballroom. He wished that Barbara could be so easily manipulated.

Left by himself, Reyne reviewed his situation, his face stoic. He, too, had been infuriated by Mr Baggeley's remarks, and ready to do anything in his power to make up to Barbara for his own part in it. Had she allowed him, his first inclination would have been to partner her all evening, in order to make it quite clear to all those who watched that he was very well satisfied with his bride. But now, seeing Barbara with Falconer, and seeing him bend to whisper something in her ear in what he felt was an over-familiar way, his good intentions flew out of the window, especially when it became obvious that most of their guests were watching him to see how he was bearing up. No more than Barbara did he appreciate being made to look foolish, and he had a strong desire to show her how easily the *biter* could be *bitten*.

Having observed Falconer dancing with Miss Chalmers, and having been introduced to her by his wife, he considered her the perfect person to help him do so, especially since he had noticed an excess of cordiality when the two ladies had greeted each other, which led him to believe that a certain coolness already existed between them. Quite deliberately, he now went over and cut in across several other gentlemen who were begging for the pleasure of dancing the cotillions with her.

He could not have hit upon a girl who could more easily annoy his wife, for Miss Chalmers was probably the only young woman in the district whom she disliked. She was considered by many to be a handsome young woman, having a high complexion, good features and a trim figure. But that was not why Lady Reyne disliked her. Having herself a nice sense of decorum, she could not admire Miss Chalmers's more forthright character and high animal spirits. For such a young woman (Miss Chalmers was just eighteen!), she was much too free in the company of gentlemen to suit Lady Reyne's more fastidious taste. Having been spoilt by her father, she was rather too sure of herself, being excessively vain and assuming that every man she met must be attracted to her. When Reyne asked her to dance, the compliment of rank should, at least, have subdued her spirits, but she considered it no more than her due, and tripped across the floor with him, holding possessively on to his arm.

When Barbara saw Reyne bring Miss Chalmers into her set, it would have been too much to expect her to endure Reyne's challenge peaceably. With every wish to the contrary, she gave Mr Falconer far more encouragement than she would ever have dreamed of before, and if he was aware of her reasons for such a delightful volte-face, it did not make him averse from taking advantage of it.

'With that young hothead of a husband of yours hovering about, I wonder if I dare tell you how charming that gown looks, My Lady,' he began, caressingly. 'But yes: I think I must be so bold, for it would be churlish not to do so in the presence of so much beauty. How thankful I am that I was able to return from Tunbridge Wells, else I'd have missed seeing you in it.'

'Since I shall undoubtedly wear it again, sir, the loss would not have been so dreadful.'

'At the risk of offending a lady, I can only say that you are wrong. Any day when I don't see Lady Reyne is hateful.'

'Then I am very glad that you have returned, sir,' said Barbara, his words going some way to ease her wounded pride. 'I should not wish you to have any hateful days. And I am glad, too, for a different reason: who else could have partnered me so well in the cotillions? I'm sure I could not find a partner who danced them as well as you do.'

'Perhaps that is because our steps match so well,' said Falconer, with a meaning smile. 'I have long suspected that, when one dances well with another, a general harmony in other things is almost certain to follow.'

'That is a very bold supposition, sir,' said Barbara. 'I'm sure that I should need to spend a great deal of time in a person's company to be able to be sure of *that*.'

'A great deal of time spent in the company of the beautiful Lady Barbara! What a delightful thought.'

'Surely you mean *Lady Reyne*, sir?' Barbara corrected him.

'Oh no, were I to have my way, that lady would be quite free from the name of Reyne, as I am sure you are well aware.'

Barbara almost gasped at his boldness and would not chance another word, but she was very pleased at the impression of intimacy such a close conversation must have been making on Reyne. She could not resist looking across at him to see how he was bearing up. Far from being annoyed by her behaviour, he didn't seem even to have noticed it. He was still dancing with Miss Chalmers, and their conversation looked quite as intimate as her own had been. Certainly it was obvious that he was enjoying her company very well: obvious, too, much to her disgust, that, during the years they had been separated, Reyne had learned to dance the cotillion quite as elegantly as Mr Falconer. From Miss Chalmers's sparkling eyes, he obviously flirted just as easily with other women as he had earlier flirted with his wife: no doubt he would kiss her as willingly, if he got the chance. It wanted only that to set the final seal on a miserable evening, and Barbara could not wait for it to end.

But it was not yet eleven: she knew from experience that it would be several hours before she could be released from it, and she had more irritation to endure from Reyne before she could go to her bed. Not content to dance once with Miss Chalmers, Lord Reyne had the temerity, later on, to ask her again, and even took her into supper. Barbara even had to endure the exquisite annoyance of seeing him rewarded with a flower from her corsage. Naturally, with such blatant provocation, Barbara could not resist Mr Falconer's supper invitation, and she took the opportunity, knowing Reyne was nearby, to offer Falconer a flower from her own corsage, though it didn't entirely satisfy her desire to get even. When Lord John Wynnon asked her to waltz with him after supper, she was in the full stream of indignation and, despite being well aware of the depth of Lord John's feelings for her, the provocation from her husband now proved too much. Knowing that he was undoubtedly the most handsome man in the room, she let the full flow of his admiration wash over her, which encouraged him so much that, for the first time, he showed openly how much he adored her, without caring what his neighbours thought.

Several of the chaperones, gathered in a knot at the side of the ballroom, were shocked by these proceedings, and quite unable to decide if Lord and Lady Reyne actually disliked each other, or whether theirs was an example of some new form of behaviour practised by young married couples in Town, a possibility which they could well believe, since, in their opinion, London was the centre for every sort of vice. They waited to see if Lord and Lady Reyne would dance together again: saw that they did not, and saw that each of them went to a good deal of trouble to dance with every presentable partner in the room. By the time the ball ended, and the last of their friends had started their drive home, under a three-quarters moon, Lord and Lady Reyne had become, once more the centre of a buzz of speculation.

As soon as the door closed behind the last of their guests in the early hours of the morning, Lord and Lady Cornford, glad that it was all over, went gratefully into the small salon, where tea had been brought. Barbara, who, by now, could not bear to be in the same room as her husband, refused it, pleading exhaustion, and picked up her own candle before her husband could hand it to her, going upstairs at once. She was in a lather of fury: the last she had seen of Miss Chalmers had been with Reyne, placing a shawl around her shoulders, and she with one of her self-satisfied looks on her face. If Falconer's adieus to herself were no less tender, it mattered little: Barbara was not amused. If Reyne dared to show his face in her bedroom, she would throw something at him.

Barbara was not the only one eager to go to bed: Lord and Lady Cornford, physically and mentally exhausted from watching Barbara and her husband hand their neighbours enough gossip to keep them happy for a year, excused themselves as soon as the rules of hospitality allowed. Lord Reyne wanted to speak to Radleigh, and deliberately held back.

After what he had just witnessed, Radleigh was quite as eager. As soon as the others had gone, he said, unusually sharply, 'I suppose there was an explanation for this evening, Marcus? Some new form of courtship of which I have never heard, perhaps? And after you had gone to so much trouble to give Lady Reyne that necklace. You were doing so well. I could almost see myself being Uncle George to a parcel of your brats. What possessed you to make up to that yellow-haired harpy?'

'By whom I suppose you mean Miss Chalmers?' said Reyne, irritably. 'Why shouldn't I dance with her, after the exhibition my wife was making of herself with Falconer? Did you expect me to stand by and let her make me look a fool?'

'Yes, on the whole I think I did,' he said, after some consideration. 'After all, you must admit it was her turn. You can't expect it always to be yours.'

'Oh, please don't joke. I'm too weary for that.'

'Who said I was joking? You heard what that old bag of wind, Baggeley, was saying. No wonder your wife was in such a mood.'

'That wasn't my fault,' Reyne protested, eager to defend himself.

'So it wasn't you who stayed an extra year abroad after Waterloo, when every officer with dependents came rushing home? And it wasn't you who stayed for those extra weeks in town rather than coming straight to his wife? I'm sorry, I must be thinking of someone else.'

'So I stayed away! That doesn't turn me into Attila the Hun,' cried Reyne. 'It isn't my fault that that hoard of gossips wouldn't let it be.'

'Do you not think so? Come now, Marcus, you might have let

her flirt with Falconer for one evening and get her own back. You owed it to her. But no, not you. Instead, you made up to one of the prettiest girls in the room and so confirmed all her bad impressions of you, as a flirt and a philanderer. It was badly done, Marcus, whatever you say. You should have eaten a little humble pie: she'd probably have forgiven you by now.'

Marcus sighed. 'You are right: I know it,' he admitted, sinking heavily into a chair. 'I shouldn't have let myself get so easily ruffled, but she drives me to distraction. I could kill Falconer. Hell, I wish I hadn't stayed away so long.'

'I think we all wish that, Marcus, especially Barbara. You've seen tonight the sort of thing she has had to put up with from her neighbours on the subject of *the husband who didn't want to come back to his wife*. I thought it was very good of her to be so friendly to you tonight in the ballroom: it showed a very forgiving nature. Good God, man, you seemed to be getting on so well!'

'We were! That's the stupid part. You know how hot it was? I took her outside. We began to talk, and one thing led to another, and she was in my arms. I was just about to kiss her, and I'm sure she wanted me to, when that blackguard, Falconer came out.'

'You kissed her! I don't believe it! Whatever made you mess it up afterwards? You'd have been in her bed tonight, have you thought of that?'

'I didn't actually kiss her, I was just *going to* when he showed up. Oh God, George, I'm back where I was when we first came here. What on earth can I do now? She's going to hate me.'

'If it weren't for the fact that we men have to stick together, I'd leave you to stew in your own juices. You don't deserve it, but I *have* put together a *soupçon* of a plan.'

Reyne looked not unhopeful.

'The old jealousy trick, Marcus my lad: it's never failed me yet. I'll let you into my little secret now, concerning Miss Waverley. I've been getting to know her, and I'm pretty certain that she imagines herself in love with Falconer.'

'Good God, another one?' said Reyne, in disgust. 'Does he make up to every girl he sees?'

'No, on this occasion you're being unfair. He *doesn't* make up to Miss Waverley. Makes up to Barbara, that is the moot point. It occurs to me that it would be a good thing were I to appear to be in love with Miss Waverly myself.'

'I don't understand. How would that help anyone?'

'Think about it. You know how often we've known civilians to get annoyed when a man in uniform flirts with their girls. And Falconer strikes me, too, as the sort of man who is much impressed by rank. It occurred to me that Falconer might very well become jealous if I make it appear that I am after Miss Waverley, and that might lure him away from Barbara.'

'This is all too complicated for me. Why should he get jealous if it's *Barbara* he's after?'

'It's my job to *make* him jealous. He seems just the sort of paltry fellow to suddenly realize he likes a girl if she's being chased by the son of a viscount: especially when that girl comes with a hefty dowry, which is sure to weigh with someone like him. Trust me. He must realize that his chances of getting at Barbara are thin, at best, now that you are home. That could tip the balance in Miss Waverley's favour.'

'It seems a bit far-fetched, George. He seems very fixed on Barbara.'

'Of course it's far-fetched, but it's the best we've come up with, unless you've got a better idea. With a bit of luck, he won't realize what's going on until Miss Waverly gets the noose round his neck. Not that he deserves such a sweet little thing as her: he's a bit too unctuous for my taste, but she seems to like him.'

'Oh, now I understand,' said Reyne, laughing. 'You want me to feel grateful that you're going to all this trouble for me, when really you just fancy a pleasant little flirtation yourself, and you've found the perfect excuse to have one.'

'I? You malign me, sir,' replied Radleigh, with an innocent expression. 'You just leave it to me. And, by the way, aren't you supposed to be upstairs? Didn't you agree to go to your wife's room each night and morning so that the maid can see you together? You'll be too late if you aren't quick.'

Lord Reyne took the stairs two at a time and, having been helped by his valet into his nightshirt and shrugged his dressing-gown over the top of it, he made to go into his wife's bedchamber, this time through their shared dressing-room. Pausing before he opened the door on her side, he had a momentary qualm. Almost he decided to go back into his own room, except that the moment when he had almost kissed Barbara had taken possession of his thoughts. She had certainly responded: it wasn't his imagination. It was that memory, that moment when she had lifted her face to be kissed which spurred him on. He turned the handle.

Stowe having departed for the night, and Barbara being already in bed, the bedchamber was in complete darkness until his candle began to throw light around the walls. Walking a few feet into the body of the room, Reyne whispered, 'Barbara, are you awake?'

There was no reply and he brought his candle nearer the bed and held it over his wife. 'Barbara, are you awake?' he hissed again, impatiently.

He sat on the edge of the bed and went to touch his wife's shoulder, but a great uncertainty held him back.

'Barbara, you can't still be asleep,' he said, thinking how foolish he must appear, but she still did not stir.

Finally he lost all patience. 'Look here, Barbara,' he said acidly, 'pretend to be asleep as much as you like: it won't trouble *me*. Just remember that I shall be in here before your maid brings in the tray! And, while you are at it, you might ponder on how much reputation you have left, if you have *any*, after your disgraceful exhibition tonight!'

And with as much dignity as he could muster, he made his way back to his own quarters, rather spoiling his retreat by tripping over the cord of his dressing-gown, which had somehow become untied.

In the darkness, Barbara's eyes snapped open and, swivelling her head toward the dressing-room, her eyes bored into the door through which he had gone. She could hardly decide whether she was more relieved or disappointed that he had gone so tamely.

And how dare he berate *her* for her behaviour! Recalling the memory of her husband placing that shawl around Miss Chalmers's handsome shoulders, she was furious with herself that she had not been quick enough to reveal that she was still awake: it would have been very satisfactory to her to have thrashed out their differences while she was still in the white heat of anger.

Despite the lateness of the hour when she had gone to sleep, Barbara was already awake in the early morning, when she felt Reyne slide in beside her. She had a great temptation to let him know that she was awake, but, after last night, she wasn't sure what he would do. Being in bed with a man when one was only in one's nightgown put one at a distinct disadvantage: she decided to pretend still to be asleep.

She was quite close to the middle of the bed and, as he moved to make himself comfortable, his body touched hers. She could feel the warmth of his thigh against hers and a shiver ran through her. She was almost sure that he knew she was awake, and the suspicion created a strange tension between them as if the aura around their bodies flowed from one to the other. Barbara hardly dared to move: she was certain that any sure indication that she was awake might lead to *anything*. Thus they lay there, perfectly still, unnaturally so, like two dolls laid in their bed by a child, until Stowe knocked on the door. The two broke away from each other, as if a gigantic hand had released them, and Lady Reyne called for her maid to enter. Today, Reyne was less sure of himself. He didn't goad her as he had on the previous morning: nor were there any kisses, much to Stowe's disappointment. Even on Stowe's account, there wasn't any conversation. He merely drank a dish of tea, ate a slice of toast, and then slipped out from under the covers, pulling his dressing-gown around him over his thin nightshirt.

Before he went out of the room, he did say, very stiffly, 'I must dress and go down, for I promised Guy that we should take the curricle out for an hour,' but that was all.

When he had gone, Barbara pushed the tray from her and, when Stowe had taken it away, she pulled up the bedcovers once more and lay down again. Staring straight upwards at the hangings, which covered the roof of her bed, she felt an overwhelming impulse to burst into tears.

It wasn't only Lady Reyne for whom the ball had been momentous, for Miss Waverley, too, had spent a very eventful evening. While her maid helped her out of her ball gown, a small, self-conscious smile played around her mouth, as she recalled the half-hour she had (quite shamelessly) spent with Captain Radleigh in Lord Cornford's lush gardens.

When the heat in the ballroom had driven them outside, they had wandered through the gardens down to the lake, to where stood a small, open-sided pagoda, erected by one of Lord Cornford's ancestors. There they had sat looking out across the moonlit water, and then back up to the house and ballroom, their eyes drawn towards an enchanting vista of lanterns and moon-silvered trees. It was very strange that she should have gone so unhesitatingly with him, for she had never done such a thing before. Strangely, she was quite certain that she could trust him: certain that he would let no harm come to her. She began to wonder if she was fickle. All these months thinking herself in love with Mrs Falconer and only a few hours in another's company had driven him completely from her thoughts.

Dismissing her maid, Mary curled up contentedly in an armchair, wrapping a shawl around her shoulders and tucking her feet up under her nightdress. She could remember only brief snatches of their conversation: he had certainly mentioned Mr Falconer, for she could clearly remember him warning her not to measure everyone by Falconer's standards.

'Look into your glass,' he had said. 'Take a very long, hard look. You are an amazingly pretty girl, you know. All this business about nobody wanting to marry you is just so much rot. You are certain to marry well.'

She had replied lightly enough, saying, with an ironical laugh, 'Oh, certainly I shall marry well. *Eventually*. Just *when* will be is more of a problem. Who knows how long it will take for Papa to winkle out a gentleman of good birth poor enough to be so good as to forget my humble beginnings?'

'To hear you speak so makes me happy indeed that I have come into Cheshire, Miss Waverley,' he had replied, unexpectedly. 'I only wish I had come before, for if all the fellows in these parts are such slow tops that they let a beautiful girl like you doubt her powers of attraction, Cheshire must be a paradise for anyone with even half the common amount of address. Even I must be in with a chance.'

'What, even you?' she had said, laughingly.

'Certainly! I may have a monkey face, but at least I know a good thing when I see it. It astonishes me that you should have reached the age of – what is it? Twenty? Twenty-one? – without having received at least half-a-dozen offers.'

'Well, I have, sir, regrettably,' she had replied, defiantly. 'Nobody wants me at all. And you do not have a monkey face. I like your face.'

And she did like his face: and more than his face, for he seemed to her to be the epitome of gallantry. After Mr Falconer's dismissive behaviour, Captain Radleigh's admiration was soothing indeed to her ruffled sensibilities.

His last words to her had been, 'If I believed that you had no admirers, I should be truly sorry – for them, not for you, for if they are such fools I would not wish one of them on to you. Only think how uncomfortable it would be to be married to a half-wit. But the truth is, Miss Mary Waverley, that I don't believe it at all. It is all balderdash. Remember that I was with you when no less than three gentlemen tried to nab you for the next two dances before I could get you out here!'

After that, nothing else had been said of her prospects. Indeed, she could remember only the flavour of the conversation which followed, not any real content. She only knew that she had never spent a more agreeable evening in any other company.

# Chapter Sixteen

'AND WHAT WILL you do with yourself while Reyne is out?' Lady Cornford asked her daughter, as they walked languidly around the flower borders, yawning now and then, from the inevitable bout of ennui following the ball.

'Reyne? What has Reyne to do with any plans I might have, Mama?' said Barbara, with a hint of impatience. 'I do not depend on him for my entertainment, and he certainly doesn't rely on me for his.'

'But Ba, surely you *should* be relying on each other for company. Time enough later to do things separately. No wonder you are looking so pale this morning, for things seem to be taking a very sad course between you. You must get Stowe to fetch some strawberries from the kitchen garden; they are very soothing crushed on the skin, especially under the eyes. There is a definite smudge of blue under yours, which I never saw there before. Oh, my dear love, I never thought to see such goings on in my ballroom as I saw last night. It shocked me, I don't mind telling you.'

'I can't imagine what you mean, Mother,' said Barbara, with a lift of her chin. 'I saw nothing unusual. And there is nothing wrong with my face which an early night won't cure.'

'You and I must have very different notions of what is usual, Barbara. And don't pretend that you are not angry with Reyne, for I can hear it in your voice. You are not angry that he has taken Guy out in the curricle? It is very good-natured of him, to be sure, though I was against it at first. Your father assures me that Reyne means to be very careful, and I spoke to Wytchett yesterday, and he said that, even if driven fast, an open carriage will do Guy no harm. Besides, Reyne promised that he should not let Guy drive fast, nor do so himself.'

'I am sure that he is everything obliging, Mama,' said Barbara, sullenly, wishing that, in that heat, somebody had thought to take *her* out for a drive. 'And of course the carriage will not hurt Guy. Whoever thought it would?'

Lady Cornford ignored the truculence in her voice. 'And Captain Radleigh, too,' she said, stooping to pinch out a brown leaf on one of the rose bushes, 'he is a very pretty-behaved young gentleman. It was vastly obliging of him to go off to enquire after the Waverleys, this morning. I was surprised, my love, that you did not accompany him. I should have thought you would have wished to discuss the ball with Mary.'

For the first time that day, Barbara's face showed animation. 'Dear Mama,' she said, taking her mother's arm and squeezing it to her side, 'I stayed behind deliberately. I wanted him to go alone, for I have a little plan, which I hope you may approve of. What think you of Captain Radleigh and Mary?'

'What think I of *what* of Captain Radleigh and Mary?'

'Why marriage, of course. What else should I mean?'

'How odd that you should say so, love. I was thinking the very same thing when I saw them dancing together last night. Indeed, I said as much to dear Grace. It would be the very thing for that sweet child, if he could be persuaded to take her.'

'Perhaps he won't need much persuading. They danced two sets together at the ball, and he took her into supper, which quite set me wondering. I saw them go out into the gardens together, too, and when they came back they were speaking so earnestly that one could not help but think that *anything* might happen! He seemed very put out when Josh Baggeley asked her to dance, for I noticed him watching them all the time he was dancing with Jane Kilpatrick, and then, you know, he sought her out again, immediately afterwards.'

'That is certainly particular, my love. I cannot remember when I have heard anything to please me so well,' said Lady Cornford, who had been too busy seeing to her guests' comfort to have noticed all the details observed by her daughter. 'It would be a great match for her, Barbara. And how delighted her dear parents would be. If I can do anything to forward it, I shall certainly not spare myself.'

'I think we should bring them as much together as we can,' said Barbara, glad to have her mother on her side. 'If only we could think up a few amusements, using Reyne's arrival as an excuse, then we might ask Mary to join us without being too obvious.'

'What a coincidence that you should say so, my love, for your father is very worried that your husband and the captain will get bored without something to do, and he has asked me to do the very same thing. Indeed, I had just this moment been considering suggesting the possibility of us all taking a carriage ride to Chester, this afternoon. Are you too tired for it, my love?' she asked, anxiously. 'I always find it the very place on such a hot day as this. So much cooler being driven than walking, and we could take a little saunter along the Rows or the walls, for there is always a pleasant breeze up so high, even in such warm weather as this. Reyne was saying last night that neither he nor Captain Radleigh has ever been to Chester, and it would not seem at all particular if we asked Mary to accompany us, for they know that she is your best friend. You young people could ramble along the walls whilst your father and I looked at the shops. I am sure that Reyne and the captain will like to see the views out to the Roodee. Or there are The Groves, now, you might have a delightful walk there.'

'I should like it of all things, Mama,' said Barbara, 'if Mary can be persuaded to accompany us. It is far more tiring moping about in this weather than taking a pleasant drive out. We could take the landau and Reyne's curricle, which will just give us enough room, if Guy will but squeeze in.'

When the others returned, the plan was enthusiastically taken up, and Lady Cornford sent a note to Mrs Waverley, requesting permission for Mary to join their party, which was graciously given.

When it came to arranging their disposition in the carriages, Lord Cornford naturally assumed that Barbara would be driven by her husband in his curricle, and had already, in private, warned Guy not to ask to be taken up instead. He was surprised, then, when Barbara said that she preferred to travel in the landau, and suggested that, since Miss Waverley had never had an opportunity to travel in a curricle, Captain Radleigh might wish to borrow Reyne's carriage, and drive her himself. Had not his wife endorsed it, Lord Cornford would have disputed with her, but when Reyne expressed himself perfectly satisfied to be driven in the landau, the matter was settled. Miss Waverley was handed into the curricle by Captain Radleigh, and, to Guy's disgust, the rest squeezed into the landau.

Their journey took them little more than an hour, and appeared shorter from everyone being anxious to point out landmarks and views to Reyne and to Captain Radleigh as they drove along. It seemed very soon that they were driving past Foregate Barrs towards the East Gate, the carriages being driven through and into Eastgate Street, where the party descended at the lower level of shops, leaving the coachman and groom to take the vehicles to the livery stable.

Climbing one of the short flights of steps to the covered galleries, which in that city are called the Rows, they felt the full advantage of this happy arrangement in taking the fashionable promenade along avenues of small shops, and from being able to enjoy to the full the salubrity of air and quaintness of scene described in the Chester guide which, it declared, *no other city in England could surpass*.

The day being so hot, they decided to take to the walls, which formed the old city boundary. Since Lord Cornford had his wife on his arm, and Captain Radleigh was escorting Mary most solicitously, it would have seemed churlish, despite last night's disagreement, had not Reyne pulled Barbara's hand through his arm. He was too well bred not to instigate some form of conversation, and being very impressed by Chester's beauty, his parents-in-law were reassured at hearing Barbara explaining to him, in reply to a question, some small part of its history. Proceeding northwards, she pointed out the Phoenix Tower, where Charles I had witnessed the discomfiture of his army on Rowton Moor; the Northgate, with its elliptical arch, and, when they had ascended by steps to the Mount, the rich views over Broxton and Eddisbury, and the Peninsula of Wirral, which stretched in the distance to the Irish Channel.

By this time, Lord and Lady Cornford, to whom none of this was new, felt that they had walked quite far enough in that heat and, since Guy, too, was uncomfortably hot, and even a little bored, they made their way to the Goblin's Tower, the lower wall of which was set round with benches. Here the three of them elected to sit down and rest until they were cool, before taking themselves off in search of refreshments, and it was agreed that the two young couples should meet them back there in an hour and a half. Lady Cornford reminded them of Mr Whittel's rope walk, and that the grove of lime trees which flourished there would provide them with cooling shade, and since Captain Radleigh wanted Miss Waverley to himself, he lost no time in taking her advice. When Reyne, just as anxious to get Barbara alone, expressed a wish to see the Water Tower and the views over the Roodee instead, Lady Cornford encouraged that, too.

It was wonderfully cool so high up. Unlike Sundays, when the walls provided the favourite walk of the Cestrians, today they were very sparsely populated, and the footpaths, wide enough to accommodate three comfortably, allowed them to wander very freely. They came, at last, to a stone seat, and, in mutual agreement, took advantage of it.

During the whole of their expedition, they had not exchanged a word on any personal subject, and Reyne wondered how to get back to the intimacy they had shared on the veranda at Hurst Park. But every word she said seemed designed to show him that she intended to keep things on a very distant footing. Thus she pointed out for him many of the principal houses of the city and told him the names of their owners; she showed him the Roodee and gave him the dates when the races were held there and she pointed to the New Tower, which she pronounced to be seventy feet in height, adding that the river ran immediately under its wall, and that in the past boats had once been fastened to it by iron rings. He soon began to feel as if he had taken Guy's tutor for a walk and, when she was still in full flow and waving her arms in all directions so that he should not miss any of the most important sights, he suddenly grabbed her hand, and pulled it towards him, holding it in his lap.

'Yes, Barbara, you have a delightful city here, and I am sure you love it,' he said placidly, 'but you and I, I think, have other matters to discuss.'

'Best not, sir,' said Barbara, with a bitter laugh. 'Whenever we discuss anything it ends badly.'

'But I want to talk to you, My Lady, and I must have my way. Actually, I would like to continue the conversation we were having in your father's gardens last evening.'

'I think that conversation was quite finished, sir,' said Barbara, colouring up.

'Whereas I think it was just coming to the interesting part,' he said, meeting her eyes, which were with every word becoming more indignant.

'Not so interesting that you did not immediately ask Miss Chalmers to dance with you, My Lord,' she said, looking away into the distance.

'Not immediately, Barbara. First I watched you, dancing with Falconer.'

'I should not put Mr Falconer and Miss Chalmers in the same category. Mr Falconer and I are old friends.'

'A good point, ma'am. Certainly Miss Chalmers and I are not old friends, but we have become good friends, and surely that is similar enough?'

'I think you will find that Miss Chalmers is good friends with several gentlemen, sir,' said Barbara, coldly.

'Including Mr Falconer, or so it seemed to me.'

Before she could stop herself, Barbara blurted out, 'Mr Falconer is not at all interested in Miss Chalmers, sir.'

'No,' Lord Reyne flashed back. 'He is too busy being interested in my wife!'

He stood up abruptly, flicked out his coat tails and walked on, leaving Barbara sitting there. His face was like a thundercloud, and he was thinking her the most unreasonable female of his acquaintance, until he recalled Captain Radleigh reminding him that, of the pair of them, Lady Reyne was the more sinned against. He was suddenly ashamed that he had allowed his dislike of Falconer to make him lose his temper again, and became determined to try once more. He ceased walking, pretending to be very interested in looking out over the walls, until Barbara eventually caught up with him. With exaggerated courtesy, he held out his arm for her to lean on and, realizing that she would only look childish if she refused to take it, Barbara put her arm through his, though with little appearance of enthusiasm. Determined, at least, to keep the peace, Lord Reyne began what he thought would be a safe topic of conversation.

'No wonder you like Chester so much, My lady. The city walls are magnificent, and it is very pleasant up here on such a hot day. I imagine you will miss it greatly when you return with me to London. We shall have to visit very often.'

'Go to London?' she protested, in a voice which disabused him of the hope that they could converse without argument. 'I don't understand, sir. Nothing has been said of my leaving Cheshire. I did not expect it.'

'You did not expect it? But of course you must come to London. I shall be living there for much of the year, and, now that you are my wife, you must live there too,' he said, gently. 'Though, naturally, we will live part of the year down at Chellings, for shooting, Christmas, and so forth. And we shall go to Brighton for the summer, which you will like. But London will, very naturally, be our usual address, though I hope we shall be able to come to Cheshire several times a year for a few days at least.'

'A few days? You are all goodness, sir. I shall want to come home for more than a few days. What should I do in London?' said Barbara, annoyed at being so summarily ordered about by him. 'I know hardly anyone in Town, we go so rarely: here I know everyone.'

'You know me,' he reminded her.

'Yes, I certainly do,' she replied, bitterly.

'And you know my mother,' he persevered, 'which is the same as knowing everyone, for she will introduce you to them all. She is the most sociable of creatures; she is hardly ever at home and, when she is, the house is never empty. Of course, you may wish her to move to the Dower House, which she is quite willing to do, but you will still be much in her company. She won't let you be lonely.'

'I can hardly be said to *know* your mother,' she reminded him, 'though she may be everything obliging. I have met her only once. And of course I do not wish her to leave her home. Just as I should not wish to leave mine.'

'But your home is in Cheshire no longer. As a married woman, you must live in your husband's house,' he expostulated.

'Why so? I have been a married woman these eight years and it has never before been a requirement.'

'Oh, surely we have said everything which needs to be said about our separation,' said Reyne, beginning to feel very heated.

'I can quite see why you might think so,' said Barbara, coolly. 'So much more convenient for you.'

He began to get very frustrated by her determination, especially since a part of him felt her logic to be undeniable.

'But, don't you see? Can't you imagine what people would say if you remained in Cheshire whilst I was living elsewhere?' he exhorted.

'Can I *imagine* it, sir? I doubt I need much imagination. I think I know very well what they would say. I suppose it would be very much what they have been saying about us this past eight years.'

'But it was your mother's wish that you should remain at Hurst Park,' he reminded her.

'Yes, for two years, My Lord, not eight.'

'But by then I was in the army.'

'So you were,' she said, pleasantly. 'And how did you get there? Were you pressed? Did your late father force you to take up a commission?'

Knowing that he was cutting a poor figure, he was forced to admit that he had not.

'I think it would be very hard were I to be obliged to live in Town, My Lord,' said Barbara. 'You might decide to go off for another eight years and I would be stuck there on my own.'

'Perhaps you would miss me, were I to do so?'

'Not at all,' said Barbara, cheerfully. 'It is what I have been used to, after all.'

'But if you would not mind if I were there or not, you might as well be in Town as here,' he said, digging in.

'But here I have my parents and my brother. I should certainly miss them,' said Barbara, firmly. 'To speak plainly, sir, London is not to my taste.'

'Then I am very sorry for you,' said Reyne, uncompromisingly. 'No doubt you will get used to it.'

Hearing Barbara gasp at his rudeness reminded Reyne that he had intended to be conciliatory. 'Well, let us agree to disagree for the time being,' he suggested. 'We can speak of this another time. The weather makes us both a little irritable. Your brother, Lady Reyne, what a delightful boy he is,' he went on, deliberately making a huge leap of topic.

'I am glad you are pleased with him, sir,' she said, bowing her head to acknowledge the compliment. 'It should be a source of happiness to you to know that you are something of a favourite with *him*. He calls you a Great Go, whatever that may be, but I suspect it to be a compliment. I hope that all this driving about with him doesn't bore you.'

'Not in the least. I find I understand him very well: he is very like myself as a lad. I flatter myself that we are becoming good friends, so at least I shall have *one* at Hurst Park.'

'Oh, more than one,' said Barbara, with deceptive affability. 'You forget that my parents like you, too.'

'A low, but worthy thrust, My Lady,' said Reyne, appreciatively, 'but trust me, I shall come about.'

'And does Guy's driving progress,' she asked, 'or are you every moment afraid that he will overturn you?'

'No, indeed, I promise you. He makes excellent progress. He is a natural with horses. What a great pity that he has not been allowed to drive before.'

'Do not say so to Mama. She can hardly bear to let him go out with you now.'

'I realize that,' he replied, 'but, forgive me, it does seem a pity to keep the boy in leading strings. He seems perfectly stout. I had a word myself with that tame physician of your mother's, and he thinks him in excellent health.'

'So do we all, except Mama,' said Barbara, sighing. 'Poor Guy has such a patient disposition that he never flies out at her as another boy might, at his age.'

'You do not fear that he will one day break out from all this coddling and get himself into some sort of mischief, if these restraints are not slackened off?'

'I am almost certain that he will: indeed I sometimes wonder if it would not do a great deal of good if he did so.'

Exploring such innocuous topics of conversation they continued on their tour as far as the cathedral before they gauged it to be time to return. Barbara had been nearly an hour and a half alone with him and, as they walked back to meet the others, she reflected, with a certain amount of surprise, that they had managed to spend the last part of their walk reasonably amicably. She accounted for it through his not returning either to the subject of Mr Falconer or of London: instead, he had put himself out to be entertaining and agreeable and, though they had not regained their previous intimacy, she was beginning to feel almost comfortable in his society. She was cheeky enough to be just going to tell him so, when a female voice, strangely familiar, assaulted her ears, calling, 'My Lord: Reyne! My Lord!'

Turning abruptly, Barbara was less than amused to see the bustling figure of Miss Annabel Chalmers hurrying towards them, dragging her father in her wake. The four made their bows, and Sir William, a round, jolly man, who had had the corners of his plebeian ancestry rubbed down, rather than rubbed off, said cheerfully, 'This is very well met, My Lord: Lady Reyne. We must all have had the same idea: isn't it grand to be up here out of the heat? I hope you suffered no ill effects from the ball, My Lady. We had an excellent evening, didn't we, Bella? I don't know when I've enjoyed myself more.'

'Indeed, yes,' agreed Miss Chalmers, staring pointedly at Lord Reyne. 'I never before attended such a delightful ball. So many excellent fellows, and they will spoil me so.'

'Aye, they do that, girlie,' said her father, dotingly. 'I thought you would be tired out after all that dancing, but you never are!' He turned back to Lord Reyne. 'Well, My Lord, this is particularly good luck meeting you like this. I was going to send a note this evening, and now I can ask you to your face instead, which is the way I like to do things. I'm rounding up a few of my tenants tomorrow, to help me to clear out some of the rooks which are making a mess of one of my plantations. I know there's not much hereabouts to entertain a couple of strapping gentlemen like you and your friend Radleigh at this time of the year, so I thought I'd give you a chance to refuse me by asking you if you'd like to join us. Truth to tell, it was girlie here's idea. She was wild to ask you, and though I know it's not what you're used to, you don't seem the kind of man to stand on ceremony. I liked a set-to of this kind myself at your age: your rook gives you good sport, if you're not too high to enjoy it. So, if you're interested, sir, we're collecting early. Grab a bite to eat and get at 'em!'

To Barbara's intense annoyance, he didn't hesitate to accept, holding himself responsible for Radleigh's acceptance, too.

But worse was to come, for Sir William, his weather-beaten cheeks beaming with pleasure, and encouraged by his lordship's friendliness, went on to say, 'And if you feel like it, you can take pot luck with us when we've done with the birds. No frills, My Lord, but I'll warrant you'll not go hungry. And I've as soft a port as you'll find anywhere, which I'm itching for an opportunity to open.'

And, since Lord Reyne was a very sociable young gentleman, with no inhibitions at all as to rank, he accepted with every appearance of pleasure, much to Miss Chalmers' obvious delight, since she counted it a compliment to herself.

Why, he has only been here two days, thought Barbara, indignantly. How dare he go off for a whole day without asking me if I mind!'

Miss Waverley and Captain Radleigh were having a far more agreeable walk in the shade of Mr Whittel's lime trees, though they took very little notice of the scenery. He had not tried to have anything more than desultory conversation while they were in the curricle, but as soon as he got her alone in Chester, Captain Radleigh said, 'How could you dare tell me that you are unpopular with gentlemen, Miss Waverley? I could barely get near you after supper. You knew that I wanted another two dances.'

'Nonsense, sir!' cried Mary, her eyes alight. 'I couldn't dance with you again when we had already danced four dances. My reputation would have been in shreds.'

'But you let Falconer have them! I thought we decided we weren't going to be kind to Mr Falconer!'

'Foolish man,' said Mary, giggling. 'I wasn't kind to him. But I couldn't refuse to dance with him. He asked me earlier to save him two and I had promised.'

'Yet you refused *me*!' he said, looking aggrieved.

'Because I was scolded by Mama. She saw us come back from the gardens. After we had the second two dances, she absolutely forbad me to let you have any more. I believe I am in her bad book.'

'Don't worry about that: I'll soon get round her, I'm good with mothers,' he said audaciously.

'Having had a good deal of practice, I imagine,' said Mary, with a roguish look.

'Don't change the subject. What did Falconer have to say to you, anyway? He seemed mighty friendly to me.'

Mary coloured up. 'Indeed, he was, sir. He flirted shamefully.'

'Dastardly behaviour! I hate people who flirt, don't you?'

'It is as well that I don't,' she said sternly, 'for I've never known anyone who flirts as much as you do.'

'But I've practised so hard to perfect it, you see. It would be a shameful waste not to use it, for I've never found anything else that I do quite so well.'

'You certainly put it to good use last night, sir,' said Mary, with some satisfaction. 'I am sure that Mr Falconer asked me to dance because you showed him that you didn't consider me too low for you. I could almost see him thinking that, if the son of a viscount didn't disdain to dance with me, he wouldn't actually catch anything nasty from me, if he did so as well.'

'What a buffoon! If I had my way, I should see that he was only allowed to dance with the daughters of dukes and princes, for every one of them that I've ever met has been a very unlovely creature.'

Remembering his promise to Reyne, Radleigh knew that he should be encouraging Mary to continue to like Falconer, and be pleased that he had danced with her. Unfortunately, a little voice kept telling him that not only was Mary a mile too good for the likes of Robert Falconer, but there wasn't a single person for whom that would not also apply.

# Chapter Seventeen

THE ATMOSPHERE CREATED by their meeting with Sir William and his daughter was almost tangible and, having said farewell, Reyne could not wait to reach the Goblin's Tower so that they could be reunited with the rest of their party. As they walked back to the others, he said everything he could think of to re-ignite the spark of amiability, which had earlier struggled into being, explaining to his stiff-backed wife that he had accepted Sir William's invitation only to be neighbourly, but to no avail. Barbara, whilst not going so far as to refuse to take his arm, or to converse with him altogether, answered only when spoken to, and then in the briefest possible terms. Her coolness contrasted strongly with the good spirits of the rest, which could be discerned, even from a distance, long before they reached them, for they were huddled together, and obviously in animated conversation. As they came in view of the tower and were noticed, Guy ran the few steps to meet them and dragged them to the others.

'Ba! At last!' he cried, in the greatest excitement. 'You will never guess! Father is going to take us on the Steam Packet to Liverpool! It is quite settled: it wants only for you and Reyne to agree and everything can be arranged while we are still in Chester.'

'Guy!' protested Lady Cornford, laughing at his exuberance. 'Calm yourself, do. Let your father speak for himself. They will be thinking we mean to go today, if we don't explain.'

Within a very few minutes, the tale was told. Lord Cornford had noticed, during the past few weeks, some advertisements appearing in the *Chronicle,* for a new steam packet, established by the Ellesmere and Chester Canal Company, for the purpose of carrying passengers on the one-hour trip between Ellesmere Port and Liverpool. As soon as he had seen the first, Lord Cornford had been seized by a wish to experience the new form of transport. Then, as if to tempt him even further, in that week's *Courant*, amongst the list of special entertainments being offered for the anniversary of Waterloo celebrations, which were to take place in only a day or two, he had seen another advertisement, this time for a public dinner which was to be held at the Royal Waterloo Hotel, near Liverpool, at Crosby Seabank, in honour of the occasion. Wonderful coincidence! He had wanted to celebrate the great victory in some special way, and had determined to make enquiries to see if they were too late to obtain places on the packet, and reservations at the hotel for an overnight stay at Crosby. Their expedition had given him the means to do so: he had been assured that places on the steam packet were still available, as were hotel reservations. It would mean quite an early start, he told them, for they would have to reach Ellesmere Port in time to catch the packet, but if they liked the idea, he was ready to close with the Canal Company at once.

'Ba! Do say you will!' cried Guy, his face ablaze with excitement. 'At Crosby we can go sea bathing! And there is to be a capital bowling green and I don't know what else!'

Could the answer be in doubt? All the animation which had receded from Barbara's face, reappeared, and she joined in the general joy which such a scheme invariably provokes.

Lord Cornford was as pleased as a schoolboy. 'I must confess,' he said, smiling wryly, 'that I should have been extremely disappointed had you not wanted to go. I am getting old, you know, and must get to see these newfangled things while I still have the time.'

His children, naturally, pooh-poohed the idea that he was old, and declared him to be the best father in the world, which only increased his good humour, and led him to ask Miss Waverley if she would like to accompany them on that trip also, should her mother be able to spare her. When she replied that she thought she could answer for her mother's willingness to let her go with them, the happiness of the whole party was assured.

Since Lord Cornford preferred to be active himself in the matter, he left the rest of his party to take refreshments and went off to confirm his arrangements, bringing back with him a printed flyer for the steam packet, which they were all eager to study.

Now that the afternoon was cooling down at last, they lingered in the environs of Chester, returning, inevitably, to the Rows. Since the gentlemen could not be persuaded to pass by a gun or pistol-maker's without walking in to see their latest wares and the ladies were drawn to every hat shop and draper's they came to, the hour was well past six before they eventually began to make their way homewards, Miss Waverley and Captain Radleigh again taking the curricle.

They retraced the route they had taken, passing out of the old part of the city towards Boughton, leaving the environs of the city and all its inhabitants, still bustling, behind them. It had been a long day, and coming on top of last night's ball, they were all feeling very fatigued: indeed, Lord and Lady Cornford were actually asleep in their corners of the landau, long before they reached Hurst Park. The atmosphere in the carriage was cordial: Guy was still studying the flyer and full of chatter, and Lady Barbara was so happy at their proposed expedition that it was difficult for her to continue being short with Reyne, though certainly, she had not forgiven him and intended to punish him if she could.

She could not have been more pleased, therefore, when, reaching the gatehouse to her father's estate, she saw, riding towards them, and obviously about to turn in through the gates, the handsome figure of Mr Robert Falconer. Barbara told the coachman to stop and spoke words enough to encourage Mr Falconer (who, having seen that they were just returning from an excursion, hesitated to impose himself upon them) up to the house. Telling the coachman to drive on, she then sat back against the cushions, very well pleased with herself. Now Reyne would learn what it felt like to be angry.

Mr Falconer had already dismounted and his horse had been led away by the time the landau pulled up at the front of the house. He was clearly waiting to hand Barbara down: instead, Reyne jumped in between them and held out his own hand, uncompromisingly, for his wife to take. Mr Falconer had no alternative but to give way, and Lady Cornford hustled him into the house.

As the others moved off, Reyne grasped Barbara's wrist and swung her round to face him. 'You were awake when I came to your room last night, weren't you?' he said, harshly. 'And this morning?'

Barbara met his eye disdainfully. 'I haven't the faintest idea what you mean,' she said coldly.

'I doubt you'd have pretended to be asleep were I Falconer!' he rasped, and Barbara gasped at his implication.

Wrenching her wrist from his grasp, she said, frigidly, 'You really should not judge everybody by your own standards, My Lord. Some ladies, and indeed, some gentlemen, have rather higher standards.' Then she moved off after the others.

It had already been decided that Miss Waverley would remain at Hurst Park for dinner, to be escorted home later and, however reluctantly, Lady Cornford felt that she had no alternative but to invite Mr Falconer as well, the only one of the party to be pleased, when he accepted, being Barbara.

Since it was so late, they decided not to dress for dinner. The ladies were gone no more than a quarter of an hour to undertake such small repairs to their toilettes they thought indispensable, before they all rejoined in the salon, where Mr Falconer made a beeline for Barbara, encouraging her to sit with him on a small sofa rather out of the way. He gave as his reason for visiting them a wish to enquire if she was quite recovered from the ball, and wondered to hear that they had all been off gallivanting.

'But it would have been far more fatiguing here, Mr Falconer, in all that heat,' she assured him. 'It was Mama's idea to go to Chester, the Rows and the walls being so cool. We didn't set out until after luncheon, which is why we are so disgracefully late, but we had a most refreshing walk.'

'I am very glad of it. And how did your husband like our city?'

'Very well, I believe – especially the pistol-makers' shops. Those he could not be dragged away from.'

'Had I known you were here until luncheon, and not still asleep, I should have come earlier. I had a particular reason for wishing to see you: I have not had a chance to bring it before – the ball not being appropriate – but I have a small gift for you. I brought it back from Tunbridge Wells.' He took from his pocket, and handed her a small package. When she had displaced the wrapping, she saw that it was a tiny, delicately designed and intricately patterned wooden box.

'It is a special type of work, made only in Tunbridge,' he explained. Then he took the box from her and flipped open the lid. Inside, to her confusion, was a folded sheet of paper. For one heart-stopping moment, she thought that he had hidden a note there, until he explained that it was a riddle for her collection. Since all the other riddles he had brought to her had hinted heavily at his devotion, she would much have preferred not to have him draw attention to this one, but it was too late. Reyne, who did not like his wife's company to be utilized by other gentlemen, had been hovering nearby, and having overheard some, at least, of their conversation, pressed his wife, while they waited for dinner to be served, to share the riddle with the whole company, so that they might all have a part in guessing. When Barbara expressed her reluctance to do so, he swooped in on the box before she could realize what he was about, picked up the paper and flicked it open with two fingers, reading it through quickly, one eyebrow raised as he caught its meaning.

'Well, now,' said Reyne, a spark of something, which was not quite amusement, in his eye. 'Let's see if we can solve this, shall we, Barbara my dear?'

His wife, already flushed, turned several shades darker. 'Not now, Reyne,' she protested. 'Not before dinner, if you please. Now is not the time for such occupations.'

Lord Cornford, who had caught none of the undercurrents, cut in and said, innocently, 'Go on, Barbara, let us try it. I dearly like a riddle myself.'

Barbara again protested, but nobody listened and, to her chagrin, Reyne began to read out loud:

*My first is meted out in high degree*
*To young ones, through a mother's smiling grace.*
*It is but a rehearsal for that time,*
*When such will issue from another's face.*

*My second is an enemy of man,*
*Which sends him off unseasonably to lie,*
*And should it not be speedily o'ercome,*
*Why then, we'll gather round to watch him die,*

*The whole can make a man forsake his friends,*
*And travel far and wide to find a cure.*
*But every grief from this at last will end,*
*When beauty smiles upon him, bright and pure.*

When he had finished reading, Reyne's face took on a comic look, which showed him to be perplexed. 'You didn't write this, Falconer, did you?' he asked, wrinkling his forehead. 'Dashed if I can make head nor tail of it!'

Mr Falconer denied that he had done so, pretending that it was written by a friend, but he said it so self-consciously, that it was obvious, to Barbara at least, that it *was* his riddle.

'Oh, but of course you didn't. Forgive me,' said Reyne, his voice as smooth as cream. 'How could you have? To write such a riddle for a married lady would be the height of indelicacy.'

'Let's see it, lad,' said Lord Cornford, holding out his hand. 'Let's see what this friend of Falconer's has written.' He ran his eye down the sheet and threw it back to Reyne, saying, 'No! Can't make anything of that!'

'Oh, surely we can solve it,' said Reyne, continuing quite unperturbed by his wife's stormy look. '. . . *meted out in high degree*? And by the mother too! That can mean only one thing to my mind: cough medicine. That's what my mother meted out to me.'

'I wonder which she used,' said Lady Cornford, catching the last part of this speech. 'Wytchett has a mixture of his own sent for Guy when he has a cough, though I sometimes use a remedy my mother had from Sarah Lennox, when it is *very bad*. A diet entirely of milk with a little gentle infusion of bark. His cough is always gone within a week when he takes that.'

'Indeed?' said Reyne, politely. 'I shall have to tell my mother, for she dearly loves a cough remedy. But I'm afraid I can't tell which is meant here. He doesn't name it.'

'No matter,' said Lady Cornford, placidly, going on with the shawl she was netting. 'Very likely it wouldn't do anyway. Guy's throat is so delicate.'

'Are you sure it's cough mixture?' broke in Captain Radleigh, who could guess how angry Reyne must be feeling at seeing his wife so openly courted, and was eager to get his share of the game, 'It could be a remedy for chills, not coughs, in which case the word might be garlic. My mother always made my sisters and I chew garlic to ward off a chill: mounds of the stuff. And it does say "meted out in high degree".'

'Good point,' said Reyne, enjoying himself hugely. 'So, the first word is either cough mixture, or garlic. Hmm. That's not at all promising. I cannot think of a phrase which could begin with either, can you, George?'

'Oh, good God, Reyne,' cried Barbara, unable to stand it any longer, and furious at seeing her favourite made to look such a fool. 'The answer is *love-sickness*! The merest baby could make it out.'

'Love-sickness? Is it?' said Reyne, looking closely at the paper. 'Hmm. Mother? Meted out in high degree? Ah, it *is* Love. Do you know, Barbara, I think you may be right. You must be an expert in such trifles. But you cannot be altogether surprised that I should not realize what it meant. One would not look for such a meaning in a riddle addressed to one's wife by another gentleman, surely?'

Lord Cornford, for whom the whole had gone completely over his head, said, fairly, 'Ah, but you are forgetting, my boy, the riddle wasn't addressed to Barbara. It was written by Mr Falconer's friend at Tunbridge Wells, and Barbara has never been there.'

'Thank you for reminding me, sir,' said Reyne. 'That's quite a relief, for I'd certainly have had to do something about it had it indeed been addressed to my wife.'

Mr Falconer could not mistake his meaning, nor could Captain Radleigh or Miss Waverley, both of whom had held their breath, Miss Waverley with none of the enjoyment which the scene had invoked in Radleigh. She had watched all with mixed emotions, amazed that Mr Falconer could so openly flout convention in giving such an amorous riddle to a married woman. She was shocked, and heartily despised him for it. Her second emotion had been one of sympathy for her friend, for to have such an explosive thing virtually dropped in one's lap and then to have one's husband discern it and make it public, seemed the height of embarrassment, nay more than embarrassment, of *suffering*. She was sure that she could not bear it, and her blame went back to Mr Falconer. While Reyne pretended to be trying to solve the riddle, and all the innocent interruptions lengthened the time Lady Barbara was held in suspense, she wished she could think of anything to spare her friend such public humiliation. Every shade of pink flowed just as strongly through her cheeks as through Barbara's and Captain Radleigh threw her a comforting smile. He felt that he already knew her well enough to guess that her discomposure was all for her friend, and he honoured her for it. She met his glance gratefully, her colour gradually receding.

Just then, Bragg announced dinner: in the confusion, Mr

Falconer sprang up and before Reyne could guess what he was about, snatched the riddle from his fingers. He pretended that he had done so in order to read it, made a pretence of running his eye down the page, and tore it into small pieces, saying to Reyne, audaciously, 'I'm not surprised you found it difficult to solve, My Lord. A very poor thing. I shall tell Collins so when next I see him, just see if I don't.'

Then, turning to Barbara, he said smoothly, 'Forgive me, Lady Reyne; I should have read it properly before giving it to you, but I caught only a glance at it. I know how much you enjoy such trifles, so when Collins was writing it in the book of a mutual friend, I could not resist getting him to copy it out for you.'

Barbara could not deny that it was a good defence. She bowed her head as if to acknowledge merely that he had not offended her, knowing that all eyes were upon them. On reflection, however, she wished that he had left it unspoken, since, somehow, in defending it, he had made the offence more. Besides, it was not the first riddle he had given her, and she had recognized the writing to be his own.

# Chapter Eighteen

IN SPITE OF the very hot weather, a distinct chill reigned over Lady Cornford's dinner-table that evening, and Mr Falconer felt her silent rebuke when she placed him the table's length from her daughter. He found himself next to Mary instead, and proceeded to engage her in conversation, which pleased neither her nor Captain Radleigh, as they had hoped to sit together. Mary was under no illusion as to why Mr Falconer put himself out to charm her: last night she had hardly been thought good enough to dance with: tonight, with no more important young women nearby for him to speak to, he sharpened his charm on her.

Most of group were fatigued from their day out and conversation was desultory. There seemed to be an unspoken agreement not to mention their Crosby plans and, in order to set up an innocuous subject of conversation, Lord Reyne mentioned how much Barbara seemed to despise London.

'Does she?' said Lady Cornford, with a puzzled frown. 'I didn't know that! Why, when we took her to London she seemed vastly pleased with it. Indeed, we went everywhere: the opera, Almack's, Vauxhall, the Royal Society. And you didn't enjoy it, Barbara? My poor girl, I wish you had said: I'd happily have brought you home earlier, for I'm much more comfortable at home. And you really didn't enjoy it? No, I'm sure you did.'

'You are mistaken, Mama,' said Barbara, holding her ground,

valiantly. 'One naturally makes the best of things, but I had much rather be in the country.'

'But my dear, you are always complaining at how rarely we get the best performers at the theatre in Chester, and wishing you were at the Haymarket instead.'

Reyne smiled a little when his wife denied it. He turned to Mary, and said, persuasively, 'I rely on you, Miss Waverley, to help reconcile my wife to Town. And I *must* get her there, you know, for I have to take my seat in the House in the autumn. My parents-in-iaw and Guy will naturally be frequent visitors in Berkeley Square, but I have been thinking how much Barbara would enjoy your company. Do I impose on you by asking that you come to us when you can? We have a good deal of room, so I could have a bedchamber made over to your exclusive use, should you be so good as to oblige us.'

Mary blushed, obviously delighted, and said, with her usual playfulness, 'Now you are entirely my idea of the perfect host, My Lord. You offer me my own room in your house and then express yourself obliged to *me*.'

'Tell her, Barbara, how much we want her,' said Reyne, knowing how it would rankle, being outmanoeuvred.

'Next to my parents and Guy, there is nobody I want more,' she assured her, throwing Reyne a challenging stare, 'Though I see no reason to go so very soon. We are just coming to the warmest of the weather, and Town in heat is never pleasant.'

'Oh yes, my dear, do go,' said Lady Cornford, pleased for Mary beyond anything, 'It will be an excellent opportunity for you. You have been too little seen. With your sweet face you will be in huge demand, I daresay, especially when it becomes known what your father means to do for you.'

'I doubt if gentlemen will concern themselves with her dowry, once they have seen Miss Waverley,' said Radleigh, gallantly.

'You are very right,' agreed Reyne. 'And when you do marry, Miss Waverley, you will still have your quarters with us, you know. What excellent times we shall all have.'

And Falconer noticed Reyne toss an amused smile at Captain

Radleigh, obviously including him in it, which gave Mr Falconer considerable food for thought. If Mary Waverley was to have the run of Lord Reyne's home whenever she pleased, and was thought good enough for Radleigh, perhaps he had been wrong to exclude her so summarily from his list. Reyne's connections were the highest in the land, and would surely give him far more opportunities than a mere Sir William.

Despite her determination not to put herself entirely at Lord Reyne's bidding a moment sooner than she must, his suggestion as to Mary had delighted Barbara. To have her as a regular visitor would be a pleasure in itself, but the chance it would give her to throw her more in Captain Radleigh's way was an opportunity that no self-respecting matchmaker could dislike. As the day had progressed, she had observed how the captain had sought out Mary: no efforts on her behalf should be spared to bring such a promising beginning to a happy conclusion.

As if her mother had read Barbara's thoughts, Lady Cornford now turned to Mary, saying, 'My dear, it is a wonder I did not think of it before. You must be fatigued: why don't you remain here tonight? I shall send a servant directly to your mama, shall I, and get your things? They can be here at once. To have to go out again after such a long day will be quite exhausting.'

Mary expressed her gratitude, and left the table, going into the salon to write a note for her mother. Lady Cornford followed her, and once out of Mr Falconer's hearing, said, 'Mary, dear, let me add a note for your mama, telling her about our expedition to Crosby, I did not want to say anything in front of Mr Falconer: I'm sure you understand why. I mean to ask her if you may remain with us, and leave for Liverpool from here, if you are in agreement? There is not the least need for you to go home: your maid will surely be able to pack anything you will need.'

Mary, naturally, was very happy to agree, and the note was sent, and they returned together to the dining-room in time to hear Captain Radleigh suggesting that, in view of the success of their visit to Chester, another drive out elsewhere might be planned for the morrow.

'Why; sir,' said Barbara, throwing her lord an arch look, 'have you not told poor Captain Radleigh that you have already disposed of his person tomorrow? That is a great deal too bad of you. Captain Radleigh is not to be bullied, you know. You are not married to *him*.'

'I hope I should not bully anybody, My Lady. I am not a monster. It had merely slipped my mind, you know.'

'How upset Miss Chalmers would be to hear you say that, sir,' she said, with a tight smile. 'Well, I shall tell you, Captain Radleigh: you are to have the glorious and noble enjoyment of slaughtering a wood full of Sir William Chalmers's rooks tomorrow. But whether you prefer that to a drive out is not for me to know.'

'A wood full of rooks!' cried the others, in unison.

'Chalmers offered it, sir,' shrugged Reyne, looking slightly embarrassed, 'and I did not wish to appear top-lofty and refuse – though, clearly, my wife thinks I have been too low.'

'I mean nothing of the sort, as well you know,' said Barbara, angry at being so misrepresented. 'I was simply surprised at your agreeing to Captain Radleigh's going without making certain that he should wish to.'

'Oh, he has always been sure that I have low tastes, My Lady,' said Radleigh, with an engaging grin.

'And you are invited to dine, sir,' said Barbara, 'so you will be able to escape seeing the ladies of *this* house, at least for a whole day, which I am sure will be a great relief.'

Lord and Lady Cornford looked along the table at each other, mortified that, after being amongst them for such a short period, their son-in-law was willing to forsake his wife for a whole day.

'Believe me, Lady Reyne, nothing I shall find at Sir William's home will compensate me for what I shall leave behind me,' said Radleigh, gallantly.

'Very prettily said, sir,' said Lady Cornford, pointedly. 'Young ladies are inclined to become resentful when they are neglected, you know.'

Being in no doubt what was meant by that, Lord Reyne

hastened to assure his mother-in-law that he had only consented at all because he thought they would wish him to be neighbourly, and that they should certainly return at the earliest opportunity.

'Don't hurry back on my account, sir,' said his wife, lifting her brows. 'I am certain that I shall be able to find something to do. I am not so lacking in resources.'

Mr Falconer, saw an opportunity at once. 'Indeed you are not, My Lady,' he said, smoothly. 'Your brother despises my poor landau, but, if you are not of his mind, I should be very happy to put both it and myself entirely at your disposal tomorrow.'

'There is not the least need for you to put yourself out, sir,' Lady Cornford speedily interceded. 'Miss Waverley has agreed to remain with us, and she, you know, will be able to keep Barbara company.'

'Then it will be an abundance of riches, ma'am,' said Falconer, smoothly. 'Two charming ladies instead of one.'

The alacrity with which Lady Barbara accepted his gracious offer left Reyne in no doubt how much he had annoyed her: he berated himself inwardly that, in his absence, he had left the field open to Falconer again. As for any help he might yesterday have hoped for from Radleigh, having watched him with Miss Waverley during the past twenty-four hours, he was sure that he could expect none. Indeed, he rather thought that were Falconer to begin to show any real interest in Miss Waverley, he would find Radleigh a formidable opponent.

Realizing that an atmosphere was building up at her table, Lady Cornford hastened to leave the gentlemen to their port, an unhappy circumstance for all of them, since Reyne could not disguise his dislike of Mr Falconer, and the atmosphere not only remained with them, but followed them back into the salon afterwards.

The evening was quickly felt to be untenable and, since it was generally agreed between them that they were too tired for music or cards, and wanted only their beds, Mr Falconer was obliged to take his leave of them, but it was with a promise to return next afternoon to take the ladies driving. Lady Reyne having enhanced this plan to include his coming for luncheon, he went away in a happy frame of mind, quite indifferent as to how her husband felt, and trying to think of ways in which, on the morrow, he might lure Barbara away from Miss Waverley.

Pausing only to ensure that Mary was comfortably settled in the bedroom she always occupied when she stayed with them, Barbara went at once to bed, wanting only to sleep. Reyne, however, had other plans: although he knew very well what had led to Barbara's provocative behaviour, he still seethed at Falconer's brazen behaviour in daring so openly to court his wife, and was determined to have it out with her. Instead of waiting until he was ready for bed to go to her bedchamber, he stormed in at once, while Stowe was still undressing her. When he entered her bedchamber, she was dressed only in her shift: he halted on the threshold, his angry words dying on his lips, while Barbara grabbed the gown just taken off and held it in front of her, her cheeks ablaze.

'E . . . excuse me, My Lady,' stammered Reyne, averting his eyes, just as discomposed as she was, 'I . . . I stepped in to tell you that, since I am to make an early start tomorrow, I shall not disturb you tonight. You'll say all that's proper to Guy for me, won't you? Poor boy, I forgot to let him know that I shan't be able to take him for his lesson. Tell him that I promise to make it up to him.'

Giving her no chance to reply, he withdrew through the dressing-room door, and thence, into his bedchamber, where, as his valet prepared his night attire, his brain was charged with the vision of his wife as she had been when he had left her. He had the strongest wish to go back to her: had Stowe not been with her when he had entered, he would not have withdrawn so meekly. He cursed himself for being so stupid as to pretend to Barbara, on that first night, that he had no wish to share her bed, since the insult made it almost impossible now, for him to ask if he might stay. It had been a lie even when he had said it, but almost from that moment, his craving for her had been mounting, until now it threatened to overwhelm him. Last night in the gardens, they had come very close to embracing: she would have let him kiss her had not Falconer come upon them. Even when she had been at her most infuriating, he had had the greatest difficulty in keeping his hands off her, and he knew now that it was inevitable that he must have her. He wanted her now; knew, indeed, that most husbands would simply have gone in and taken what was theirs, and had an overwhelming desire to do so. But his feelings for her had now become so impassioned, that he could not countenance their coming together until she was as eager as he was himself.

# Chapter Nineteen

MUCH AS LORD Reyne and Captain Radleigh enjoyed helping Sir William rid his lands of the plague of birds in his woodland, they excused themselves from staying for dinner, pleading as their excuse the early start they had to make for Liverpool next morning, Reyne being anxious to please his wife, Radleigh just as anxious to return to Miss Waverley. Riding back to Hurst Park, Reyne was full of good intentions: tonight they wouldn't be plagued by unwanted guests, so perhaps they might even begin to return to some sort of intimacy.

Walking into the house, having thrown their reins to the grooms, none of the family was anywhere to be seen. Enquiring of Bragg, they were informed that Lady Reyne and Miss Waverley were taking refreshment in the garden and, pausing only to tell Bragg to inform Lady Cornford that, after all, they were dining at home, they went in search of them.

The scene, which met their eyes would probably have been thought attractive by anyone of an artistic temperament, but it was viewed by Reyne with dismay, for there, in the shade of an ancient oak, against a pile of cushions, sat Lady Reyne. Lying on rugs and cushions very close to her were Mr Falconer and Lord John Wynnon, each propped up on one elbow, listening admiringly to whatever it was that she was saying. It was very obvious, from where they stood, that Barbara was enjoying their attentions.

As the two gentlemen came into view and Barbara saw them, she broke off in mid sentence and stared across at her husband with a satisfied look, which said, 'And do you see now, sir, that when you neglect me, I am perfectly able to find somebody else who will amuse me?'

She looked comfortable enough seated there against the bank of cushions, the skirts of her gown, made of some floating material, ruffling in the slight breeze which made the heat pleasant, and with her two cavaliers at her feet. The two gentlemen were less so: seeing Reyne they jumped to their feet at once, for they could see from the dark look which crossed his features that he didn't enjoy finding them there on his return.

Whilst Captain Radleigh joined Miss Waverley, where she had stationed herself somewhat apart from the rest in order that she could sketch them, Lord Reyne went in amongst the others until he stood above his wife.

'So, My Lady,' he said, striving to keep his face pleasant, 'you see we are home. You made so much fuss about my going to Sir William that I dragged Radleigh back betimes. Now I see I need not have bothered.'

'You came back for me?' said Barbara, with exaggerated surprise. 'How you do spoil me, to be sure. I must be the luckiest woman alive to have such a considerate husband. But I did tell you not to bother. We have had such a delightful day, and I should not have wished you to spoil your day with Miss Chalmers.'

'Had I known you were so well entertained, I should certainly not have done so! And I think you mean my day with Sir William, don't you? It was he who invited us, you will remember. Indeed, he had gone to considerable trouble to provide for our entertainment. But there were several other gentlemen present, so I hope we won't be too much missed. And so much was made by you of our going.'

'Thoughtful, and modest too,' said Barbara, opening her eyes very wide. 'I am sure you underestimate your importance to Miss Chalmers. And to Sir William, of course: we must not forget good old Sir William.'

The two gentlemen with whom she had been whiling away the afternoon in gentle flirtation, could sense the *frisson* of discord, and Mr Falconer was pleased to see it, for it made up in part for much of the disappointment brought by a day which had not, so far, lived up to his expectations. As promised, he had come early to drive out with Lady Reyne. After luncheon they had taken a carriage ride and a pleasant walk along the shady riverbank, but any chance that he might be alone with Lady Reyne had been thwarted by Miss Waverley, who stuck so closely to her friend's side that he had not had Barbara to himself, even for a moment. That was bad enough, but, when they returned to Hurst Park, his frustration had increased tenfold to find Lord John waiting for them. It was not altogether surprising, therefore, that the tones of discord, which showed through every word of the Reynes' exchange, were like music to his ears. Despite the fact that the hour was now quite advanced and he hadn't been invited to dinner, he decided not to take his leave just yet, and seeing him sink back down on to the cushions and rugs, Lord John followed suit.

Reyne, who expected them to go now that he had returned, was extremely put out when they showed no inclination to move. When Barbara excused herself and went up to the house to see Bragg about bringing more refreshments, he strode after her without even attempting to excuse his behaviour in leaving Radleigh to play host. Waiting until they were out of sight of the others, Reyne caught up with Barbara.

Walking along beside her, he said, steadily, struggling for composure, 'You seem to have had a pleasant day without me, My Lady.'

'Should you have preferred that I had *not*?' said Barbara, arching her brows. 'That is not very gallant.'

'Perhaps I might feel more gallant had I not come back to find that my wife has been entertaining two unmarried gentlemen in my absence,' said Reyne, visibly annoyed.

'Should you?' said Barbara. 'But how was I to know that? You cannot expect me to be conversant with your wishes, My Lord:

you have spent so little time in my company. Indeed, I suspect you have spent almost as much time with Miss Chalmers as you have with me. All those dances at the ball: and then, your attendance on her today. I daresay she knows your little preferences far better than I could ever do, by now. Perhaps I should ask her what they are? No doubt that is why you went there so eagerly today. And who am I to blame you? It is so much more soothing to the spirit to be in the company of persons who understand one. I certainly find it so.'

'You certainly do, ma'am, as I have seen this afternoon. No doubt Falconer is very soothing to your spirits.'

'Certainly Mr Falconer is a good friend,' said Barbara, as if considering the matter, 'but then, so is Lord John.'

'Strange that so many of your friends seem to be male. Do you think it acceptable for a married woman to flirt with unmarried gentlemen?'

Barbara pretended to be shocked. 'My dear sir, I do *not*!' she said, emphasizing the last word. 'But then, I am of the opinion that it is extremely bad *ton* for married people of *either* sex to flirt with anybody but his spouse, though it is clear that not everyone shares my opinion.'

'If you are accusing me of going to Sir William's house in order to flirt with Miss Chalmers, you are miles out,' said Reyne, heatedly, very annoyed to find the tables turned on him so neatly. 'I went to shoot with Sir William and for no other reason. I saw Miss Chalmers only at luncheon – and I certainly didn't flirt with her.'

'So, you didn't flirt with Miss Chalmers and I didn't flirt with Mr Falconer. What a very virtuous day we have both spent,' said Barbara, with exaggerated cheerfulness. 'I'm so glad that is sorted out. How pleasant to find ourselves in agreement. We must, we simply must have more of these little talks.' And, with that, she walked away, leaving Reyne a prey to many emotions, the chief of which was a desire to wring her neck.

So annoyed was he that he determined to rid himself of their visitors before Lady Reyne could return and prevent him. Going back to them almost immediately, having paused only long enough to send to the stables for their horses to be saddled and brought round, he shocked Miss Waverley and Captain Radleigh by saying to Barbara's two visitors, 'Gentlemen! Still here, I see. Then I'm sorry to be the bearer of evil tidings. My wife has sent me with her apologies: a sudden, fearful headache. She intends to lie down before dinner in the hope that it will pass. I've sent for your horses, and I'll bid you good day, for I must go to her now to make sure that she has all she needs.'

There was nothing for them to do but leave as graciously as they could and, to make sure they went, Reyne walked up with them to the house, where Lord John's horse and Mr Falconer's carriage, were awaiting them. But they were not alone: Guy, who had been pestering the grooms in the stable when Reyne's orders had been received, and hearing that his hero had returned, rushed round in the hope that Reyne might, belatedly, offer to take him out in his curricle. Thinking to get himself in Lady Reyne's good book, Falconer offered himself instead, saying that he would take Guy up and let him take the reins of the landau just to the edge of the Park. Remembering Barbara's strictures on good manners, Guy swallowed his disappointment, agreeing with what cheerfulness he could muster.

The two gentlemen and the boy were only just out of sight when Lady Barbara returned from her errand, surprised to find that her guests had gone. She was suspicious at once that her husband must have had a hand in it and, when she looked toward Mary and Captain Radleigh and they refused to meet her eye, she was sure of it.

When Reyne told her that Guy had gone with Falconer in his landau, she was much gratified, saying, 'How very good of him, to be sure. I mentioned to him earlier how disappointed Guy was when you neglected him in favour of Miss . . . Sir William.'

'I *didn't* neglect him. I told you to tell him that I should make it up to him,' Reyne protested, feeling, however, that he had indeed let Guy down, and finding himself oddly anxious not to have been supplanted in the boy's affections.

'But we go to Crosby tomorrow. It will be three days before another chance offers,' she pointed out, rubbing salt into the wound.

'Then I shall take him out when he gets back now. There is still time. I'll have my curricle sent round.'

'There is not the least need,' Barbara hastened to assure him. 'Not now that Mr Falconer has taken him up.' And she turned cheerfully on her heel and went back into the house, leaving Reyne to stroll back down to the lawns, where he surprised Mary and Radleigh in close conversation.

As he came into sight, Radleigh called to him, 'Good God, man, that was polite of you, getting rid of them like that! I've been assuring Miss Waverley that you are not usually so boorish. She will be thinking that her friend has made a very sad match.'

Reyne had the grace to apologize, adding, 'It was unpardonable that you should see such an exhibition of bad manners. I'm not usually such an oaf, but it was the sight of those locusts hanging about my wife.'

'Indeed, sir,' she said, anxious to reassure him, 'you had no need to concern yourself, I have been with Lady Reyne every moment. And if I hadn't,' she continued, lifting her chin bravely, 'you still need fear nothing, for she is known as much for the modesty of her behaviour as for her beauty.'

He bowed, acknowledging her reprimand, then, feeling himself very much *de trop*, wandered off by himself in the shrubbery, until it was time to dress for dinner.

Watching his friend's retreating back, and left alone with Mary, Radleigh said, 'I shall be very happy when those two have settled their differences and come together as they should.'

'You think they will, then?' asked Mary, looking hopeful.

'Do not you?'

'It is a strange and a mighty battle, but, yes, I think it is inevitable.'

'I shall be very glad of it, for then they will move to London and you shall have that little room in Berkeley Square. How comfortable that will be.'

'Is it, then, such a comfortable house?' said Mary, mistaking his meaning.

'Certainly it is, but I wasn't thinking of the house. I was speaking more of my own comfort.'

'But how can that affect you, sir?' said Mary, in some confusion.

'Why, because I shall ask my man of business to find me some rooms in St James's Street,' he said cheerfully, 'and then I shall be able to see you every day whilst you are in Town.'

'Oh!' said Mary, covered in confusion.

She would not chance another word, and soon excused herself to change for dinner, but a fierce spurt of pleasure sprang up within her, which she could scarcely contain.

Conversation at dinner was, again, a desultory business, with Reyne and Barbara saying hardly a word to each other and the rest trying to disguise the fact that they had noticed it. When the party separated for bed, very early so as to be fresh for the long day ahead of them, Barbara wondered, briefly, if her husband would come to her room and undertake another battle royal. But, when her candle had been blown out for a full half-hour and there was still no sign of him, she knew that he would not come, and pretended to herself that she was glad. Nor did he come to her bedchamber next morning. Indeed, the first she saw of him was when the family met downstairs for an early breakfast before leaving for Crosby Seabank and the Waterloo Hotel.

# Chapter Twenty

THE WEATHER REMAINED clear and bright as the party from Hurst Park left their carriages at Ellesmere Port and boarded the steam packet which was to carry them, their luggage and a few of their servants across the Mersey. They had begun their journey very early, passing through villages and hamlets along the way, all ringing with the sound of church bells in thanksgiving for the allied victory at Waterloo, and clearly in a mood for celebration. Even there, on the quayside, they were still almost deafened by bells as every nearby church competed with its neighbour to sound most joyful. Every person was dressed in his best clothes; each face wreathed in smiles.

The packet boat proved to be very spacious, for it had been built to accommodate very large parties. As their own party boarded, and Lord Reyne handed his wife on to the gangplank, she could not resist a dig at him, saying, 'How disappointed Stowe was this morning, sir, when you failed to appear in my bedchamber. I'm sure that she quite depends on seeing you there, you know, such a romantic as she is.'

Lord Reyne looked up quickly, hoping her expression would show that it was really his wife who had wanted him there, but one glance at her satirical look led him to answer her in kind.

'I was disappointed myself, Lady Reyne,' he said with a grin. 'You must know that to have Stowe make sheep's eyes at me every morning quite sets me up for the day. But what of you,

Lady Reyne, I hope you were not too disappointed that I did not come?'

'I?' said Barbara, staring as if such an idea was completely impossible to consider. 'Now that would be absurd. Certainly I steeled myself to expect you, since you had set so much store by it, but when you failed to arrive, disappointment was not quite the word I would have used to describe my feelings.'

'You steeled yourself?' said Reyne, quizzically. 'Why? You were in no danger from me, I assure you.'

'Now that I am wide awake, naturally I realize that. But remember, I was then still rather drowsy and had quite forgotten that you seek quite different company nowadays. Certainly I should not have expected to see you in my bed: I shall not do so in future, you may be certain.'

'If by *different company* you mean Miss Chalmers, I should not like to mislead you into thinking that my having visited her would keep me from my wife's bedchamber whenever I wished to enter it. I failed to come to you today because I knew that you and Stowe would be completing your packing, and for no other reason. I shall certainly expect you to keep to our bargain.'

Barbara could not trust herself to answer him civilly and, throwing him a look of loathing, she hurried after Lady Cornford as the boat slipped from its moorings and steamed out into the River Mersey.

While Barbara sent Stowe to search out the private apartment set aside for women, the ladies were beguiled into watching the scenery along the banks, as their boat steamed past the elegant Tudor house at Speke, with its fine black and white exterior, on one bank, and on the other bank, the high ground of Bebbington, sloping gradually down to the town of Birkenhead on the point of the Wirral. None of the ladies had ever before been on any boat larger than a punt, and they found the whole experience more exhilarating than they could ever have imagined.

The gentleman wanted nothing so tame as scenery. While the ladies ordered that their coffee be brought to them on deck, the men started on a tour of the boat, the engine being, naturally, its chief attraction. When, half an hour later, the whole party met up again, Guy and Lord Cornford were full of its wonders. Guy had been very much impressed with Lord Reyne who, on his travels, had seen more than one steam engine and was able to explain some of its intricacies. He continued to fire questions at his brother-in-law, which soon threatened to exhaust Reyne's slender knowledge, and Lady Cornford, who wanted Reyne to spend time with Barbara, quickly took her husband and her son off to the mixed salon to find refreshments. The two younger couples wanted nothing, and were free to wander at leisure, being soon separated from each other by the fashionable crowds milling around them.

Having manoeuvred shamefully to get Miss Waverley to himself, and the two of them finding a snug corner from which they could watch the progress of the little steam packet as it cut its way across the running tide, Captain Radleigh said to Mary, 'Am I imagining it, or do I again sense a chill in the air between our illustrious hosts?'

Mary sighed, admitting that they did seem as much estranged as ever. 'Poor Barbara,' she said, miserably. 'I had so hoped that by now they might be reconciled.'

'Poor Barbara. What about Reyne? He is just as miserable.'

'I am sorry if their misery is equal,' said Mary, unable to hide her indignation, 'but I cannot feel that the cause is as equal. You can have no idea how much she has suffered in all this. Why, from the very first, when her father married her off at sixteen, it has been a disaster for her. If you had a sister, would you wish to see her married so young, and to a stranger? I hope I shall always give Lord Cornford every respect, for he has been very kind to me, but I shall ever think that he used his daughter very ill.'

'Indeed, you are very right,' Radleigh readily agreed. 'A monstrous thing to do, but do not forget that the same thing befell Reyne. He was not much older himself.'

'I do not forget it, sir, nor do I blame him for being miserable, but to run away, leaving his wife to bear the brunt of all the criticism, that was not kind. Had he come when she was eighteen, as he should, instead of going off to war, all would probably have been well by now. Can you imagine how poor Ba felt when Reyne finally came back to England and was in London for those weeks, knowing full well he should have been in Cheshire? And to have every newspaper writing of it, as they did! Poor, poor Barbara. To know that she might have been married to any one of half-a-dozen men, had her father not made her marry Reyne must rank as a considerable irony when it is obvious, from his behaviour, that the man who was lucky enough to marry her doesn't even want her.'

'But I think you are wrong: I am sure he does want her,' said Radleigh, sincerely. 'That is why I say poor Reyne.'

'Then he has a very odd way of showing it. You were not aware of it, I know, but Miss Chalmers has been one of the most cattish of all those who have smiled behind Barbara's back. Had Reyne planned to make their estrangement as conspicuous as possible, he could not have chosen better. And then to go to her house for almost a whole day, so soon after he had finally come into Cheshire, that was surely infamous.'

'I like your loyalty, but you need not be angry with me, for I said much the same to him myself. But, you know, when he first came home from France, he was very nervous as to how he would be received by her: it is not altogether surprising that he was a trifle reluctant to put it to the test. Yet I know, for a fact, that he came with the best of intentions: only think of that necklace. Even had she been plain he would have made an effort to try to make her happy, but he was shocked at finding her so beautiful. Then, when he saw how Falconer was hanging about her skirts, naturally, he was angry. Nobody acts rationally when they are jealous.'

They sighed, simultaneously, watching as their destination came ever closer: the bustling city of Liverpool, with its docks, which housed a multitude of tall ships from all parts of the world, as well as the more humble vessels which plied back and forth across the Mersey.

'We must do something, Captain Radleigh,' said Mary, at length. 'Women like to be wooed, you know. I think Barbara feels that she has been had too . . . too cheaply. It was bad enough when she was sixteen, for she always felt that much was wanting, but now she knows what men are capable of. She has a standard by which to judge his behaviour towards her. She has had admiration from others which she should have had from her husband.'

'It is the very devil of a situation.'

'Could you not try to get Lord Reyne to take a more conciliatory stance, sir?' said Mary. 'Lady Reyne has been used to receiving compliments, and trinkets, and to be driven out to picnics – oh, any manner of pleasant things.'

Radleigh smiled, congratulating himself on, at least, learning which things might make Mary more disposed towards a gentleman who wished to ingratiate himself into *her* good book.

'I do not know what ladies are like on the other side of the Channel, sir,' she continued, with magnificent understatement, 'but I do not think Lord Reyne did his cause a great deal of good in describing them so minutely to his wife. You will excuse me for saying so. Indeed, I am much inclined to think that was his biggest mistake. Could he not show a little humility? No, not humility, I do not ask for humility, but a little less confidence, perhaps?'

Radleigh laughed out loud at that. 'You are very right, Miss Waverley. He is a good deal too sure of himself. I am afraid it is the ladies themselves who are responsible for that. Such a great handsome brute as he is! He is not used to having to fight to be admired.'

'Nor is Barbara, sir,' said Mary, drily. 'Perhaps it is not reasonable to expect either of them to humble themselves. How I wish I could think of something to help them. And you, sir, could you not impress on Lord Reyne the need . . . oh, the desperate need, sir, for a woman not to feel that she is taken for granted.'

To Mary's surprise, Captain Radleigh took her hand from the boat rail, and pressed his lips to her palm. 'You are a very good friend, Miss Waverley,' he said gently. 'And I shall certainly do my best to help in the difficult matter of bringing about two of the most stubborn individuals to be met with anywhere.'

Just like Mary and Captain Radleigh, Lord Reyne and his wife were leaning on the boat rail a little further along the deck, watching as the steam packet took them nearer to their disembarkation point. All around them, fashionable people seemed to be enjoying themselves, and, after he had been with his wife for some while without them having exchanged a word, Reyne eventually said, in desperation, 'Look, Barbara, can't we agree to call a truce while we are at Crosby? It won't be pleasant for the others if we spend all our time either arguing, or ignoring each other. After all the trouble your father has gone to in order to see that we all have a pleasant time, it seems a little harsh that we should repay him so meanly. And it *is* the anniversary of Waterloo. We should be celebrating, not getting cross.'

Barbara, who had been thinking much the same thing, could only agree and, if conversation between them was still hardly amiable, at least nobody listening to them would realize that there was any real enmity between them.

Truth to tell, Barbara was glad to agree to Reyne's wishes, for she felt most extraordinarily happy to be out on the water. It was all new to her, and she found that she loved the feel of the sea breeze against her skin, the tug of it through her hair, the excitement of approaching unknown country and seeing it emerge from the distant haze. Their journey across the River Mersey between Ellesmere Port and Liverpool would take little more than an hour, but Barbara wished that it could last all day. She knew that when eventually they disembarked at Liverpool, they still had to take another packet boat the short distance to Crosby, but that would certainly be drawn by horses, which would not be half so exciting as the steam packet.

Her feeling of exhilaration was mirrored in her face: her eyes sparkled with pleasure; her skin had become delicately flushed from the breeze. Looking back at a moored boat, which they had just passed, she noticed Reyne looking at her intently. Her skin took on a deeper shade, when he said, 'I am glad we are going to be friends today, Barbara. When you look as delightfully as you do at this moment, it is very difficult to quarrel with you.'

'Very pretty, sir,' said Barbara, with a mischievous smile. 'But there is not the least need to overdo it. You only have to be nice to me when others are nearby. You will have a seizure if you try to be pleasant to me all day, and I could not bear to have that on my conscience.'

'I only said you were in looks, Barbara,' he said, wishing he hadn't given her a chance to put him down. 'Did your mother never teach you how to take compliments graciously? I certainly can't compliment you on any noticeable difference as to character, for that is very much what it was.'

'Since most people see nothing wrong with my character,' said Barbara, impudently, 'I can only say *thank you*, sir.'

A laugh was surprised from Reyne. 'You really are the most impossible woman, aren't you?' he said. 'Two days of being sweetness and light – how shall we manage?'

'I have grave doubts that it is possible,' said Barbara, joining him in laughing, 'but if we ignore the subjects of nuptials, letter-writing, living in London, and gentlemen callers, perhaps we may make a fair fist of it?'

'Haven't you missed the subject of Miss Chalmers off your list? You surely don't want me to speak about her?'

'You are very right, sir,' said Barbara, with a distinctly frigid glare. 'We shall find it very difficult indeed to get through the next two days!'

Having disembarked, reluctantly, at Liverpool, the family hired carriages to take them the short journey to join the *Lancashire Witch*, a packet boat belonging to a rival canal company, the Leeds and Liverpool. As Barbara had guessed, though it was a very well-appointed boat, it was horse drawn and much slower than the steam packet. Since there was a postilion on board, whose job it was to sound a horn to warn of its coming, the journey was also decidedly noisy, and none of the party was sorry when they reached their destination.

Guests making for the Royal Waterloo Hotel were obliged to disembark at Endlett Lane and take carriages for the last part of their journey across the sands. Just to see the full panorama of the seaside had put them all into high spirits and Guy, who had never seen even such a modest place as Crosby, could not wait to get into the water.

But it was already approaching two o'clock by the time their carriages halted in front of the handsome, three-storeyed hotel, standing just behind the sand dunes, which was to be their resting place for the night, and the celebration dinner was due to begin at four. Despite all Guy's pleas to be allowed at least to put his feet into the water before they went to their rooms, his mother was anxious, since he was to be allowed to stay up late, that he should take a nap so as to be refreshed for the evening.

'I wish you will not always treat me as if I were about five years of age, Mama,' said Guy in exasperation, for once not being able to control his irritation. 'I don't need to take a nap like a baby. You spoil *evcrything*!'

Seeing Lady Cornford's face crumple on hearing such harsh words from her beloved boy, but at the same time very much understanding Guy's frustration, Reyne went in to heal the breach.

'It's too late, boy, for a really satisfactory bathe. We'd have to get out almost at once. We'll do it tomorrow, when we can spend more time in the water. Your mama's quite right, you know. I'm feeling dashed tired myself. Think I'll get my head down for an hour, get a cool bath, too; this heat is deuced uncomfortable.'

Lady Cornford threw him a grateful glance at seeing her son become his usual tractable self, and as they went up to their suite of rooms, Barbara murmured her own thanks, saying, 'You are very good, sir, pretending to be fatigued. You really don't have to come up if you don't wish it. As soon as Guy goes to his room, I wish you will go down again.'

'What makes you think that I don't want to go to bed, My

Lady?' said Reyne, deliberately provocative. 'There are some occasions when it can be very agreeable indeed to spend a couple of hours lying down in the afternoon.'

Catching his meaning at once, Barbara refused to utter another word, but pushed on ahead, still hearing him chuckling as she slammed her bedchamber door behind her.

# Chapter Twenty-One

MUCH AS LADY Cornford wanted them all to rest before dinner, it was not to be. As she lay down against the cool sheets, so much noise and bustle issued from the crowds which had made the journey to Crosby and taken to the beach, that it quickly became apparent that they might just as well begin to dress for dinner and go downstairs again.

The gentlemen had only to bathe and change, but for the ladies it was a more leisurely business: they had noticed numbers of very fashionable women arriving at the Royal Waterloo and had no intention of being thought dowdy. Nevertheless, by the time they were ready, they found they were still a good half-hour early for dinner and rather than wait in the hotel lounges, they decided to join the gentlemen in taking a walk along the footpath which edged the sands, in order to see what the little resort had to offer.

Although the hotel was a new venture, Crosby Seabank had begun to have a reputation for its expanse of golden sands, clear waters and fine open spaces from the time, nearly half a decade earlier, when the Great Crosby Marsh was enclosed. Before that, Crosby had been little more than a small, isolated collection of farms and fishermen's cottages, but in the past few years, having been advised by their physicians of the excellent benefits of sea bathing, more and more visitors had begun to be attracted to its coast. Today, the resort was bustling with people. Not all had come to stay at the hotel: some were local people come to the hotel merely to dine; others came to bathe; many had come just to have their spirits lifted by the fine views of the Dee and Mersey and out to sea, and of the Welsh mountains and the Cheshire coast.

There were other attractions too: as promised in the flyer which had first caught Lord Cornford's eye, a handsome bowling green had been built near to the hotel and, although they had yet to see it, they had been assured by a waiter that the promised billiard room was already in use. Most important of all, Mr Rodie and Mr Horsfall, the hotel's far-seeing proprietors, had recognized an opportunity really to put Crosby on the map, and had arranged for the setting up of bathing machines, which were nothing more than wheeled, wooden bathing huts in which gentlefolk could change, these being then pulled down to the water by horses so that their occupants could emerge directly into the sea.

Men and women naturally bathed separately, the gentlemen at one end of the long sands, the ladies at the other, well out of the way. From where the Hurst party stood, they could just about see the huts away off in the distance, but Guy noticed that some of the younger gentlemen had brought telescopes with them and were training them on the fair bathers as they made their way from their bathing machines into the enveloping sea. Guy thought this a wonderful idea and pleaded to be allowed to purchase such a telescope, an idea his father squashed at once by telling him, in no uncertain terms, that some men were gentlemen, but others clearly were not. That, on the face of it, seemed to be *that*, but the alluring idea failed to be banished from his mind for the very good reason that he happened to have an unusually large sum of money by him just then and could afford the not inconsiderable cost of such a fine piece of equipment, which he was sure he could put to good use in any number of ways, even when they went home. In general he was not the recipient of large sums: if he went to Chester, or to the village shop, his father might give him a few small coins to spend as he chose, but since Lord Cornford invariably bought for him everything which he might need, there was very little need for regular spending money. The journey to Crosby, however, had made Lord Reyne, always very free with his money, think last night of giving him some guineas to spend during their trip, recalling how irksome it was to have to ask for money for every small purchase. Since Captain Radleigh had been present when he thought of it, he, too, gave Guy some spending money, and the two sums together added up to more than he had ever before had all at once. Later, when he had gone to his bedroom, lying on a table next to his bed was a little note from Barbara, which said, simply, *So that you may have a really splendid time, Love B*. On the note rested a further two guineas. By that time Guy's head had been spinning at gaining such largesse, but when, just before they left the house, ready for Liverpool, he had received a not inconsiderable sum from his father (with the order not to make a nuisance of himself by hinting at his guests to treat him!), and a half guinea from Miss Waverley, he felt himself to be as rich as Croesus. He determined if he could, to wander off on his own next day in case he should accidentally come across a shop where he might purchase a telescope without his family being aware of it.

That afternoon, the path in front of the hotel was packed with smart people, and there was a fashionable squeeze along the edge of the sands. Lord Cornford and his party sauntered with the rest, revelling in the afternoon sunshine and salty breeze. Since they were all now very formally attired, they could not actually go on to the sands, and they found themselves wishing that they, too, might join the numerous groups of visitors who had set up little picnics in the dunes, while they watched their children running in and out of the waves, or building castles from the sand.

In view of the fact that his greatest wish was to go sea bathing, Guy was feeling particularly frustrated and he began to lag behind, wondering if anywhere hereabouts he might find a shop selling telescopes. To his disgust, not a single such establishment could be seen: indeed, apart from one or two cottages where small gifts and refreshments could be purchased, there seemed to be no shops at all on the seafront. It was a bitter blow, and he was just wondering whether he might sneak off next day back to Liverpool, where he had noticed a good many shops, when he heard a voice calling out from somewhere above him, to one side of the path. At first he could not locate from whence the sound had come, but then he noticed a high stone wall, which had been built to separate the garden of a small, but very pretty cottage from the promenade, On top of the wall was perched a handsome boy, dressed in nankeen breeches and a shirt, his jacket carelessly flung down on a nearby rose bush, whilst he precariously kept his balance. The fact that he looked to be sufficiently near enough to Guy's age would have made Guy wish to know him: the fact that he had, tucked under his arm, a fine, brass telescope was enough to make him Guy's best friend! Without giving his family a second thought, he dashed over in order to become acquainted.

The boy's name was Arthur Sefton and, since he was staying at the cottage with only his mama and a few servants, he was more than willing to meet up with someone of his own age. He understood at once what was needed to cement their friendship, and helped Guy to climb up next to him, where he immediately handed him a rather fluffy sugar bonbon from his pocket, then stuffed the telescope into his hands, pointing out where the ladies bathed. Just at that moment, a lady of very large proportions, dressed in a multitudinous bathing wrap and cap made up in a florid shade of cherry, was being helped to descend from one of the bathing machines and into the sea, by one of the formidable female bathing attendants who made their living by helping those who could not manoeuvre themselves. That the sea water was colder than it looked became apparent at once when that lady let out a huge cry and clung on like grim Death to the poor unfortunate bathing attendant, who was pulled beneath the water with her client, a sight which seemed to Guy even funnier from the fact that they were so far away that only the telescope enabled him to see it at all, and he could not actually hear the screams which emanated from the horrified mouth. He thought it a huge joke as the two women floundered about in the water, coughing and spluttering, before they managed to get back to the safety of the steps and climb out, and soon found himself much in charity with Arthur, who apologized that he could not offer him better fare that day, since most of the ladies who usually bathed were getting ready for the evening's entertainment at the hotel. He assured him, however, that they would certainly be back next day, and very amiably invited him to join him on his parapet. He also promised that, since he and his mother always dined at the hotel, he would look out for Guy, since they were certain to be bored by all the speechifying which would inevitably follow. Guy thought he had never before met anyone with whom he agreed so well, and the two were on the way to becoming firm friends when Lord Cornford, who had finally noticed his son's absence, came in search of him. Giving him a well-deserved dressing down for scaring his mama, and another for getting dirt on his breeches and his coat, he rushed him away, hardly allowing him to say goodbye to Arthur, though that enterprising young gentleman called out that he would be sure to see him later, before going back to his vigil on the ramparts.

Naturally, it was necessary for them all to return at once to the hotel so that Guy could be brushed down, and by the time he had been scolded sufficiently to put him into a very discontented mood indeed, dinner was being announced.

The Waterloo's proprietors had done their visitors proud: the dining-room, laid out in rows, refectory style, was bedecked with huge bowls of flowers and hung with the flags of the allied nations, and even before the main courses were brought in, side-boards and dressers already groaned with side dishes elaborate enough to whet the fussiest appetite. Those gentlemen still under the flag, including Captain Radleigh, were naturally dressed in their best regimentals, their bright red coats standing out against the more sober frockcoats worn by civilians, and the ladies in their silks and muslins.

The whole affair was very well organized. Since nearly 200 people had to be seated, ushers with seating plans were ready to lead them to their places and, as they moved into the body of the room, a quartet began quietly playing from a raised dais in the corner. The party from Hurst Park had been placed close to the speakers, seated at the front, and they congratulated themselves on being near enough to have a very good view of the proceedings. To everyone's relief, speeches were relegated to the end of the meal and they could all settle down first to enjoy the fine dishes and wines.

They were all talking animatedly together, and Reyne, determined to talk Barbara into a happy frame of mind, had just raised his glass to her when his face froze and he let the glass fall again. Leaning his head towards her, he said, in an angry whisper, 'Had you told me that you wished your admirer to accompany us, I'd have issued him with an invitation myself.'

Bewildered by his sudden change of mood, Barbara, who had hoped to get through the evening without too many disagreements with her husband, followed his gaze. To her complete amazement, she saw that Mr Falconer was taking his dinner at a table further down the room.

'Are you seriously suggesting, sir, that I asked Mr Falconer to come here today?' asked Barbara, in freezing tones.

'Madam,' he replied, equally frosty, 'are you seriously expecting me to believe that you did not?'

# Chapter Twenty-Two

WHEN, A FEW moments later, Lord Cornford caught sight of Mr Falconer, he, too, was rigid with anger. Turning to his wife, who noticed Falconer at much the same time and with similar horror, he hissed, 'Now do you see what comes of encouraging gentlemen to pay court to young married women, ma'am? You will congratulate yourself on the outcome, I suppose, when your daughter's husband seeks to divorce her. Too fragile to be allowed to consummate her marriage? I think not! Indeed, I never saw anything more *coming* than my own daughter meeting up with one of her cicisbei at a seaside resort, and in the same room as her husband and her parents.'

'Hush, Husband,' she hissed back at him. 'You surely do not think Barbara planned to meet Mr Falconer here?'

'Do not you? I hardly know what other interpretation would account for his being here.'

'Neither do I, foolish man. How can either of us know what brought him to Crosby? I am, however, quite certain that Barbara can have had nothing at all to do with it. You do not really think a daughter of ours would behave so dishonourably?'

'Until tonight,' he replied, heavily, 'I'd have staked my fortune on it. But I'll tell you something, madam, I intend to find out! And until I do, be sure never to leave her out of your sight. I'll make certain that any plans that gentleman has have no chance of developing, if it's the last thing I do. I don't want to find myself fighting duels at my time of life, for my daughter's honour.'

'Surely, were there any truth in this speculation, that would fall to her husband, my dear?' she said, dipping her head in Reyne's direction.

'You are supposing that he would think her worth the trouble,' he said irritably.

And, certainly, to see the way that Lord and Lady Reyne were studiously ignoring each other did not inspire them with confidence. Lord Reyne, preserving an icy front, had his eyes fixed firmly on Mr Falconer who, realizing that he had been noticed, sent him an insolent bow.

On the opposite side of the dining-table, Captain Radleigh, aware of it all, said to Miss Waverley, behind his hand, 'That's torn it! Surely Lady Reyne did not ask him to come?'

'Don't be ridiculous, sir,' said Mary, indignantly. 'She hasn't been alone with Mr Falconer since the arrangements were mooted. I was always at her side when he was in her company, and I can vouch for the fact that she said not a word to him about our coming here. I'd have heard had she done so. But she would not; she simply would not.'

'Then I'd like to know how he came to hear about it. It can hardly be a coincidence.'

'I could more easily believe it to be a coincidence than to imagine Barbara doing anything dishonourable,' said Miss Waverley, unequivocally.

At every other table people seemed to be enjoying themselves prodigiously, whilst on Lord Cornford's table all pleasure seemed to have departed: the excellent dishes were like dust and ashes in their mouths. Amongst them, only Guy, who had not noticed Mr Falconer and was therefore quite unaware of any atmosphere, continued to eat with unabated greed. The interminable meal dragged on, to be followed by even lengthier speeches, until finally it was all over. Never had a party of pleasure turned more sour, but, eager as they were to escape from it, Lord Cornford's party had been placed at the very front of the dining-room, whilst the doors leading to the other rooms were at the back. They had therefore to wait patiently in the wake of the crowds edging their way out, so that it took nearly ten minutes before they found themselves seated in one of the crowded drawing-rooms, where music was being played again by the quartet which had entertained them earlier.

Almost immediately, Guy spotted Arthur across the salon, where he was seated with his mama, amongst a crowd of friends. Pointing them out to Lady Cornford, Guy begged to be allowed to go across to him, scarcely waiting for her permission before he was off across the room. Seeing him vacate his chair, Mr Falconer, who had single-mindedly tracked them down, made straight for Barbara. Her horror at seeing him would have been amusing had she not looked quite so tragic. With increasing indignation she was forced to listen to the lame excuse he had invented for coming to Crosby, which was in the nature of a supposedly prearranged visit to his lawyer in Birkenhead on a business matter of some importance. Having learned of Lord Cornford's intention to attend the celebrations at Crosby, and knowing that he would be nearby himself, it had been irresistible, and he had decided to surprise them there. He added that, whilst he had managed to get a place at dinner, he had been unable to secure a room at the hotel and had, instead, found an hotel in Liverpool, to which he must later return. It was a flimsy excuse at best, and most of the party were sure that it was an outrageous lie.

'So, you thought you would surprise us, sir,' said Barbara's father, stiffly. 'What a strange world we live in nowadays, to be sure. In my day, as I remember, we waited to be invited before joining a party.'

It was the nearest thing to rudeness anyone had ever heard Lord Cornford, that most punctilious of hosts, utter. Falconer had the grace to look discomforted, but he quickly rallied, saying with a charming smile, which sent the dimple scurrying to his cheek, that, since they were all such friends, he had been sure that they would not wish him to stand on ceremony. He added that he was mortified if he had offended them, and would withdraw at once.

After such a handsome apology, there was nothing to be done but to bring him in. A chair was brought for him; he flicked up his coat tails, and sat with them, squeezing his chair between Lady Cornford and her daughter.

Even Mr Falconer found himself a little abashed at all the disapproval he felt around him, but he could not be sorry that he had come, for he had determined that this would be his last throw for Barbara before he moved his attentions elsewhere. Indeed, he would hardly have come now, but for the fact that, when he had left Hurst Park on the previous afternoon (had been almost thrown out), Barbara and her husband had seemed to be on such very bad terms. It was obvious that Reyne was no complacent husband, but Falconer still could not gauge whether his jealousy would cause him to cling more tenaciously to his wife, or make him repudiate her entirely: and if there was any chance at all that Barbara *would* be repudiated, it would be foolish indeed to lose her, after all his months of hard work. This trip to Crosby would seem to give him a perfect opportunity to see if he still stood a chance, without exposing his interest to his neighbours. And, if Lady Reyne *should* finally be lost to him, Crosby would be the perfect place in which to find out whether he could charm back Miss Mary Waverley, for that, too, he preferred to do away from the prying eyes of his neighbours, especially the beautiful blue eyes of Miss Annabel Chalmers.

While Mr Falconer was busy plotting, and the others were joined in spasmodic conversation in order to disguise the very great divisions amongst them, Guy came running back to his parents, being so much involved in delivering his message that he failed even to notice Mr Falconer amongst them. His mission was a simple one. Some of the local villagers had made an effigy of Napoleon and had been given permission to burn it that night on the common. Most of the village was going off to watch; there were to be one or two other amusements, and Mrs Sefton was willing to take Guy with them if his parents agreed that he might go. Lady Cornford was very happy to agree, and went over to meet Mrs Sefton, whom she found to be a very modish, very genteel sort of woman, whom she did not object to know better. She agreed at once to entrusting Guy to her charge and would have gone with them herself, had it not been necessary to keep an eye on her daughter's behaviour towards Mr Falconer, and indeed, on her husband, who was steadily becoming more and more surly with every word Falconer uttered. She hinted as much when she returned to her group, and Mary and Captain Radleigh, picking up the hint which had gone completely over her husband's head, good-naturedly joined Mrs Sefton's party on the common.

By now, there was a distinct *frisson* between Reyne and Barbara, for he was watching her closely for anything with which he might take issue, and she was furious that he so obviously felt that it was necessary. It was an insult past bearing. And, as for Mr Falconer daring to crash in on them in such a way as to make everybody think she must have arranged it with him, it was insupportable. She began to realize that she had thought far too highly of him all these months, for a gentleman would never have placed her in such an invidious position.

Lord Reyne broke in on her thoughts by saying to Mr Falconer, with false affability, 'You'll have to watch the time, I daresay. I understand that the last packet goes back to Liverpool quite early, and you won't want to miss it.'

Mr Falconer bowed his thanks, but said, with what Reyne chose to think was complaisance, 'You are very good, sir, but, being aware of that, I came by carriage.'

'Still,' said Lord Cornford, adding his mite. 'You can't be too careful, sir, if you intend to take that path across the sands. You'll need to do it while it is still perfectly light. You'd be a fool to chance it in twilight: you've only to get a wheel off the track and you're certain to get stuck. It'll be the devil of a job to get yourself out again.'

'I am grateful for your concern, My Lord,' said Falconer, gently, 'but I believe there's still an hour or so left of daylight.'

'It can be very deceptive, Mr Falconer,' said Lady Cornford, seeing her husband glower at his response. 'It appears light, you know, from all the lamps they have hung about the gardens, but when you are driving that path across the sands, I daresay you may not be able to see a hand in front of your eyes.'

Since it was palpably still daylight, Barbara was moved to protest, irritably, 'I am sure that Mr Falconer knows quite well what time the packet returns to Liverpool, Mama, and that he can drive a carriage quite as well as anyone across the sands. I am even reasonably confident that he is able to ascertain for himself how dark it is. Let him make up his own mind as to his means of returning to his hotel.'

But when, in response to her outburst, Mr Falconer threw her a triumphant look, as if he felt that he had scored points against her family, she fell irreparably out of charity with him.

'You will excuse me I hope, Mama? Papa? I find I have the most dreadful head again,' she said, feebly. 'The unaccustomed travel, perhaps, and this heat. I shall go up now, if you please. I'll bid you goodnight, Mr Falconer.'

Her parents were delighted to see their daughter separated from Mr Falconer and applauded her good sense when she left them immediately, making her way up a nearby crimson-carpeted staircase to her room. She was followed, a few moments later, by Lord Reyne, who caught up with her partway down the corridor, which led to their suite of rooms.

'How dare you encourage Falconer to meet us here,' said Reyne, standing in her path and preventing her from going on. 'Did you really think I should allow it? Forget what you owe to me: what of your parents? How do you think they must feel?'

'If you think I am capable of such an outrage, I rather wonder that you imagine I would worry about what my parents think, for surely I must be dead to all sense of decency.'

'And I should need to be stupid, indeed, were I to believe that you didn't persuade him to come here,' he said, defending himself stoutly.

Barbara's temper, which she had been determined to keep in check, now fell entirely into disarray, for she was furious not to be believed when she spoke the plain truth. 'Believe what you wish!' she threw at him. 'I did it! I did invite him! Why, I . . . I wrote him a letter! I went down on my knees to get him to come! Whatever you will! I care not a jot what you think!'

And with that, she stormed off down the corridor to her room, slamming the door behind her.

Shaken by her outburst (which, strangely, convinced him that she was quite innocent), Reyne sought his own room next door, ashamed at having lost his temper. Since there was an adjoining door between their bedchambers, he had just made a step towards it, ready to apologize, when he heard from her side the click of a key being turned sharply in the lock.

His temper was up again at once. He had been magnanimous enough to be prepared to apologize, but if she was such a termagant as to dare to lock him out, he would certainly not demean himself by knocking.

# Chapter Twenty-Three

OUTSIDE, ON SOME common ground close to the hotel, Miss Waverley and Captain Radleigh had joined the crowd of villagers and visitors enjoying the savage spectacle of a huge effigy of a very obese Napoleon Bonaparte, made of flour sacks and dressed in full French uniform, being burned on a massive bonfire. Close by, a fiddler had set up to play, and five or six couples from the village were performing a country-dance in the orange firelight. Further from the bonfire, a circle of village elders were seated, smoking their clay pipes and drinking ale around a pig-roast on a spit, the delicious aroma wafting on the night air.

Radleigh and Miss Waverley were very glad to be out of the atmosphere which Mr Falconer's arrival had brought down on them all, and with Guy engaged with Arthur and Mrs Sefton, they felt free to enjoy each other's company, much as they had been doing almost every day since they had first met.

The sea air had brought a healthy glow to Mary's cheeks: the excitement of the bonfire, and being with Radleigh, brightness to her eyes. She looked very lovely in the half light, and the affection for her which Captain Radleigh was supposed to have been inducing in Mr Falconer, but which had, instead, crept up unawares upon himself, presented itself now, full grown. He was in no doubt at all as to the wishes of his heart, and, perhaps he might then have spoken to her but that, on chancing to look across at Guy, he saw that he and Arthur had joined a group of village boys prodding the fire with long sticks. It looked very dangerous, and since Mrs Sefton was speaking to a gentleman nearby and Captain Radleigh was not confident that she had noticed, he bad Mary wait for him, while he hurried across to lead the two boys away to safety, out of the way of the hail of sparks crackling and rising into the night sky. Almost as soon as he left her side, Mr Falconer seemed to appear from the shadows beside her, making her start.

If everybody else who had come out to see the bonfire seemed to be enjoying themselves, the same could not be said of Mr Falconer, since tonight he had finally admitted to himself that any hopes he might once have entertained regarding Barbara had been nothing but pipe dreams. He had watched her with Lord Reyne very carefully that evening, and what he saw between them had not pleased him at all: he knew enough of men and women to recognize, as Barbara and Reyne had still to recognize, that a flame had been lit between them which would not be easily assuaged. They were still at the sparring stage, but, so far as Falconer was concerned, the outcome was not in doubt. But even that had not decided him to leave the field as much as his realization that, in coming to Crosby, he had overplayed his hand with regard to Lord Cornford. Many of his hopes had rested on the foundation of that gentleman's approval for which he had a healthy respect. He now knew that, even if Reyne could be brought to discard his wife, Lord Cornford disliked him too much to allow him to take Reyne's place. It had not taken him more than a few minutes after Lord Reyne had followed his wife upstairs, for Falconer to come to his decision, and, bidding Lord and Lady Cornford an obsequious farewell, he had gone outside in search of Mary to see if he could do any better there. Outside, a charming scene met his eye, in the light of a good moon: tables and chairs had been set up in the hotel grounds for the convenience of its guests, and everywhere groups of people were either seated enjoying the warm evenings and the sound of the quartet emanating from the hotel, or were sauntering along the promenade towards the common, listening as they went to the distant sounds of the fiddle and to the crashing of waves as the sea spread itself slowly up the beach towards the hotel. Mr Falconer joined the promenaders to the common, and soon saw Mary in the firelight, being quick to join her when Captain Radleigh left her for a moment.

When Mary saw him, she gave a gasp of surprise.

'I've found you at last, Miss Waverley,' he said, coming close. 'I hope you are pleased with the bonfire. What a deal of bloodthirsty children live in Crosby, to be sure. Poor Boney would be mortified, could he see them.'

She had to remind herself that, as little as a week ago, his seeking her out would have been delightful to her, for now she felt nothing more than a brief impatience.

'Indeed, sir,' she said, without agitation, 'Captain Radleigh and I have been enjoying it immensely.'

'Radleigh? Well, and why not? He is a good sort of fellow, I suppose, if you like these military types,' said Falconer, with insufferable condescension, pulling her hand through his arm as if it was an everyday thing, and he had a perfect right to do so. 'But I am glad, nevertheless, to see him go, for I have been hoping to have you to myself since I arrived. You cannot know how inconvenient I have felt his presence to be.'

Mary eyed him with dislike. 'We are obviously not of the same opinion, sir,' she said firmly. 'I find Captain Radleigh to be a charming companion.'

He felt her rebuke, and would have said something soothing, but that Mary gave him no opportunity to do so, saying quickly, as if it was something she had saved up to say to him, 'Mr Falconer, I pray you will leave Crosby. I have always, 'til recently, thought you a man of honour, but to turn up here! How could you try to make mischief in such a way? Whatever made you come?'

Mr Falconer gave a curt laugh. 'Why should I not come, Miss Waverley? It was a mere spur of the moment decision. You'll remember that I took young Guy up in my poor despised landau, last evening. He told me all about your trip. Believe me, it was irresistible.'

'Then it should not have been, sir,' she scolded. 'I am shocked that you should try to compromise Barbara in this way. Go home, now, I beg you. What can you expect to gain by it? You are upsetting dear Lord and Lady Cornford for nothing. Perhaps you have been misled by the few differences Barbara and Lord Reyne have had, but these are quite settled now, I do assure you. You have come here for nothing. And if Lord Reyne suspects you of any base design, he will surely call you out for it.'

'But I have the best reason in the world for coming here. You seem quite certain that I came to see Lady Reyne, but that simply is not true.'

And with that, Mr Falconer went on to positively declare himself interested in Miss Waverley, obviously expecting her to believe that she had created in his heart an unequalled attachment to herself, and that it was her he had come to see.

Miss Waveerley's astonishment knew no bounds; indeed, at first, she could hardly suppose him serious, and several times tried to draw her hand from his clasp in exasperation. But, when he pressed her for an answer to his proposal, she began simply to be cross, for she could not account for such a change in his treatment of her.

'Mr Falconer!' she cried, at length. 'Please let go of my hand!' She drew back from him. 'I know not what silliness you have got into your head, but I should tell you that this type of flirting I find very unpleasant.'

'But l am not flirting, Miss Waverley . . . Mary. You must surely know how much I love you?'

'Must I, indeed? Was it your behaviour in writing riddles to Lady Reyne which should have alerted me to your intentions, sir, or should I have recognized the depth of your ardour when you ignored me in favour of dancing with Miss Chalmers?' she said, throwing him an indignant scowl.

'I am all astonishment,' said Falconer, with a crooked smile. 'Do you really think that I had any serious intentions as to Lady Reyne? How could I? She is a married lady. We have had a delightful flirtation, but that is all. I honour Lady Reyne, but our relationship was never meant to be anything more than friendship.'

'Your idea and mine of the meaning of the word *friendship* must be very different indeed, sir, not to mention *honour*,' said Mary, seriously.

'You are very severe, Miss Waverley. Surely you realized that I flirted with her so as to give myself an opportunity to be near you!'

She turned her eyes on him reproachfully. 'You wished to be near me, sir? Certainly, when you left me stranded in the middle of Lady Cornford's ballroom a few nights ago, that impression wasn't uppermost in my mind.'

'I am sorry you misread my intentions, Miss Waverley,' said he, with a ghastly smile. 'When a man finally finds the woman to suit him, he is naturally careful of her reputation. I did not wish to draw attention to my affection for you until I was sure you wished for it.'

'You must certainly have been very successful in that, sir. I doubt that anybody seeing me left there, without a partner, while you went off elsewhere in search of somebody you thought good enough, would have been under the impression that you were struggling with the passion of your life. Do not add lies to your insults, sir. Any *gentleman* would naturally have asked me to dance on the music starting up. And I use that word advisedly.'

Her words hit their mark, and even he had the grace to blush. He saw that she was staring across at Captain Radleigh.

'You mean Radleigh, I suppose,' he said, bitterly, as her father's fortune began to look in danger of slipping away.

'Certainly Captain Radleigh has behaved in a very gentlemanlike way to me,' she agreed, calming herself with difficulty.

'If you think to get Radleigh,' said Falconer, his anger making him less than wise, 'you'll be caught out. He'll not be content with a wife from merchant stock.'

'Thank you for that, Mr Falconer,' said Mary, coldly. 'but now I think that you have said enough! Indeed, you have been kinder to me than you have to yourself, for you have saved me from even feeling sorry for you.'

His own hot temper had led him to betray himself, and he tried to redeem the situation by saying, humbly, 'My feelings for you are such as to lead me to use any means to try to separate you from any other man who shows an interest.'

'Then I am very sorry for you, sir,' she said, icily, though she would not have been human had she not known a moment of triumph, 'for mine are quite different.'

She was never to know what else Mr Falconer might have said to try to get himself back in her good book since Captain Radleigh chose that moment to return to her.

Though Falconer was the last person he wanted to see with Mary, he greeted him in his usual friendly manner, adding, 'You still here? Thought you'd taken yourself back to Liverpool.'

'No, not yet,' said Mr Falconer, seriously annoyed at being interrupted at such an unfortunate juncture. 'I have been having a conversation of some moment with Miss Waverley, if you will excuse us, Radleigh.'

'There is not the least need for that, sir,' said Mary pointedly, putting her arm through Radleigh's when he offered it. 'I think we have said all we need to each other, don't you?'

'I think what Miss Waverley is saying, Falconer, is that you are decidedly *de trop*, old fellow,' said the captain, with an impudent grin.

Not to be outdone in impudence, Falconer gave them one of his famous, dimpled smiles, and bowed very low, in a picture of elegance. 'I perfectly comprehend. Your servant, Miss Waverley. And yours, sir,' and with that he turned and left them, sauntering across the grass, his thoughts already ahead of him, chasing onwards towards Miss Chalmers, whom he would be certain to call on as soon as he got home, though he could not quite banish a slight *frisson* of regret that Miss Waverley had not been rather better born, for even now he was certain he would have charmed her had he been able to come at her at the outset.

As Mr Falconer passed the hotel on his way to the livery

stables, he was in time to see Lord and Lady Cornford, just coming out in search of Guy.

'What, you still here, young man?' cried Lord Cornford, somewhat pointedly. 'I shouldn't have thought there was anything to keep you here.'

'No,' he agreed, flatly, 'There is nothing to keep me here now.'

'I think, you know, there never really was,' said Lady Cornford, gently.

He gave her a crooked smile and, somewhat unexpectedly, kissed her hand. 'I think ma'am there may be much in what you say,' he said wryly, turning on his heel and walking away from them into the twilight.

As he went on his way, Lord Cornford watched his departure with a good deal of satisfaction, saying gruffly to his wife, 'Now perhaps we can get some peace around here.'

Meanwhile, where they continued to stand around the glowing remains of the bonfire, Captain Radleigh was deep in conversation with Mary. Indeed, he had just plucked up his courage and said, 'I tell you what, Miss Waverley, when we are married, I don't want that fellow skulking about.'

Mary looked up at him in astonishment, her heart bounding with happiness and gratitude, which increased still more when, in place of his usual easy confidence, his face displayed every sign of anxiety as to her answer.

'You have not yet asked me, sir,' she reminded him, laughter lighting her face.

'No, and if you dashed well think I'm going to here in all this crowd, you are heartily mistaken. Not my style at all. I intend to find somewhere much more romantic, but I give you warning of my intentions. Then, if that fellow Falconer comes sniffing round you again, you may tell him you are spoken for.'

It was just about then that Lord and Lady Cornford reached the bonfire, and Lady Cornford spotted them at once. There was something in the way they were standing a little apart from everyone else, and in the way they were looking deep into each other's eyes, which made her congratulate herself very particularly on her clever idea of bringing Mary with them to Crosby.

Guy, meanwhile, had seen his parents, and came over to them, Arthur and Mrs Sefton in his wake.

'My dear Mrs Sefton, how good you have been to bear with this young man,' said Lord Cornford, giving her a hearty handshake. 'Perhaps we may return the favour and take young Arthur sea-bathing with us tomorrow?'

'Sea-bathing?' cried Mrs Sefton, holding up her hands in horror. 'You do not seriously intend to allow Guy to bathe, sir?'

Lord Cornford intimated that such had been his intention.

Mrs Sefton turned to his wife. 'Oh, my dear Lady Cornford,' she said, in a voice of doom. 'Reconsider, I pray. I never allow Arthur to do so. My cousin Pellow allowed her son to go sea-bathing at Brighton two years ago, almost to the day. Her physician had told her that it was the very thing for a weakness he had in his chest. Ten minutes, and no more, was he in the water and he went down with an inflammation of the lungs that very night. My dear ma'am, he was dead within a sennight!'

Lady Cornford stared at her in horror, and the result of this consultation was a foregone conclusion.

# Chapter Twenty-Four

DURING THE NIGHT the weather underwent a considerable change, and when Barbara awoke she looked out on a leaden sky, a grey, choppy sea topped with white horses crashing on to the shore, and fine spumes of sand being blown about from the peaks of the dunes. It all seemed very apt, since it matched her mood, which was decidedly grey, though at first she could not recollect why. Then she remembered her argument with Reyne and shuddered.

She was just putting the last minute touches to her toilette when there came a tentative scratching on the outer door to her bedchamber, which slowly began to open.

'Are you alone; my dear?' said Lady Cornford, urgently, her head showing around the door.

'Of course, Mama. Why should I not be?' said Barbara, somewhat bitterly.

'Why, Reyne, dear. I thought Reyne might be here, you know.'

'You have always been an optimistic soul, Mama,' said Barbara, cryptically, though Lady Cornford was in no mood to decipher her meaning, her concern, that morning, being centred on her son. Since Barbara had already gone to bed when Mrs Sefton informed Lady Cornford of the ill-effects to be had from sea-bathing, she knew nothing of her mama's determination that her son should not be allowed to expose himself to the elements.

Being informed of it now, and hearing that Guy had thrown a

fit of pique, Barbara sighed. 'But Mama, he has thought of nothing else for two days. You surely do not mean to disappoint him?' she said, anxiously.

'I know how much he has looked forward to it, love, but you would not wish him to be put at risk?'

'Is it such a terrible risk? Everybody else seems to think it beneficial for their children.'

'Everybody's child is not prone to whooping cough, my love,' her mother reminded her.

'How do we know if Guy is still susceptible when he has never been given an opportunity to find out? Mr Wytchett seems happy enough with his constitution. Do you not think you dwell too much on illness, dearest?'

'What are you saying to me, Barbara?' asked her mother, indignantly. 'You think I'm a hypochondriac, don't you?'

'No, Mama!' said Barbara, horrified to see the mortification which spread across her mother's face. 'But perhaps you should try not to think about illness quite so much. Could you not try to be a little more like Papa? He sometimes has such agony with gout in his poor leg, and yet he never complains of it.'

'Of course he doesn't, Ba,' said Lady Cornford, knowingly. 'He has a wife to do so for him. He merely lets us see his pain when he is sure we are watching and all the while pretending to hide it. He may then have the luxury of having his aches and pains fully discussed and worried about, as we all wish to do, but with the added happiness of being thought a hero.'

Barbara, who had never considered her father's stoicism in that light before, thought that perhaps there was much in what Mama said.

'Dear Mama,' she said, trying to placate her mother, now in the full stream of indignation, 'I don't think you a hypochondriac at all, it is just that you have worried about Guy for so many years now, that perhaps it is a little difficult to give him the freedom a boy of his age needs.'

'You think I have mollycoddled him,' said Lady Cornford, indignantly. 'Well, I never thought to see you so unfeeling,

Barbara. I am shocked that you should be so callous with regard to your brother. I have heard of siblings not caring very much for each other, but I never thought to see it in my own family.'

'Mama! Don't be silly. Of course I care for Guy, which is why I do not wish to see him unhappy.'

'This conversation is pointless, Barbara,' said Lady Cornford, drawing herself up to her full height. 'Even could I have been brought to allow it on a fine day, on such a cold, blustery day as this I should be a strange mother indeed, were I to agree to it. I have prevailed upon your father to cancel our tickets on the later packet and we are to take carriages back to Liverpool first thing this morning, so as to get the early boat back to Eastham. Stowe must pack your things whilst we are having breakfast in order to be ready.'

'In that case, Mama, we must all think ourselves fortunate that Guy has such an excellent disposition, since you are determined that he shall miss entirely his chief reason for coming here. I know many a boy who would rebel at such treatment.'

'Indeed, I have been particularly blessed in my children,' said Lady Cornford, sublimely unaware that Barbara was gently scolding her.

But, by the time they had been five minutes at breakfast with Guy, it was apparent that she was to be blessed no longer. He shambled up to the table with none of his usual cheerfulness: his face was moody; he initiated no conversation; and he answered only in monosyllables until, driven to it by his father saying that he was making a good deal of fuss about not very much, he was moved to say to his mother, in exasperated tones, that he thought her to be the most unkind mother he had ever heard of.

Seeking for the most hurtful thing he could think of, he went on to say that he wished he could have a mother such as all his friends had, since every one of them had been allowed to go bathing. 'I am the only one who has never been,' he flung at her plaintively. 'It just isn't fair!'

'Arthur wasn't allowed to go,' his mother reminded him.

'Just because *his* mother is a featherbrain, *you* don't have to be one,' cried Guy, now really in his stride. 'Because some unknown boy died, it doesn't mean that I should.'

'But only think, darling, how cold it is,' pleaded his mama, her mouth all a'quiver at his disdain, she who had hardly heard a sour word pass his lips before.

'If you had let me go in before dinner yesterday as I wanted to, it wouldn't have been. But no, you had to forbid it as you do everything I want to do.'

Whatever Lady Cornford said in her own defence, he was not to be placated, and he went on like this for several minutes more until Reyne, who wasn't in the best of moods himself, said, 'Don't be a bore, Guy. Your mother says you may not go and there's an end to it. You shall have to make the best of it.'

Guy flushed to the roots of his hair at being so berated by his hero and, seeing it, Barbara, who had already been feeling mortified for Guy, threw her husband a darkling look and said, tonelessly, 'What a very helpful suggestion. Why didn't we all think of that?'

Unfortunately, Lord Cornford, who had been trying to read his newspaper and, in the way of many gentlemen, was taking little interest in this domestic argument, was not so complacent when he heard Barbara's words and said firmly, 'Apologize to your husband, Barbara. Naturally he does not wish to endure the tantrums of a spoilt boy at breakfast. Why should he?'

'There is not the least need, sir,' said Reyne, hastily, seeing obstinacy flow through every contour of his wife's face.

'On the contrary, sir, there is every need,' said Lord Cornford. 'I did not have my children brought up to raise Cain at breakfast and spoil my appetite.'

The whole party, with the exception of Miss Waverley and Captain Radleigh, who had their own insulation from unhappiness that day, was thrown immediately into the worst of tempers, and not a word more was spoken until Lord Cornford, having read his favourite pages in his newspaper, looked at his pocket watch and declared that their carriages would be awaiting them within twenty minutes and he expected them all to be ready. Their servants and baggage were rounded up and the carriageway across the sands to Liverpool traversed, without any of them falling victim to any of the accidents they had prophesied for Mr Falconer on the previous evening.

A fine drizzle had just started as they joined the line waiting to board the steam packet back to Eastham, and the whole party crowded into one of the salons as soon as they boarded, enduring, with the other wet passengers, a miserably choppy crossing across the estuary. Although the rain had stopped again by the time the packet steamed into Eastham, they were very glad to get back on shore and thence to Hurst Park, not long after two in the afternoon, for Guy's temper hadn't improved and the sight of his face set stolidly into a hang dog expression induced agreement amongst them all that the trip had not been an unqualified success, though Radleigh and Mary, at least, could never regret that they had come.

But even for that couple, all the doom and despondency was a little dampening to their mood and, since he wanted to get Mary to himself, Captain Radleigh offered to escort her home, which had Barbara and Lady Cornford exchange knowing looks.

The party left behind was a sad one: Barbara and Reyne were still not speaking; Guy received a dressing down from his father for spoiling everyone's holiday, and Lady Cornford went off to cry in her room for being thought by her son to be a dragon. Seeing Guy show no remorse for his bad temper, and seeing Lord Cornford holding his temper by only a huge effort of will, Lord Reyne good-naturedly took Guy off to the lake for some fishing so as to stop him from driving everyone mad. Seated by the lake, each with a line in the water, they seemed to be on their usual good terms, which made Lord Reyne say, confidentially, 'I am on your side boy, you know, though I am sorry that you have hurt your mother. I think you have been very hard pressed. I promise you that it shall be my business to see if I cannot get those apron strings loosened.'

Although Guy appreciated the gesture and thanked him, even that promise wasn't enough to put him in a better frame of mind, and he added, 'It's too late to sea-bathe, sir. You can't do that around here. You will never know how much I longed to do so.'

'Foolish boy! There will be heaps of occasions for you to do so. You can go again to the seaside, you know.'

It was late afternoon by the time Lord Reyne and Guy returned to the house, and Reyne asked at once for Radleigh, being surprised to hear that he had not yet returned from taking Mary home. He finally showed himself at around six o'clock, and they saw, to their surprise, that he was not alone. Not only had Mary returned with him, but her parents had come too. The reason was quickly and joyfully explained when Captain Radleigh told them that he had asked Mr Waverley if he might pay his addresses to his daughter, and that Mary had accepted him.

Naturally, Lady Cornford could not bear to hear of them going home before she had been appraised of all the details of their courtship, and she at once invited them to stay to dinner.

It was a very happy party which collected together. Before they had to sit down to their meal, Barbara, overjoyed to see her friend form so excellent an alliance, took Mary to her bedchamber, so as to hear all the delightful details of how the match had come about. Mary explained that on their way to her parents' house, Radleigh had driven the carriage off the road and come to a halt by the river, where he had proposed to her in good form.

'I hope he went down on one knee,' said Barbara, laughing.

'Actually, he went down on two,' said Mary, her face a picture of mirth. 'I said I could not take him for anything less.'

Mary also told Barbara how Captain Radleigh had warned her of his intention to propose whilst they were at Crosby and, very naturally, Mr Falconer's part in the proceedings featured very prominently in her narrative, for Mary felt that Barbara should not be kept in ignorance of Mr Falconer's perfidy. Barbara was sure that she should feel not only angry but hurt, and found herself strangely unaffected.

Mary caught a plaintive look cross Barbara's face and, putting her arms around her impulsively, she hugged her, saying, 'I wish I could see you as happy with Reyne as I am with Captain Radleigh, my love.'

Barbara snorted inelegantly. 'Very likely, my love,' she said drolly. 'That sweet man had the gall to blame me because Falconer came to Crosby yesterday. He actually accused me of arranging an assignation.'

'He didn't! But Ba, dearest, how foolish of him, to be sure. It was Guy who told Mr Falconer of our trip, for I had it from Mr Falconer himself last night at the bonfire. You must tell him so.'

'I'd die, rather. If he chooses to believe that of me, let him do so. I'm not going to defend myself against an accusation so base.'

But Mary did not think that anything could be served by Reyne's not being in possession of all the facts and, when they returned downstairs to the rest of the party, she sought out her fiancé to tell him to make sure that Reyne learned the truth.

Dinner that night should have been perfectly happy, and would have been were it not for Guy, who continued to nurse his discontent. It was perhaps inevitable that, when once he had begun to protest, that protest should be long and hard, but Mrs Waverley, unbeknown to herself, actually made things worse by saying, to the table in general, 'How delightful your trip to Crosby must have been. Sea-bathing is sublime: I went into the sea at Brighton, you know, and I must say, it set me up for the whole winter. I never felt so well before.'

Mr and Mrs Waverley, who had never seen Guy in any but the most complaisant of moods, were shocked when he cried out to his mother, 'There! You see, Mama! Even Aunt Grace thinks sea-bathing is good for you! It is only mollycoddling ladies like you who like to see a fellow's enjoyment shot to pieces.'

Even so, they had a certain amount of sympathy in hearing the cause, since they had long considered that Lady Cornford babied him beyond what a boy of his age could tolerate.

But Lord Cornford's strict rules of etiquette could not allow his son to cast a shadow over Miss Waverley's celebrations, and giving him no opportunity even to apologize, Guy was sent to bed while it was still light, and ordered not to leave his room until he had learnt to mend his manners.

Although the ladies all felt for Guy, it must be admitted that the party benefited from his absence in a considerable lightening of atmosphere. Lady Cornford's chef produced some choice dishes; Bragg brought up from Lord Cornford's cellars several bottles of his finest Champagne, and there was a good deal of joyful conversation.

One particular snippet was especially interesting, and again, it was Mrs Waverley who introduced it to the room at large, by saying, 'I think that romance must be in the air, you know. Have you heard the news of Miss Chalmers since you returned from Crosby?'

They had to confess that they knew nothing of Miss Chalmers's news.

'Why, she, too, is engaged to be married. We heard about it yesterday. What a shock it has been to everyone, for nobody knew anything of it. Apparently it has long been understood that she is to marry a distant cousin of hers. A man of rich estates in the north.'

Barbara could not help but look at Reyne to see how he was taking it: he saw her look and laughed over at her.

'I am very glad to hear it,' was his only comment, but there was meaning in his look.

And Mary could not help but say to herself, with a little giggle, 'Poor Mr Falconer: Barbara; myself; and now Miss Chalmers. I wonder who will be the next poor unfortunate he will pursue.'

It was almost two o'clock before the party finally broke up and the Waverleys departed but, even if the hour was very late, Lady Cornford could not go to bed until she had made her peace with her son, though her amiable husband advised her to leave him to stew until breakfast-time. This she could not bear to do. For the past couple of hours, she had been haunted by a vision of him lying on his bed, imagining all their enjoyment in the salon, and feeling sorry for himself. It would not do to wait.

Stopping only to collect from the kitchen some macaroons and a glass of milk, for Guy had missed his pudding, she made her way to his bedchamber.

Barbara, who was very tired, had gone up before her and, while she was taking down her mistress's hair, Stowe, knowing what an interest she had always shown in that gentleman, said, 'Oh, m'lady, did you hear that Mr Falconer is to give up the lease of Garthwaite Manor? They say that he proposed to Miss Chalmers, but that when she told him she was already betrothed, he was mortified. He has already left the house and has gone to some watering place or other, where his mother is staying. Mr Plimstock, who came this evening to bring the essence of Olympian Dew which we ordered, said that it is all over the neighbourrhood that he is to return no more.'

Barbara was about to chastise her for gossiping but, at that moment, they were interrupted by an almighty series of screams, which seemed to be emanating from the other end of the gallery. Barbara ran out of her bedchamber and followed the screams to Guy's room, where she found her mother prostrate on the floor in a half swoon, her hand across her eyes and forehead. Telling Stowe to fetch her father, and to bring some *sal volatile*, she loosened her mother's clothing.

'Mama,' she cried, urgently. 'What is it my darling? What is wrong?'

Lady Cornford let her hand fall from her face: her eyes met Barbara's in a look of dismay.

'Oh, Daughter, it is all my fault! He is not here: his bed has not been slept in. Guy is gone!'

# Chapter Twenty-Five

THEY WERE, AT first, unwilling to suppose that Guy could have gone very far. Lord Cornford, who was ready for his bed and in his dressing-gown and nightcap, was inclined to be cross, and thought that his son must be hiding so as to worry them. But when a thorough search had been made of every part of the house – including cupboards, dressing-rooms, stables and outhouses – and no sign had been found, Lady Cornford fell into strong hysterics and her husband, too shocked to be of any use, sat heavily down in an armchair, his face in his hands.

'He has been stolen away by gypsies,' said Lady Cornford, her face muffled in her handkerchief. 'It is like that case at Oxford we were reading about, Barbara.'

'Nonsense, Mama. It is far too soon to think any such thing. Besides, they could not get into the house.'

'Barbara is right, ma'am,' said Reyne. 'You must calm down, you know, else you will make yourself ill. You will find that it is pure mischief. He has felt himself very ill-used today.'

'Indeed, Mama, it is the sort of thing that all boys do at some time or another, only that Guy is usually so good that we have not come to expect it of him. I think we did not quite comprehend, you know, just how important it was to him that he should be allowed to bathe at Crosby. We shall soon have him back, darling, and then, you know, we must let him go back to Crosby as soon as we get any settled weather.'

Lady Cornford, who was by no means as sanguine as Barbara concerning her son's imminent return, would, at that moment, have allowed him to scale a mountain or swim an ocean so long as she knew of his whereabouts. The search of the house was extended to a search of the estate and of the neighbourhood, with Reyne and Captain Radleigh taking on most of the responsibility for organizing the servants and calling on the help of Lord Cornford's tenants, Guy's father being entirely cast down by fear. He was left, with Barbara, to look after his wife, when Reyne and Radleigh rode off on horseback to see if they could hear of any sightings of the boy.

As they rode their hunters out of the gates, Radleigh called out to Marcus, 'This boy is beginning to be a bit of a nuisance! First he tells Falconer of our plans to go to Crosby, and spoils it for everybody, and now this! I tell you, Marcus, if I didn't know how all that namby-pambying by his mother had chaffed on his spirits, I should be inclined to give him a good thrashing.'

Marcus abruptly reined in his horse, and grabbed Radleigh's rein to pull him up.

'What? What are you saying?' he said, urgently. '*Guy* told Falconer? Are you quite certain of that?'

'Falconer himself told Mary that it was so. There can be no mistake. Why? What is it, man?'

'Oh, God, what a fool I've been. I accused Barbara of asking him to meet us there. No wonder she was so angry.'

'So, you continue to handle your personal affairs with your usual panache, eh Marcus? What a masterly way you have with that woman.'

A strangled laugh was surprised from Reyne. 'Oh God! I accused her of . . . I don't know what I accused her of. Would that I had half your aplomb, then I might be basking in the light of a woman's smiles as you are, instead of being thought the most miserable worm in England. You are a very fortunate fellow, George. Mary Waverley is charming. You could not have chosen anyone better – though you seem to have entirely forgotten that you planned to marry her to Falconer for me.'

'Ridiculous notion, wasn't it? I tell you what, Marcus, I was never so glad of any invitation as this to Cheshire. It does not bear thinking about that I might never have met her.'

'And now I suppose I must endure seeing you walking around smelling of April and May, while I languish in my room to one side of that blasted dressing-room, and my wife sticks pins into my effigy from the other.'

'Certainly, you can do that if you like. I doubt that I should be so willing to be shut out. For goodness sake, man, go to it! Mary is convinced that Barbara only needs to know you love her before she admits to herself that she likes you too. You *do* love her, don't you? Or have we both got it wrong?'

Reyne rubbed his hand up and down his cheek, and said, with a rueful grin, 'Of course I love her, you fool. She is the most annoying woman of my acquaintance, but of course I love her.'

By the early hours of the morning, the search had been widened as far as they thought Guy could possibly have travelled on foot, without any result, and Lord Reyne and the captain began to think that the boy must have somehow obtained access to some transport. Leaving all the willing volunteers to continue the local search, the two gentlemen returned to the house where only Barbara and Lord Cornford were to be seen, Lady Cornford having been sent to bed by Mr Wytchett with a draught of laudanum, so as to deal with the irritation of her nerves. Barbara came to meet them with a pitiful look of hope on her face and, when Reyne shook his head, she too, sank into a chair, her head in her hands.

But Reyne had been turning over in his mind all the possibilities, and instead of allowing Barbara to wallow in her misery, he bade her tersely to *buck up* and suggested that she and Stowe should search Guy's things to see if anything was missing. She looked puzzled, but when he explained that if Guy had taken some clothing with him it was an indication that he had gone at his own volition and had not been spirited away, she went at once, knowing how much comfort such a possibility would give her parents, They found that a pair of nankeen breeches, a shirt and a nightshirt had gone, as had a small valise.

'Wicked, wicked boy!' cried Barbara, as one weight at least slipped from her mind. 'How could he put Mama through such a nightmare?'

'Yes, yes,' soothed Reyne, noticing how pale she looked and pouring her a glass of wine from a decanter on a nearby table. 'I shall let you give him the drubbing of his life when we have him safe. Meanwhile, we have still to find him.'

'He can't have gone far,' said Lord Cornford, who had rallied a little on realizing that it was unlikely that his son had been kidnapped. 'He hadn't enough money.'

'Indeed, no,' said Barbara, 'for I gave him only two guineas when we went to Crosby, and he can't have gone too far on that! Not with travel costs being what they are.'

'You gave him money, Barbara?' said her father, in some alarm. 'There was not the least need for you to do so, I had already given him more than enough.'

It was inevitable that the whole tale of the money should be forthcoming, and it quickly became apparent that between them they had given Guy more than ten guineas.

'And he couldn't have spent any at Crosby,' said Barbara, 'for there weren't any suitable shops to spend it in.'

'So we must come to terms with the fact that he has money enough to take him a good distance,' said Captain Radleigh.

'That being the case,' said Barbara, grimly, 'I'll wager he's gone back to Crosby. It's the only thing which makes any sense.'

'He can't have,' Lord Cornford insisted. 'How would he get there? He couldn't even get to Eastham very easily.'

'But any passing carter would give him a ride to Chester, sir,' Reyne reminded him. 'Remember that flier? That gave him all the information he needed. He knows he can take a boat from Chester to Eastham and pick up the Liverpool boat from there. With money in his pocket he'll have no problem.'

The more they thought about it the more it seemed to make sense and, since it was already nearly nine o'clock, Reyne settled it that he and Radleigh should lose no more time, but should take the curricle across country to Eastham and intercept the boat when it arrived there. He recommended, curtly, that in their absence, Barbara and her father should try to catch up on some sleep.

A little more than three hours later, Reyne and Captain Radleigh were back at Hurst Park, but without Guy. They had met the boat, but Guy wasn't on it, the whole vessel having been pre-booked for a large party.

They were now in a quandary as to what to do next, and Barbara and her parents were in despair. They were still debating it whilst eating a hasty breakfast, when Bragg came into the breakfasting parlour and, hovering by the door, gave a hesitant cough. In normal circumstances, nothing could have induced him to interrupt Lord Cornford's breakfast, but today wasn't normal, and when Jem Prophett came with news of Master Guy, even he could not ignore him in favour of life's niceties.

Jem's story was a simple one. He had left in his cart in the early hours of the morning on his usual weekly ride to Chester, taking in some of his cheeses with which he supplied some of the best grocers' shops in the city. Partway there he had come upon Master Guy on the road, and he'd naturally, taken him up and given him a ride into Chester. When he got home and heard all the fuss about Master Guy, he'd come at once to tell Lord Cornford that he had nothing to fear.

Jem Prophett, one of Lord Cornford's poorer tenants, was a simple man, and rather slow: when Lord Cornford berated him for not making Guy come back with him, he scratched his head in a puzzled way, and excused himself by saying that he was a poor man, and he didn't hold with poor men interfering with the ways of their betters.

'Did he say what he intended to do when he arrived in Chester?' urged Barbara, anxiously, realizing from past experience, that Jem was unlikely to understand the enormity of letting a young boy go off on his own.

'It weren't rightly my business to ask him, I reckon, My Lady,' said Jem, rubbing his hands down the front of his smock, anxiously. 'If Master Guy wanted to get to Chester, it were my duty to get him there, I'd say. 'Tweren't for me to tell him what to do when he got there.'

In the face of such bovine reckoning, there was nothing more to say, and Lord Cornford sent him off to the kitchens to get himself some food and a tankard of ale for his trouble.

'Guy must have gone to Chester, intending to go to Crosby,' said Reyne, 'but then he must have found, like us, that the boat to Eastham was full. He'll either wait for a later boat, or he'll have gone elsewhere. He'll never come home with his tail between his legs, that's for certain. Not in the mood he was in. I'll borrow one of your teams for my curricle, if I may, sir, and Radleigh and I will go to get him back for you.'

But Barbara intervened, insisting that she, and not Radleigh should go with him. Reyne's first inclination was to refuse, but one glance at her pale, anxious face, convinced him that she would suffer more from waiting than she would in being bounced about in a curricle being driven at speed. Within less than a quarter of an hour Barbara was ready to travel, having replaced the evening dress she still wore from last night with a more serviceable dimity cotton and a warm, full-length pelisse which she could wrap around her. Pausing only to put on a stylish close bonnet and to pull on some tan York gloves, she hugged her father to her, promising that she would not return until they had Guy safe.

It was fortunate that the biting cold and drizzle of the previous day had been replaced by more settled weather: the journey, even at the cracking pace Reyne set, might yet have been pleasant had not dreadful uncertainty made it impossible that they should enjoy it. As it was, they drove to Chester almost in silence, their minds fixed on finding the runaway. If, as they drove ever nearer the city, Reyne thought of apologizing to his wife for having suspected her of luring Robert Falconer to Crosby, a few moments' reflection told him that now was not the time and he remained silent.

As soon as they got to Chester and rid themselves of their carriage, they went to the booking office from which Lord Cornford had arranged their own trip to Crosby, in order to enquire if anyone remembered seeing Guy. The young man behind the counter remembered him well, because of his youth, and remembered, also, that, finding the packet to Crosby full, he had taken the early coach, instead, all the way to Barmouth on the Welsh coast, the clerk having told him that at Barmouth he would find sea-bathing, bathing-huts, and everything he had left behind him at Crosby.

'Did you not think to stop him, man?' said Reyne, impatiently.

'My business is to sell tickets, sir, and that is what I do, to whoever has the money to pay for them. You'd be surprised at how often children are sent to travel alone.'

'Not that sort of boy, I think, sir,' said Reyne, stiffly. 'When I am at leisure I shall have words to say to your employers. If anything happens to the boy, I shall hold you responsible.'

'I am sorry you see it that way, sir,' said the clerk, with deceptive humility. He then added the rider, 'Mayhap, sir, you should have taken a little more responsibility for the boy yourself.'

Seeing Reyne stiffen up, Barbara took him by the arm and pulled him away from the counter. 'He is very right,' she said quietly. 'Guy is our responsibility, not his. Arguing will not bring him back.'

They speedily ascertained the route taken by the Barmouth coach, and Barbara heard Reyne making arrangements for a carriage to send her back to Hurst Park. She absolutely refused to go, insisting that she must be allowed to go with him to Barmouth.

'You will be very uncomfortable in an open carriage on such a long journey,' Reyne pointed out. 'You have suffered enough from the speed I was forced to travel coming here, but the clerk said that the route to Barmouth is fearsome. Rough roads; potholes; hardly suitable for a gentlewoman. And you've had no sleep.'

'Neither have you,' she flung back at him.

'I'm used to it. In war you learn to take sleep as you can.'

'I can sleep in the curricle. We shall send a message to Papa to put his mind at rest and tell him what we plan.'

Contrary to Barbara's expectations, the intolerable nature of the rutted roads running through to the Welsh coast, once they had crossed the border, made sleep impossible, and some six or seven hours later, they were in an exhausted state. Reyne was impressed by the way Barbara continued stoically to cling to the straps, allowing him to halt only briefly to change horses and to take some brief refreshment, but by the time they reached Bala, the little grey stone town situated between the mountains and the lake, a grey sheet of water, Barbara's face was ashen with fatigue. Reyne insisted that she must rest overnight, but that they would continue their chase at first light.

Barbara protested, but when she tried to get down from the carriage and almost fell, she had, reluctantly, to admit that she could go no further. Making Reyne promise that he would not leave her in bed and go on without her, she allowed him to lift her down from the carriage.

# Chapter Twenty-Six

WHEN BARBARA AWOKE early next morning in her large, cheerful bedchamber which was the best the White Lion Hotel could offer, she found a maidservant awaiting her, with a china pail of hot water and, laid across the dressing-table, a number of items, which included a brush and comb, some soap, a toothbrush and some undergarments, which were obviously new. Enquiring of the maidservant from whence they had come, she was informed that My Lady's husband had, on the previous evening, as soon as she had gone to bed, sought out Mrs Ellis, the landlord's wife, and had given her a great deal of money to procure them for her in the village, though the hour had been so late.

Remembering the previous evening, her exhaustion and Reyne's inestimable kindness, this extra sign of his consideration could hardly surprise her, and she felt herself to be more in charity with him than she had ever thought possible.

At the hotel he had hired not only their large and comfortable suite of rooms, but he had insisted that before she retired, she take supper with him in a private parlour where, having sat her down and filled her plate with the best of everything, he had generally fussed over her as does a mother hen her chick. When it was time to go up to her bedchamber, he behaved with every delicacy. He had loaned a nightgown from their kindly landlady for Barbara's use, had had a maidservant sent up to help her undress, and seemed determined to keep out of her way so that she should not feel that he intended to take advantage of their situation. After the way she had behaved towards him in recent days, she felt that he had been more generous than she deserved.

She had gone to sleep as soon as her head touched the pillow, but she knew that during the night he had come in at least once to check that she was comfortable, for she was aware of him at her bedside, and felt him tuck the covers, which had partly slid off the bed, up around her shoulders once more. Had she had the energy to open her eyes, she would have thanked him, but she had been too fatigued to lift lids which seemed weighted down. Nonetheless, his protective gesture left her feeling warm and contented, and this morning, the feeling lingered.

He had ordered breakfast and was waiting for her in their parlour when she went downstairs, having first put on the new underwear and her outer clothes, now freshened and pressed. When she entered the room, he rose from his seat and came to fetch her to the table, staring hard at her face as if to search for any signs that she was not feeling quite the thing. What he saw obviously satisfied him, for he gave a brief nod, and then drew back a chair for her to be seated.

Her first task was to thank him for his thoughtful provision of all she would need to be made to look respectable again.

'It is wonderfully encouraging to find one's husband so conversant with ladies' undergarments,' she said, pertly.

'I thought you would be pleased,' he said, with a deliberately smug look.

While they were speaking, Reyne had been helping himself, generously, from some silver chafing dishes set out on a table, and he brought the filled plate and set it before Barbara, who protested that she never ate a cooked breakfast.

'But you will humour me in this, Lady Reyne?' he said, pushing the plate a little nearer. 'I intend to get to Barmouth as quickly as possible, but from what the landlord tells me, it'll probably take us four hours and more, because the road worsens. Thank God the weather is good, and won't hold us up, but

Guy has already had one night on his own, which is enough for any young lad. I don't want to have to stop for food.'

She began to eat at once, saying only, 'What a paltry creature you must think me, if you imagine that I should let my own comfort stand in the way of finding my brother. As for the road, I don't care what it is like, as long as it gets me to him. If only he is safe, I shall have nothing left to wish for.'

'Nothing?' said Reyne, with a quizzical look. 'I would have to cavil at that. Whilst I, too, wish to find him unharmed, I cannot pretend that when we have done so, I shall have *nothing* left to wish for.'

The implication was unmistakable. Hastily, Barbara asked him to show her the route to Barmouth on the map, which he had borrowed from the obliging landlord.

The toll road between Bala and Barmouth was hazardous and fatiguing, not only through the crookedness of the roads, but from the surfaces being clogged with mud and encumbered with large stones. By the time they reached the bridge at Llanelltyd, ready to begin the final part of their journey, along the beautiful Mawddach estuary to the sea, they had already travelled for more than three hours.

At Llanelltyd, the river-bed splayed widely. When the tide came in, it flowed within a small distance of the arched, stone bridge, which straddled the width of the estuary, forming the road which crossed it. It was largely as a result of this tidal phenomenon, and a ready supply of oak, that so many boatyards had been built along the northern shores of the estuary, at Llanelltyd itself, at Maesygarnedd, at Storehouse, and on the southern bank of the river at Llyn Penmaen, for, once the vessels were built they could be towed or floated downstream at high tide, ready to be fitted out at one of the three boatyards built at Barmouth, near the harbour quay.

Each boatyard the travellers passed seemed a hive of industry, vast numbers of vessels of every shape and size in various stages of construction being worked on by ruddy-face carpenters, the sounds of sawing, hammering, shouting, laughter, even singing, echoing in the crystal air. Large as some of the boats were, they looked like toys beneath the spine of Cader Idris, which lay along the south bank of the river. One could almost imagine a giant Gulliver peeping his head over the top of the mountain, ready to come and steal them.

The journey along the estuary was breathtaking. Reyne and Barbara were travelling along the north bank and, though Reyne was fully occupied in controlling his horses, Barbara had every opportunity to appreciate the brooding presence of Cader, opposite, its head, in spite of its being a fine day, stuck in wispy cloud which obscured the summit. Looking west, towards their destination, the estuary broadened, the river meandering rather than rushing, the grassy banks and reed beds playing host to a multitude of seabirds. To Barbara, it seemed that every direction provided a picture of the most outstanding beauty, the aspect and the light subtly changing with every bend that they rounded, until finally, they could just make out the sea between the gap where the two banks seemed almost to join, at the mouth of the river.

'Perhaps I shouldn't be thinking this now,' she said, turning to her husband, 'but surely this must be the most beautiful countryside anywhere? It is worth any trifling inconveniences of travel to be allowed the privileges of seeing Nature like this, in all its magnificence.'

'We must see it again, on a more pleasurable occasion,' said Reyne, fully in sympathy with her sentiments.

They were now on the last leg of their journey and Barbara was peering eagerly into the distance, where she could see the sails of many ships moored up, and which she knew must be the harbour at Barmouth, when Reyne suddenly halted the team.

'I don't know what we may find when we get into Barmouth, Barbara, so before we go into the town, I must get something off my chest, if you will allow me?'

Barbara looked up at him, surprised by his uncertain tone. She indicated that he was free to say whatever he pleased to her.

'It is about our trip to Crosby. I insulted you there. I was insufferably rude. My accusation, it was entirely uncalled for. I have since discovered that it was totally without foundation. Indeed, my own knowledge of you should have told me as much, without my having to have it confirmed. It *has*, however, been confirmed by someone; by a very good friend; by Miss Waverley, in effect. She told Radleigh that it was Guy who informed Falconer of our trip, and Radleigh told me. I am deeply ashamed. My behaviour was uncouth: ungentlemanly. I cannot look back on it with anything other than abhorrence, and I hope that you will allow me an opportunity to prove to you that I am not always such a fool.'

'I think you have already done that, sir,' said Barbara, generously. 'And, besides, I am not sure that the behaviour of either of us in the past few days would bear up to much examination. Perhaps we have both been in some part to blame.'

No more was said, and Reyne flicked the ear of his leader to get them on their way again, but, had she looked at his face, Barbara would have seen that he was looking considerably more cheerful.

The little seaside town of Barmouth was situated near the base of some high mountains, many of its 200 or so houses being placed on their steep slopes, one above the other, in such a way as to give those who resided at the upper levels an opportunity of seeing down the chimneys of their lower neighbours. It stood proudly on the sea-shore, where the Mawddach met the ocean and, in season, since the Napoleonic wars had made the Grand Tour impossible and people had had to look for adventurous holidays in the remoter parts of Britain instead, was full of members of the gentry, who came to the little resort for the purposes of sea-bathing and sightseeing. Recent years had produced an excellent hotel in the shape of the Corsygedol Arms, a small parade of showy, fashionable shops had sprung up, and in the season there was an assembly twice a week.

But Barmouth had more to offer: an exceptionally fine and extensive sandy beach, challenging mountain and river walks, bathing machines and warm, sea-water baths all made it a magnet for the Midlands gentry; so much so that the same families returned year on year, taking the same lodgings for the two or three months which comprised the season.

As soon as they had arranged rooms at the Corsygedol Arms in the High Street, and rid themselves of the curricle, they rushed to the sands, which were so close that on windy days they spread themselves on to the street, and where they had seen from their hotel windows several brightly painted bathing machines. Even from the edge of the sands they could see several gentlemen braving the waves, and Barbara was certain that amongst them they would find Guy. When she didn't immediately perceive him, she felt a knot of anxiety form in her breast.

Leaving Barbara near to the roadside, Reyne dashed down to see if Guy was in any of the gentlemen's bathing machines, but, finding no sign of him, the anxiety which had been gripping Barbara transferred itself to him. Determined to remain calm, he said merely, on rejoining her, 'No, he isn't there. I suppose we were being too optimistic to expect to find him in two minutes. He has obviously gone for something to eat. We will walk along the beach until we find him.'

His matter-of-fact voice calmed her, and to keep her so, as they strolled along the fine sand away from the harbour, he pointed out how indifferent were the bathing machines, having no wheels to move them like the ones at Crosby, which must mean that the tide had to be just right before people could bathe from them.

Their walk along the front took them past several boatbuilders' yards, and past an area of fishing boats, where nets were being mended by a group of fishermen in navy-blue smocks, seated on barrels and shabby stools. In the distance, three local urchins were cavorting in the surf, dressed only in their breeches, splashing one another and throwing handfuls of sand.

Reyne said to Barbara, 'Stay here. I'll ask those lads; they are bound to have seen him.'

The boys noticed Reyne's approach and turned to stare. One

of the boys, an extremely grubby lad from the drying sand which stuck to his limbs and chest, stopped in his tracks and looked aghast.

'Hello Guy,' said Reyne, coolly. 'What a fine dance you have led us.'

Reyne looked back at Barbara and waved, then pointed at Guy, upon which, heedless of dignity, Barbara ran across the sand to her brother, and pulled him into her arms, despite his protests.

'Wicked, wicked boy!' said Barbara, laughing and crying together. 'I have never been so glad to see anyone in my whole life.'

# Chapter Twenty-Seven

AFTER CAUSING THEM so much trouble, Guy should probably have received more of a scolding, but, once they were back at the hotel and having tea, Barbara said merely, when he protested that he had only wanted some fun like other boys, 'But dearest, think of Mother! She had hysterics and had to be put to bed with laudanum when we found you missing. We were sure that something dreadful would happen to you. Where did you sleep last night when you came off the coach? Not on the beach?'

'I'm not stupid, Ba,' he cried, indignantly. 'Why should I sleep on the beach when I had plenty of money? Some people on the coach mentioned that they were staying at the boarding-house next door, and I followed them there. Actually, it's very nice. There are lots of people boarding there and they all sit down to dinner together at one table. It's the jolliest thing: they have a harpist playing and I don't know what.'

'Didn't anyone ask you why you were on your own?' she asked, faintly, intrigued by the ease with which Guy had been able to rent a room without the protection of an adult.

'Of course they did, they're not fools. But I told them my parents had been held up and that I'd come ahead.'

'And they believed you?' cried Barbara, incredulously.

'Not *everyone* is suspicious, Ba. *They're* really nice. As a matter of fact, I've never had such a good time in my life. And the landlady and all her family speak Welsh to each other all the time. It's so jolly!'

Hearing his pleasure, Marcus said mildly, 'I suppose you were due some fun, young 'un, but you scared your parents half to death, so don't make a habit of running away, will you? It's a dead bore having to come after you.'

Guy promised, thickly, through a cucumber sandwich, that he would not and then he left his sister and his brother-in-law to decide what they should do next, while he addressed himself to a plateful of cakes.

'First we must get a message to your parents,' said Reyne. 'I'll find a horse and rider if you'll write something to reassure them. And I'm inclined to let Guy have tomorrow morning here before we start back, if you agree. He's bound to get a drubbing when he gets home, but I'd say he's earned his adventure.'

'I'd say he's earned a drubbing,' said Barbara, her severe demeanour changing suddenly to a giggle. 'Atrocious boy! But, yes, let him have an extra half day.'

'If you are agreeable, we could travel back in easy stages and get a proper look at some of that beautiful country we passed coming down.'

Barbara, nothing loth to agree, reminded him that neither of them had any spare clothes with them, a difficulty quickly disposed of by Reyne, who reminded her of the host of small shops clustered near to the hotel, which would surely provide all that they would need for a day or so.

It was decided, too, that once their shopping was done, Guy should be moved into the Corsygedol, but, when Barbara said that she would have a truckle bed made up for him in her own room, her brother protested vehemently, saying that if he couldn't have a room of his own, he'd stay where he was.

'A very sensible suggestion,' said Marcus, a grin playing around his mouth. 'I shouldn't at all wish for you to share your sister's room tonight. You are much too old for a truckle bed. And if you've managed to get yourself all the way down here, I'm sure you deserve your own room.'

'You will be wanting to give him a medal next for putting us to all this trouble,' Barbara protested, refusing to acknowledge by any change of expression, that she suspected that Marcus had any purpose in mind other than placating her brother.

'I may yet find myself grateful enough to present him with one myself,' said Marcus, driving his meaning home.

'Why should you wish me to have a medal, sir?' said Guy, their enigmatic exchange having gone entirely over his head.

'He is being silly, love,' said Barbara, hastily, picking up her reticule and rising from her seat, throwing Reyne an indignant glare. 'Quite nonsensical.'

Their purchases were quickly made, and Guy, fidgeting all the while at having to waste so much good bathing time, moved into a room close to Barbara. He was still protesting at having wasted so much time while it was still warm enough and light enough to go into the sea, by the time they had settled him in. Marcus was not proof against his pleading looks and offered to take him, Barbara being happy to see them go, for she found the strange sensation of anticlimax which had enveloped her once she knew Guy to be safe, had left her exhausted, and she welcomed the opportunity to lie down before dinner.

'And shall *you* bathe, sir,' said Barbara to Reyne, as they left, a glimmer of laughter in her eyes.

'Naturally,' said Reyne, catching her mood. 'I never miss an opportunity to do so.'

'Perhaps I should have purchased a telescope as Guy wished to do at Crosby,' she said, impishly.

'Would you like me to purchase one for you before we leave?' said Reyne, provocatively.

'Odious man!' she threw at him, but there was not the least hint of malice in her voice.

Barbara hadn't realized just how exhausted the long journey had left her: once she lay down on her bed, she went to sleep at once and woke only on hearing someone enter the room. At first she thought it must be a maidservant with hot water so that she could wash before dinner, but when the lower corner of her bed went down, her eyes flew open and she sat up indignantly.

She felt herself pressed firmly down again, and in the half-light from the closed shutters, she made out the outline of Reyne's face hovering above her.

'It's only me,' he said, unnecessarily. 'I came to tell you that we're back.'

'There was not the least need for you to do so,' said Barbara, exasperated at his cool assumption that he had a right to be there. 'What are you doing in my room?'

'Why? Who else were you expecting?' said Reyne, smiling broadly.

'I wasn't expecting anyone, sir,' she said, grinding her teeth.

'Then that was very foolish of you, my love,' he said, with maddening calm, leaning down and placing his hands under her shoulders to pull her up towards him. Bringing her face close to his, he kissed her mouth, deeply and unhurriedly. So surprised was she that she hadn't even begun to protest when she found herself responding.

Almost at once, he let her fall back again against the pillows, wearing an infuriating look of satisfaction. 'You see, Barbara, you are glad to see me after all. I was sure it could not be otherwise. I shall be back in an hour to take you down to dinner.'

Barbara was too embarrassed that it had been he and not she who had pulled back first to say more than, 'You took me by surprise, sir.' which sounded weak even to her own ears.

He turned back from where he was now standing in the doorway. 'I did, didn't I? Perhaps I should warn you that I shall very likely do so again, so it is as well you should be ready.'

'Coward!' she called, as the door closed. But the pout she wore soon became a smile, which lingered around her lips as she continued to lie there.

An hour later, Lady Reyne left her room to find her husband awaiting her outside. He was leaning nonchalantly against the wall opposite, his arms folded, and as soon as he saw her, he made her a low bow. Then, glancing along the corridor and finding it empty, he again pulled Barbara to him and kissed her, without so much as a *by your leave*.

Pulling herself away from him, Barbara was all indignation.

'You took advantage of the fact that we are alone, sir,' she cried crossly. 'I will not be used so.'

'You surely do not expect me to kiss you when others are present? My dear Lady Reyne, I am shocked. I never expected such an indelicate suggestion from one so gently bred as you!'

She pulled herself away from him and held herself rigid. 'You know perfectly well, sir, that I meant no such thing. I do not want you to kiss me at all. Remember, we agreed on it.'

'Ah, I do remember some such thing, now you remind me of it. I wonder if there is some form of temporary insanity in my family of which I haven't heard, but which might have led me to agree to such a ridiculous pact? I can certainly not account for it in any other way. Content yourself, however, that I am myself again, and I can't be held accountable for any agreement made when I was out of my wits.'

'You might have changed your mind, sir, but I haven't,' said Barbara, swelling with fury. 'I repeat, I will not be used so!'

Standing away from her, Reyne shook his head, smiling, then, pulling her hand through his arm, he pulled her after him along the corridor towards the staircase, saying, 'Yes, yes, I am a very terrible fellow, aren't I? You shall tell me all about it later, once your brother has gone to bed.'

Guy was awaiting them downstairs at a table near to the window from where they could see the distant sands and the ocean. The proprietor, Mr Barnet himself, handed them the bill of fare, which was surprisingly extensive, and they ate an excellent meal, Guy being responsible for most of the conversation, while Barbara and Reyne eyed each other across the table, the atmosphere between them almost tangible.

As they were finishing their meal, Barbara pointed out to the others that the gradually setting sun had turned blood red, and Guy dragged them outside so that they could go on to the sands for a better view. Looking across Cardigan Bay towards the peninsular of the Llyn, they watched the sun sinking, imperceptibly, until it began to dip beneath the water. The calm sea had changed to a milky white, intercepted by crimson beams from that decreasing orb above, which slowly turned the mountains to mere silhouettes. Then, quite suddenly, the sun was gone, and it was dark. The strollers, who had stopped to watch the sheer beauty of the sunset, resumed their promenade, and Reyne, noticing that Barbara shivered slightly from a breeze which had blown up, steered them back to their hotel.

Looking down at her brother, Barbara saw that, though he would die rather than admit it, he was very fatigued, and she said without thinking that she would go with him to help him get ready for bed.

Seeing Guy's glare, Reyne said hastily, 'He's not a baby, remember, Barbara. I'll go with him to see he has everything he needs, but he is perfectly capable of seeing himself to bed.'

Barbara apologized at once, and giving Guy a penitent peck on the cheek, left him with Reyne, while she made her way to her room, where one of the hotel maidservants was awaiting her. She had done little but help Barbara remove her jewellery and begin to take down her hair, when Lord Reyne came, unannounced, into the room, having entered through the adjoining door.

'I'll help my wife now,' he said coolly, flipping the maid a coin and shooing her from the room before Barbara could find her voice.

'You can't possibly have seen Guy to bed so quickly,' she protested, feeling mild panic, as their eyes met in the mirror.

'I should not dream of insulting him by doing so,' he said firmly, 'since he is perfectly capable of putting on his nightshirt.'

'But at home Mama always makes sure that he has blown out his candle properly. Young boys are apt to be careless.'

'Since I used to be one myself, I know very well what boys are capable of, my love, but he has promised me that he will take every precaution with his candle,' Reyne assured her, moving so that he stood directly behind her. 'And I felt that *you* needed me more than he did. All those buttons.' He let his fingers run lightly down the row of tiny buttons, which fastened her dress at the back.

'I had a perfectly capable maid to do that, sir,' she protested, now feeling very vulnerable. 'She will surely come back if I ring for her. There is not the least need to put yourself to the trouble.'

'But I want to do it,' he said, taking out the rest of the pins with which she had earlier secured her hair, and letting the heavy auburn tresses fall about her shoulders. 'I assure you it is not the least trouble.'

He took up her hairbrush and began to stroke it rhythmically through her hair from root to tip. 'How many strokes must it be?' he said gently, his voice a caress. 'Remind me. A hundred?'

'I am sure you know only too well how many strokes are usual, sir,' said Barbara, tartly. 'So conversant as you are with all those little matters concerning ladies.'

'Hush! Don't scratch at me, little cat. I'm counting,' he said, soothingly.

The rhythmic brushstrokes continued for several minutes until, against her will, Barbara found herself fighting lassitude. Her eyes began to close, her skin tingling languorously, where, as he lifted her hair to the brush, his hand stroked her neck and shoulders.

'There, that should do,' he said finally, putting down the hairbrush. 'And now for the buttons. Why *do* ladies have so many, I wonder?'

At his words, Barbara, who had fallen into an almost hypnotic state, opened her eyes abruptly, and sat up, very erect.

'I believe I can manage quite well now, sir. I *have* put myself to bed before.'

'I'm sure you have, but it's much more fun this way,' said Reyne, starting to attack the twenty or so tiny buttons which ran from neck to waist.

'More fun for you, you mean,' said Barbara, trying to pull away from him.

'Oh, undoubtedly,' said Reyne, putting his hand across her shoulder to bring her back against him, 'though I have heard it said that many ladies enjoy the experience too.'

She wriggled in his grasp, and he pulled her closer towards

him. 'Keep still, little termagant. I'll never get these wretched things undone at this rate.'

Knowing that it was impossible that she should be able to get away without an undignified scuffle, Barbara sat rigidly still, while his fingers wrestled with the teasing little buttons and loops. Suddenly, she heard him say, 'Oh, to hell with this,' and she felt him rend all the buttons undone by the simple expedient of ripping the two sides of her gown apart.

Barbara's eyes blazed, as he dropped the gown from her shoulders, leaving her in her petticoat. Again their eyes met in the mirror and, to her fury she saw that he was laughing rather shamefacedly, looking absurdly like Guy when he had been caught out in some prank.

'My dress! How dare you! You have ruined it!' she cried, her rage overcoming her nervousness. 'You are the most uncouth, ungenteel, ungallant *savage* it has ever been my misfortune to meet!'

'And you are the most adorable, delightful, beautiful woman it has ever been my good fortune to marry!' he said, pulling her up from her chair, so that the gown fell to the floor around her.

Giving her no time to answer him, he picked her up in his arms and carried her to the ornate tent bed dominating the room, laying her down gently against the pillows before joining her there, and pulling the curtains around them.

As once before, Barbara backed away from him, but this time he reached out his arms and brought her back towards him.

'No, my love,' he said, with a twisted smile. 'Not this time. It is time that you and I made our peace.'

And with that, he kissed her, gently at first, but, on feeling her response, ever more deeply and then down to her neck and her breasts until they were entirely lost to the world outside the curtains.

Much later, their desire satiated for the moment, they lay entwined, and Barbara said to him. 'You have treated me abominably, you know.'

'Have I?' he said, fondly, twining one of her curls around his finger as he gazed lovingly into her eyes.

'What do you mean, have you?' cried Barbara, her voice raised half an octave. 'You know you have. I have been a laughing stock for my neighbours for eight years.'

'Falconer did not seem to think you a laughing stock, as I remember,' said Reyne, sternly, 'Nor did that slowtop Wynnon.'

'No, they didn't, did they?' said Barbara, with a delicious gurgle of laughter. 'And he is not a slowtop. He is perfectly charming. And he knows how to treat ladies, which is more than can be said for you.'

'I'm not sure I like the idea of other men knowing how to treat my wife,' said Reyne, a crease appearing between his eyes.

'I doubt you will have convinced them of that by flirting with Miss Chalmers at our ball. Many of our neighbours are even now quite certain that you have come to claim me at last only because you cannot think of any more excuses to prevent it.'

'Do you think it would help if I let them see that I adore and worship you, my love?' said Reyne, coaxingly, kissing her shoulder.

'Perhaps it might help a little,' Barbara conceded. 'A very little, though such an impression will not easily be overcome.'

'Oh, but surely, it is I who should be pitied. My own stupidity has led me to lose six years of life with you. All those fellows who have been chasing you must think me a complete half-wit not to have been protecting my own.'

'Humph,' said Barbara, mildly placated. 'Very prettily said, sir.'

'Oh, I try,' said Reyne, disarmingly.

'And even now, I cannot tell whether you really want me, or you only remain with me out of duty,' said Barbara, with a sigh. 'It is the most infuriating thing imaginable.'

'You cannot tell?' he cried, incredulously. 'When I have been giving my all to leave you in no doubt!'

'Is that your all?' said Barbara, smiling teasingly into his eyes. 'I had not thought it possible!'

'Then my performance must have been very remiss. I can see

that I shall have to do very much better so that you may be assured that I intend to love and cherish you for the rest of my days.'

And with that, he proceeded to begin to make up for every earlier omission.